MOON GAR~~DEN~~

Wendy Mewes is a writer who just managed to squeeze
in sixteen years of teaching Latin and Ancient History,
various administration jobs, three revealing spells in
industry, lots of canine contacts and some fairly
significant emotional experience in a west country
tourist office. After a couple of life-changing years in
Glastonbury, she now lives with her family in France.

MOON GARDEN

by

Wendy Mewes

RED DOG  books

MOON GARDEN
Red Dog Books
ISBN 0 9536001 1 4

British Library Cataloguing-in-Publication Data
A catalogue record for this book is available from the British Library

Red Dog Books is based in Axbridge, Somerset and in Brittany.
Enquiries should be addressed to the editorial office at
Red Dog Books, Kerjezequel, 29450 Sizun, France.
Tel. 00 33 (0)298 24 15 19
email: reddogbooks@wanadoo.fr

www.reddogbooks.com

Cover illustration: 'Wendy's Garden' by David Brayne RWS
© David Brayne
photographed by www.ikonstudios.com

Printed and bound in Great Britain by
Cox & Wyman Ltd, Reading, Berkshire.

For BB, BB, GB and BB
que je vous aime

ACKNOWLEDGEMENTS

Special thanks to the following special people:
Janet Laurence for her incisive comments on the
manuscript and all she has taught me about the
writer's lot over the years;
Maggie Makepeace for her suggestions,
encouragement and much-valued friendship;
my good friend David Brayne for the wonderful
painting on the cover;
helpful friends Rosemary Alexander and Les Keen;
Elaine Barry for a lot more than she realises;
Joan Field for many years of loving support;
Sue Gregory for being who she is (including the finest
friend imaginable);
my editor at Red Dog Books and the non-executive
directors for their relentless input.

Chapter 1

He was disappointed to hear that the house wasn't haunted. A ghost might have been one last frail hope of salvaging something from this stupendous disaster. Spectral shenanigans under his own roof had an undeniable cachet and friends who wouldn't come from the city for his sake might be wooed by a whiff of plasma. Without it, Mean Cottage was nothing more than its name suggested.

Rufus drained his glass and stared moodily at his feet, barely listening to some prattle about local legends the old boy beside him at the bar was still jabbering on about. He couldn't remember how much whisky he'd had, but his shoes seemed an awfully long way down, as if his legs had stretched several inches during the night. Perhaps they had. Nothing could make the total and utter cock-up of the last few days any worse: a bit of surprise leg growth was nothing to worry about in comparison. He wondered idly if he was anywhere over six foot now and how this would change his outlook on life. For the better, he hoped. Being five foot eight hadn't done a lot for him in the last thirty-six years. Not that he'd been five foot eight at birth, of course, although his mother would have been glad enough to add that outrageous statistic to her litany of grievances.

A week ago he'd been fine. Abandoned by his wife and without a livelihood, true, but apart from that he'd felt perfectly well and at ease with the world. Just days later here he was in Creech, a place only a ghost would warm to, the not-so-proud owner of a semi-derelict ruin. No-one was going to believe him. After all those plans, everything he'd told people, the pretty pictures he'd flashed about... and now this.

His legs came back sharply into focus and unmistakably at their normal length. It was one disappointment too many. He lumbered off his stool, mumbling about calls of nature and made an erratic exit from the bar, unaware of the grins exchanged between his drinking companions.

Outside The Green Man, sharp country air enveloped him. Rufus stumbled down the three stone steps from the doorway and fell into the road. A savage pain wrenched his left knee. His initial instinct was to howl like a dog, but suppressing this, he speculated momentarily whether his legs, if not longer, were actually now of different lengths. He couldn't think how else he'd ended up down here, but then a lot of other things seemed pretty inexplicable from where he sat. It was beyond belief. What had been a strong and positive decision, to make a new start after the fiasco with Alison, had turned into a nightmare of mammoth proportions. If only he hadn't met up with Charlie before going to the auction. If only he hadn't drunk quite so many toasts to his exciting new future. If only the auction hadn't been conducted in a barn-like hall with dodgy acoustics. If only the alcohol hadn't stripped him of at least two of his senses. Then perhaps he might not have bought the wrong bloody house.

Rufus hauled himself up and began to saunter down the road, trying to look casual, inconspicuous and sober. There was no-one on the street to see him, but he imagined them all inside the white rendered cottages, smugly pointing him out, people unknown to him but well aware that he was the ludicrous outsider who'd been stupid enough to buy that godforsaken place on the outskirts of the village. Old crones shaking their heads and chuckling with delight at the ill-fortune bound to attend his folly, young girls giggling slyly behind their hands whilst their mothers exchanged knowing glances. Rufus stopped dead, fists clenched in sheer frustration. Why was he so totally incognizant, so unbelievably insensible of what went on around him, whilst the rest of the world clued in effortlessly to the true state of affairs?

Take the dogs coming along the empty street towards him now, for example. There were three of them, one a glossy chestnut brown, two jet black, all running hard and straight at him. What was the obvious, harmless explanation of their behaviour that he was missing? His sudden fear translated their approach into slow motion. Screwing up his eyes into the face of the sun, Rufus watched, mesmerised by the rise and fall of their huge paws on the tarmac, muscular flesh rolling forward along their bodies with each bound.

He roused himself to turn nervously, hoping to see a clear goal in the road behind him - their master jangling a fistful of good strong leads or a roe deer doing a bit of hapless window-shopping in the high street. There was nothing but him in sight.

Rufus felt his thigh muscles trembling and knew the uselessness of flight. Not that he wanted to be chased like a rabbit. He'd been thinking lately about getting a dog, but decided, as the marauding pack came on, jaws wide and slavering in anticipation of a feast, that he might well change his mind if he survived the coming encounter.

His own mouth opened and closed in silent fear. They were six foot from him and he had half-turned away from the onslaught, one arm raised to shield his face, when a piercing whistle split the air like an arrow. Two of the dogs stopped dead, claws clenching into the tarmac. Their heads swung this way and that, searching for the source of the summons and then they were off again, veering across the road and disappearing from view between the houses.

It was too late to stop the lead dog who had launched itself at Rufus a split second before. Its body lurched sideways in mid-air, instinctively responding to the sound of the whistle, whilst still twisting its muscular neck greedily towards Rufus. He waited for the snap of pain as its jaws closed, but only his sleeve caught in the hound's teeth, pulling him backwards as the dog thudded down to earth. Through the ripping sound of his jacket, another penetrating whistle echoed along the street. The dog barely paused to extract its jaws from the strips of ruined fabric before making off after its fellows down an alley without so much as another glance at Rufus.

Silence returned to the street. Silence except for the blood rushing inside Rufus' head and his heart going like a frenzied drum solo. The thought of all those eyes peering out from behind the curtains prevented him from dashing wildly about cursing and looking for someone to hold responsible. He could hardly go back into the pub in this state as if nothing had happened. He would just have to carry on, pretending to continue his stroll along the road as if this incident was nothing more than a normal daily occurrence. For all he knew, in Creech it was.

He tentatively put one foot in front of the other and was relieved to find his legs still working, at least to the extent of a gentle totter. He'd escaped death on this occasion, and felt absurdly grateful - to what or whom he didn't know - but, as his heart rate slowed and his distance from the scene of the assault increased, he felt it was vaguely humiliating to be the object of such avid attention one minute and then totally rejected at the tug of a more important tie. It was not the first time it had happened to him. He felt himself doomed to a life of fleeting significance.

His rather shaky steps brought him to the end of the main street. Rufus stood for a moment gloomily at the old stone bridge over the busy little River Huele, and took stock of his immediate position - torn jacket, twisted left knee, bruised pride - and the wider picture: his likely bankruptcy and divorce. He looked down at the glinting water, which smiled back up at him eagerly. It's easy for you, he thought. Very pleasant just to skip along over a few smooth stones, babbling banalities. Your course is all marked out for you. Nothing to worry about or battle against.

'What about the chemicals dumped upstream by those bastards at the dye factory?'

Rufus spun round. He hadn't spoken aloud - had he?

An old woman with coarse grey hair in long braids around her head sat astride a bicycle, one foot propping herself upright at the kerb beside him. She deftly finished rolling a reefer and jabbed it firmly behind her ear whilst Rufus struggled to gather his thoughts.

'I was just...'

'Talking to the river. I've given you its answer. Now its your turn.'

'Sorry?'

'The art of conversation. You say something to the river, it replies, you reply to the reply and so on.'

'Except the river can't talk.'

'Who says it can't?'

'Well, I...'

'You?' she interrupted fiercely. 'You' - she looked him up and down, without the least glimmer of approval - 'say the river can't talk? What do you know about it? Did it ever occur to you that perhaps the river *can* talk, but you *can't* hear?'

Before he could think of any possible answer, she

swung her leg nimbly over to the pavement, propped the bike up and took one stride towards him. Rufus was surprised to see how tall she was. Taller than him certainly. He shrank back a pace, but she ignored him altogether, leant over the parapet and spoke towards the water in a hoarse whisper.

'I'll come back later when there are fewer interruptions.'

Ignoring Rufus, she mounted her bike again and pedalled off towards the village.

He was left speechless by her rudeness, although a village full of unpleasant weirdoes would be entirely in keeping with the rest of the scenario from Hades he found himself in. He looked over the bridge again. This time he noticed a small patch of brown sludgy foam caught among sticks at the side of the stream, whilst the river shimmied on, all innocent amusement, as if nothing had happened.

'I'm sorry about the chemicals,' Rufus said, aloud this time. 'But how the hell did she know what I was thinking?'

He crossed the bridge, taking a lane to the left shortly after which would lead him to Mean Cottage. The first sight of the house earlier that morning had sent him straight to the pub in the village without even getting out of the car. He had to force himself to go back for a proper look. Now or never, he thought. All you can do with nemesis is face it.

The sun was getting hotter by the minute and Rufus took off his ruined jacket, scrunched it into a ball and stuffed it into a hawthorn hedge to await his return.

It was cool and shady in this green tunnel of overhanging trees and after a short while he realised that the oddness he sensed was an absence of sound, human or mechanical. He could not remember the last time he'd heard silence or rather the depth of silence that has no surrounding sense of repressed sound at its edges. In his agitated state, it wrapped around him like a comfort blanket. He began to think that perhaps everything wasn't as bad as he'd feared. The cottage might turn out to be habitable, or maybe with a few small improvements he could hope to sell it at a profit and start all over again.

For this had been his new start, this purchase of a house in the country. He needed so desperately to make things different, partly to give himself something and partly to make an impression on others. Especially Alison.

The thought of his wife made Rufus sigh and his neck muscles tense.

They had been married for nearly six years and the idea that a time might come when they were not together had never entered Rufus' head. It had taken weeks after she told him she'd met someone else for the true situation to sink in and by the time he came out of shock, their London house was sold and Rufus was sleeping in a friend's spare room.

The mechanics of it all were still a mystery to him.

In moods of anger he blamed Alison, and only looked for his own accountability when sad or self-pitying. Had he really been such a bad husband? He'd always tried to think about her happiness, listened to her problems and gone along with her ideas. And yet that wasn't what she wanted ultimately, or she wouldn't have gone off to set up home with one of her colleagues from the school. A man, Rufus thought with sour satisfaction, resembling a bilious basset hound.

A flashing image of the back of Alison's head, hair dark, straight and glossy assailed him. She was turning slowly to face him, eyes shining into a warm smile, so pleased to see him. It was distressing now for him to remember that there had been a time when he had provoked such a response from her. He closed his eyes only to see her face close to his, mouth opening to receive his kiss, black lashes a lacy web on her pale skin as her lids closed in anticipation of pleasure.

Enough, he told himself sternly. Alison was the past and he deserved better. Things were not that desperate. He had work, after all. Charlie and his new partner Rita were swanning off round the world for a year and they'd asked him to look after her bookshop in Bruford, which was only four miles away from Creech. At least, Charlie had asked him. He hadn't actually met Rita yet, but the opportunity to work at something he knew in a new location had been the impetus for this move in the first place. He had seized the chance to distance himself from his old life, to lick his wounds and to rise again from the ashes of Alison. All he had to do was get the cottage habitable and he'd be fine. It was just about rediscovering his own resources. Rufus suppressed the wave of fear that rose from the pit of his stomach at this insight, willing himself not to give in to it.

Mean Cottage lay just up ahead, across the bridge over a tiny tributary of the Huele and round a sharp right hand bend. He walked quickly towards his goal, waiting for the first glimpse of the cottage on his left across the stream. There it was, the gable end just visible through a screen of willows. Rufus took a deep breath, dragging the air up from his diaphragm and then dropping his shoulders on the exhalation. He had to make a success of this venture, despite the inauspicious start, he thought, closing his eyes for a second to muster his determination. He opened them again to see a bicycle come hurtling around the corner towards him. It was moving too quickly for Rufus to get calmly out of the way. He caught the briefest glimpse of orange plastic helmet and lime green lycra before hurling himself onto the steep bank where he lay in a clump of nettles, winded, listening to the metallic clatter of rider and bike swerving into a resounding collapse.

The cyclist hopped to his feet at once, apparently unconcerned about the blood streaming from a gash on his knee. He bobbed towards Rufus, wrestling with the strap of his helmet, which he finally managed to release to reveal a small shiny egg-shaped head. There was something familiar about his baby alien face.

'Are you alright?'

He was smiling affably, currant eyes twinkling, hand outstretched.

Rufus took advantage of the hand to yank himself upright again.

'Yes, I think so.'

He looked down at the man's calf-length once white sock, now drenched with blood to a madder brown.

'What about you?'

'Oh, that's nothing. A mere scratch. Bugger of a corner, daresay I'd have come off even if you hadn't been in the way.'

Before Rufus could protest, his hand was clasped again and shaken enthusiastically.

'Dennis Braithwaite.'

Rufus' heart sank. He wondered if he could get away before the little man remembered that they'd met before.

'Rufus Keene,' he muttered reluctantly.

A smile of delighted recognition came over Dennis' face.

'Of course you are. You were interested in buying Mile Cottage over in Critch.'

It's not fair, Rufus thought. You don't expect to be mown down by an estate agent wearing lycra shorts and a tangerine cycle helmet almost outside a house you've just bought by mistake from someone else.

Dennis was still talking.

'I was quite surprised to hear you'd bought this old place instead.'

Should I explain, Rufus asked himself wearily. Should I tell him I went to the auction to buy Mile Cottage in Critch and ended up buying Mean Cottage in Creech because I was completely bladdered and couldn't hear properly?

'You must have been very keen to go so high for it.' Dennis cast a disparaging backward glance at the stony façade of Mean Cottage. 'I'm not sure you'll get your investment back after all the restoration costs. Still, money no object, I expect? Perhaps you've had a stroke of luck since we discussed your budget?'

He hunched his shoulders forward in eager interest.

Rufus cringed inwardly. He'd sold his cramped little bookshop in Fulham to an interior designer who was even now busily engaged in knocking down every internal wall. Too big a chunk of that capital had gone on buying the pile of money-sucking rubble in front of him. He doubted he had enough left over even for a new roof. The house he had planned to buy was half the size and in ten times as good a state. He only hoped he'd never find out what piddling sum the other place had gone for.

'And to think you could have had Mile Cottage for fifty thousand.'

Dennis shook his head sadly. Then he patted himself down, podgy hands stroking the clinging lycra almost tenderly. 'Well, I must be going. Clients to meet.' He picked up his bike from the tarmac and trotted a few paces alongside it before swinging a leg confidently over the saddle.

Rufus watched in disbelief as the white hairless legs,

bottom-clenching shorts and bloody socks moved off erratically along the road.

'Best of luck!' The bike swerved as Dennis threw a cheery wave into the air.

It seemed to Rufus as if the world was united in a conspiracy to taunt and humiliate him today. His failure to cope with the simplest transaction, to make wise use of his money or to take a single positive step in a forward direction brought back Alison's strictures at a time when the thought of her face in any mode seemed to cause him acute pain. But she was no longer his ultimate tormentor. That special place in his pantheon had been usurped by the heap of detritus in front of him.

Mean Cottage was well set back from the lane. He crossed the rough stone slab that spanned the stream alongside the road and reached what was now his front gate. Rust coloured paint peeled from the splintering wood and he had to lift the thing almost off its hinges to get through.

A stone path ran straight to the front door from the gate, with unruly grass and bushes on either side. He stopped to look at the house itself. It was of local grey stone, cold to look at even under the day's bright sun, decidedly lopsided with one chimney on the point of collapse and the other mostly missing. Walls buckled under the strain of holding up the thick stone slates of the decrepit roof, thick with algae, which undulated like a glaucous wave to Rufus' slightly hung-over gaze.

What have I done, he thought morosely. A new life in a new environment, stimulation, excitement - that was the plan. Something better than just soldiering on, pretending I didn't mind being deprived of my wife and home, content to come and go monotonously at the shop, working longer and longer hours because I'd no idea of how to make anything else happen in the way my friends seemed so unerringly to do. This was the one and only grand gesture of my life and it's a ludicrous failure.

His reverie was interrupted by the metal plate bearing the name Mean Cottage falling off the gate onto his foot, causing him first to yelp with pain and then to slump down on the nearest grassy patch in a sprawling gesture of total defeat. Locked in the nadir of his day's fortunes, he didn't notice the crescent shaped carvings now faintly revealed on the wooden batten of the gate where the sign had been.

This new assault felt like a personal insult, carefully saved up for the moment of his arrival. He rubbed his foot and then began to massage the lingering soreness in his left knee. That little tumble outside the pub seemed a pleasant nostalgia compared with all that had happened since. He sat there brooding. There was little point in going on up the path and getting his head sliced open by a roof-slate. Was it feasible that the house reciprocated his feelings of loathing and was rejecting his first attempt to establish ownership?

There must be a more sinister interpretation than mere drunken imbecility for events since he arrived in Creech. It was as if something in him had been activated - a mysterious effect of recent traumatic events - something that was responsible for the magnetic attraction of blood-crazed dogs, insane old women, lunatic estate agents and now malicious ghostless houses? Something he appeared to have no control whatsoever over. Something, Rufus felt, which could only lead to barking madness.

He scrambled up. The dilapidated sight of the house was unavoidable. It was even more disastrous than he'd thought. He could never afford to do up this place and, what was worse...

This time he heard the sound of the bike before it

appeared and swung round, fearing another encounter with the dreadful Dennis. Instead it was the old woman he'd met on the bridge, her basket now full of foliage cascading perilously close to the front wheel.

'Of course you can,' she said derisively as she passed him. 'Don't be so ridiculous.'

As he watched her pedal away, Rufus felt a nervous tremor run right through him. He must be talking aloud without realising it, impossible though that seemed. What was worse, he'd been thinking, was that Mean Cottage was in such an awful state he wouldn't be able to live there.

Hastily, he leapt back onto the road and began to run after the old woman as fast as his wretched knee would let him, calling desperately to her.

'Stop! Wait!'

No response. She pedalled on serenely, fifty yards ahead of him. At her age, he thought, she's probably deaf to sound from behind.

The bike stopped suddenly. The snake's nest of plaits bobbed angrily round towards him.

'You think I'm deaf?' Her tone was one of outraged contempt.

Rufus' nerve faltered as he came up to her, panting, his face heavy with sweat. He wanted to demand to know how she seemed able to read his thoughts. One look at the fierce grey eyes put him off this temerity.

He looked down at the road.

'I just wondered what you meant,' he mumbled sheepishly, 'considering the state of the place.'

Marginally less hostile, she considered him for a moment, ignoring what he'd said.

'So you're the new owner. What do you think?'

He dreaded her scorn when he admitted that he hadn't actually had the courage to risk the interior.

21

'Well, I haven't been in yet, but...'

To his surprise, her voice was suddenly kinder as she interrupted him.

'It's not as bad as you fear. Roughing it a bit bother you?'

'No,' he said uncertainly and then considered the idea. Would he mind a leaky roof and faulty plumbing? Or did she mean take a spade and dig your own toilet in the wood kind of roughing it?

Her tobacco-hued laugh came with a rasp. 'There is a bathroom, of sorts.'

Rufus suddenly felt exhausted and not up to this kind of challenge.

'I'll just have to manage,' he said sadly. 'I'm stuck with the house now.'

'It's more a case of the house being stuck with you, I'd have said.'

She produced a box of matches from the folds of her long skirt, took the reefer from behind her ear and lit up. 'And it's not just the house that's important.' Through a haze of smoke he saw her face, heavily lined around the sharp eyes. She was looking at him thoughtfully, as if weighing up an important issue or calculating whether he was worth the effort.

Rufus stood feebly wondering if he had the energy to deflect another broadside.

'I wonder what you'll make of the garden.'

Her question took him by surprise, except that it wasn't really a question.

'The garden?' he said. 'It's a bit overgrown, I know. But not too bad.'

She snorted derisively.

'Not that strip of nothing by the road. The real garden.'

'Oh.' He hadn't a clue what she was talking about and was ashamed to admit he'd bought a property without even looking at it. There must be more land behind the house somewhere.

'I haven't had a chance to look at it properly yet.'

For some reason, this answer seemed to amuse her mightily. He saw the laughter in her grey eyes as she gave him another searching look.

'Perhaps you never will,' she said before resuming her journey down the lane at a steady pace.

Chapter 2

Rufus went back to the gate, puzzling over her remark and trying to peer through a thick screen of elder on the right of the cottage to the territory beyond. That must have been what she meant, that it was so overgrown and neglected he'd have a job to see that anyone had once tended a proper garden there. What else could it be? Inept and useless he might be, but surely he'd manage to see his own garden? Cryptic remarks from strange old women were really a bit much to cope with after all he'd been through in one day.

Hot and desperately thirsty, he wandered across the unruly front lawn to the stream, which swung away from the road and bordered Mean Cottage. It was a strange feeling to walk on his own property like this and to dip his hands into his own cool water, rinsing the taut skin of his face, the drops as balmy as a touch of nectar.

Soothed, he turned back towards the house. He was surprised to see that from this angle it looked really quite attractive, both soft and sturdy, like a fighter run to seed, as if it had changed its mind and decided to present a more appealing face for him. Even the roof didn't appear so much in need of emergency surgery. He went hesitantly to the door, fumbling in his pocket for the key and then had to give the solid oak a good hard shove.

He couldn't see anything inside at first, stepping into the dim interior from the glare of the sun. Three small windows let in little light through their ivy coats, but he soon began to get the outline of furniture ahead, a doorway and a wooden staircase rising from the far corner of the room. The table and chairs disconcerted him. He hadn't thought of the house as having former owners or being a habitation at all: in his mind it had related only to him, that stack of rubble, a massive mistake. In fact, there was a good-sized room, occupying all the ground floor of the original house.

Rufus wandered around, initially confused to sense something far from ruin beneath the cobwebs and the dust. A strong sense of life underlay the cool, peaceful atmosphere that lingered even in the powdery air as he rested his hand on the back of an old armchair. The notion of dereliction fell from his mind. In spite of the practicalities and financial strictures of his situation, Rufus found himself suddenly at ease for the first time that day. He looked at everything, savouring the signs that this had been a home for generations before him: from the mysterious significance of cross-hatched carvings on one of the oak beams to the humdrum worn patch on the rug in front of the fireplace, a dog's habitual place of warmth.

A childhood phrase came back to him: "where we live and move and have our being". Why this should have popped into his head here and now in Mean Cottage, he didn't know, but far from the roof caving in or a beam falling on his head, Rufus had the strangest feeling that he was welcome.

That feeling persisted even through an inspection of the lean-to that straddled the back of the house, containing an unappealing room with nothing but peeling walls, one cupboard and a badly stained stainless steel sink which he took as an attempt at a kitchen. The smell of mould from an even smaller bathroom made him feel slightly nauseous, but he told himself resolutely that it only needed a good scrub and a couple of coats of paint. It was the sort of thing his mother would have said in front of others with forced jollity and then got someone else to carry out.

He was still half-smiling and only slightly daunted

when he skipped onto the stairs for a quick look upstairs and came to a sudden halt as the screech of splintering wood filled the room. He looked down to see his calf protruding from the dark recesses of the second tread. Hopping on one leg in the struggle to extricate his trapped foot, Rufus refused to succumb to his previous mood of persecuted despair, and decided to take it as the house's little joke. He wouldn't push his luck, however. He was hungry and thirsty and already late for meeting Charlie in Bruford. Better to get out now while he still had reasonable use of all his limbs.

He was looking forward to seeing a familiar face. He and Charlie were opposites in every way, but their friendship had thrived since schooldays when Rufus spent as much time as he could in the easy-going Snow household. He had helped out every holiday in the little bookshop belonging to Charlie's uncle, drifted back to its familiar security after university and eventually bought it himself with money inherited from his parents when Andrew Snow was ready to retire. Charlie and his wild schemes, usually involving money or women, had been the most constant feature of Rufus' life, now he came to think of it. It was not only the risk-free vicarious pleasure of his friend's successful wheeling and dealing in the antiques world and even more successful stream of female conquests that he enjoyed: Charlie had been a loyal and supportive friend when Rufus' parents died within months of each other, and after his recent split from Alison. In fact, he could be relied on in an unreliable sort of way.

The late afternoon sun filtered across the lawn as Rufus came out of the house and stopped at the gate for a last look at Mean Cottage. He allowed the smallest glimmer of hope to override all the recent despair. It wasn't as bad as he'd feared, just as the old woman had said. Although there was a lot to do, he felt that he could cope, that it wasn't beyond him to sort this out. The prospect of coming back the next day was almost attractive, although he might be better off in full armour or with the support of a team of strapping builders.

Rufus set off on the long walk back to the village and his car. He suddenly remembered what the old woman had said about the garden. It didn't really matter that it had slipped his mind earlier. There was plenty of time, he thought, plenty of time.

Charlie did not seem to share this view.

'Where the bloody hell have you been? I've been here nearly half an hour.'

This was rich, Rufus thought, coming from Charlie, who did exactly what he wanted the second the fancy took him. A chancer and a ditherer made a surprisingly fine pair of friends, although, as Rufus reminded himself, it was thanks to Charlie that he'd bought Mean Cottage. But that might still turn out well with a bit of overdue luck.

'Sorry, sorry,' said Rufus, as he brought over the drinks. 'I've been at the cottage, it's really not...'

'No time, mate. Change of plan, I'm afraid. We're off tonight.'

Rufus thudded down onto a stool.

'What do you mean, *off?*'

It was a pointless question. He knew exactly what Charlie meant. Years of experience had taught him to recognise the signs of his friend's alarming spontaneity. The problem of this particular case was that it affected Rufus rather more directly than usual. He was quite used to Charlie disappearing for a few months after a girl in Brighton or a trail of antique fairs up north. The man had an equally alarming propensity for attracting women and making money when he felt like it that both horrified Rufus and endeared Charlie to him. Women thought Charlie would be trouble and he never let them down. But Rufus was supposed to be spending a week at Rita's shop learning the ropes before taking over in her absence. They couldn't just bugger off and leave him to it. He didn't even know exactly where the shop was.

Charlie lit a cigarette and squinted at Rufus through the smoke.

'Travel agent's cock-up. Flights cancelled, had to rebook.'

'Crap. You're not very likely to be rebooked a week earlier than planned.'

'Oh, alright.' Charlie gave an exaggerated sigh. 'It's Rita. She has to get away now.'

Rufus felt the alarm bells ringing.

'No problem with the bookshop?'

'What? No, no, nothing like that.'

'Some jealous ex-boyfriend she hasn't told you about?'

'No, everything's fine with Rita. It's just her daughter that's the problem.'

'Her *daughter*? She's going off round the world with you for God knows how long, dumping her daughter on someone else?'

Charlie looked affronted.

'Tara's grown up,' he said. Rufus raised his eyebrows. 'Well, seventeen, anyway.'

'And?'

He recognised that shifty look. Charlie was keeping something back.

'She's not staying with anyone else. Rita thinks she'll be OK at the flat.'

Rufus' snort of horror sprayed a mist of beer foam over the table.

'Would this be the flat where I was going to stay until the cottage is a bit more up together?'

28

'Yeah, but...'

'Oh, great. And this girl will be left there all on her own?'

'Yeah, but she'll be out at college...'

Rufus held up his hand.

'So I'm taking over a business I've never even seen without meeting the owner and with a kid home alone in the flat over the shop that was supposed to go with the job. It's perfect. I couldn't be happier. Why don't you just run along and have a fantastic time on the beach in Bali or Oz or wherever, and don't give a single thought to your poor dim-witted friend back here juggling all the balls you've left behind.'

Charlie leaned forward and clapped him on the shoulder.

'Thanks, mate. I knew you'd understand.'

He means it, Rufus thought sadly through an enormous gulp of liquid, he really means it. How wonderful to go through life like that, cutting swathes through stuffy notions of consequence, responsibility and duty. He doubted whether Charlie could even define those words. When he wanted to do something, he just did it, all the obstacles and complications of normal life falling aside like dominoes in a neat knock-on sequence, clearing his path. It seemed an unacquirable skill to Rufus, and one that sent a wave of weariness through his very being at every new encounter.

'Has Rita sent me any instructions at all?' He may as well try to salvage a scant scrap of realism from their plan.

Charlie leapt up and with some difficulty extracted a bunch of keys from his very tight jeans. He laid them on the table with a smile, like a child giving a gift in the hope of praise.

'Is that it?'

'Well, Rita's not much of a one for writing.'

'For Christ's sake, Charlie, she runs a bookshop, doesn't she?'

'Yeah, but it's not that sort...' He broke off suddenly and looked around the bar as if hoping for diversion.

Rufus began to panic seriously at this ominous hint.

'Not that sort of what exactly?'

His heart was fluttering wildly. He'd cleaned up a few of Charlie's messes before, but never been on the receiving end himself.

A loud group burst in through the street door, eddying around the small table where Rufus and Charlie were sitting.

Charlie took advantage of the noise and hubbub to get up and give Rufus a valedictory pat on the shoulder.

'Oh no you don't!' Rufus was on his feet like lightning too, fear galvanising him into the speedy action of gripping his friend's arm as tightly as he could with one hand, whilst trying to put his glass back on the table with the other.

For a moment they wrestled with each other, Charlie grinning into his face as Rufus struggled to keep his hold.

'Just open up, sell them what they want and take the money, mate. Nothing to it!' He broke away easily. 'Be in touch!' Then he was gone.

Rufus went to the bar in a daze, waiting his turn as the rowdy boys in front were served. He looked down at the new bunch of keys in his hand. Not even an address label on them. He didn't even know where the bloody shop was!

It was his turn at last.

'Triple scotch,' he said to the barman, who regarded him carefully.

'Not driving are you, sir?'

'That reminds me,' said Rufus. 'Have you got a room for the night?'

Bruford was a small town, the oldest part with its smattering of medieval buildings trickling down one hillside to a tiny market square, with modern development lapping up the slopes of more gradual green hills on the other side. It looked a prosperous, well-kept little place to Rufus as he set off from the pub the next morning, purposefully jangling Rita's keys in his pocket. The shop fronts down the main street were old-fashioned, well-painted in smart, dark colours. Across the road he could see the old walls surrounding the abbey ruins in their parkland.

His spirits, becoming used to roller-coaster movement, rose. All he had to do was find the shop. In a place this size, it could hardly be like looking for a needle in a haystack or even a bookstack in Hay.

He reached the square at the bottom of the hill. Gift shops, picturesque cafes and pubs lined the cobbled street beside a swift narrow river. It was obviously the main tourist centre of the town, although quiet this early on a Sunday morning. He looked around hopefully for a bookshop, and saw a narrow frontage with 'Books' in dark green italic lettering above the window, just the sort of thing he would have chosen himself. He went over and admired the display of carefully stacked leather bound rarities, before stepping into the doorway to unlock the door.

At the same moment he realised the key didn't fit, he saw the words "Neville King" painted on the glass of the door and then realised he was looking into the unfriendly eyes of the man himself, presumably, who had been in the process of unpacking a box of books just inside the door.

The door was flung open.

'Can I help you?'

Neville King was large and choleric. His belligerent

tone belied the sincerity of the question.

'I'm sorry.' Rufus stepped back smartly. 'I'm really sorry. I thought this was the bookshop of a friend of mine.'

Christ, what was Rita's surname? He didn't even know that much about her.

The man raised one sardonic eyebrow, a magnificent gesture Rufus himself had once spent hours trying to perfect, without a flicker of success.

'Indeed.'

'Yes, um, Rita's place,' he said lamely. 'I'm looking after it while she's away.'

'I see.' A slow smile of merriment replaced Neville King's sneer.

Rufus had no idea how to interpret this change of expression and soldiered on regardless.

'I used to have a bookshop in London, a bit like this one actually ... look, I'm sorry I bothered you.'

He turned away.

Neville King stepped out into the street behind him.

'No problem. Try the alley on the right down there,' he said helpfully.

'Thanks,' said Rufus in puzzled gratitude.

Five minutes later, he understood completely.

Rita's place could only be described as a bookshop by someone with as free and irresponsible an imagination as Charlie's.

The predominant impression of the shop from the cobbles of the alley was one of purple, inside and out. It was the sort of colour that gave Rufus an instant headache. Above the door, in a vibrant shade of lilac, was the name The Craft Shop. Bloody silly name for selling books, was Rufus' initial reaction to his new business.

From the window, a huge face gazed out at him through

a mass of foliage. Rufus couldn't tell if it was a man or a tree, moulded in terracotta and mounted on a green velvet covered plinth. There was something disconcerting about the large, raw features, something knowing, shrewd and unsettling.

He was relieved to open the door and step inside until he met the welcoming wave of stale incense. The air of Mean Cottage, uninhabited for many years, had smelt fresher than this. He reluctantly closed the door behind him, and decided against turning on any lights in case anyone saw him inside and thought the shop was open. He looked around, wondering just how bad things were going to be and shuddered on quickly scanning the notice-board inside the door, which was crowded with posters and hand-written adverts for reiki massage, whatever that was, meditation classes and vegan catering.

The counter along the right-hand wall held cases of silver jewellery, Celtic style, and stands of similar earrings, as well as a modern electronic till. The opposite wall had shelves with figurines, packets of incense, bottles of scented oils and a wide variety of crystals and stones arranged in small woven baskets. He picked up one of the sculpted figures and then put it back down with alacrity. Vastly experienced with women he was not, but the grotesque renderings of female pudenda were unavoidably explicit.

On the back wall of the shop there were, undeniably, books. In the middle of rows of shelves, a door with a poster of fairies sliding down a moonbeam led to the dingy kitchenette and toilet out the back. Off this was a small room packed with stock. Rufus rummaged through the bags and boxes. It was all clean, neatly arranged and totally unfathomable. There was nothing suitable for craftwork - no embroidery kits or strips of balsa wood.

For a moment Rufus wondered if he might not have enjoyed a quiet hour or so making model aeroplanes.

But he had to admit that Rita must have some idea of business, and the account books locked in a cupboard next to the wheezy fridge suggested that there was a living to be made, extraordinary though it seemed to Rufus, from all this crap.

A sound from overhead made him jump guiltily as if he'd been caught with his hand in the till. Footsteps thumped on the boards above his head. He'd forgotten all about Rita's daughter. He waited tensely, but there was silence again and he went back into the shop to look at the books.

There were quite a lot, both new and second-hand, all arranged in what he soon saw were clearly marked and discrete sections. Most of them were of what Rufus regarded as the fringe lunacy ilk - crop circles, modern druid practice and the tarot - but there were a few books he had had in his own London shop from time to time. With the relief of familiarity he took down a copy of Robert Graves' The White Goddess and flicked through the pages.

'...when black bulls were sacrificed to Hecate, so that the ghosts could lap their gushing blood, they were wreathed with yew.'

He read on, momentarily and uncharacteristically engrossed in the world of exuberant matriarchal fantasies.

Someone came swiftly down a flight of stairs and threw open the door in the corner nearest to him. A creature emerged from the doorway. It was basically adorned in black, apart from two large mauve sweeps around the eyes, black lips and nails, long greasy black hair and a floor length black leather coat swirling over further layers of black clothing. Coming straight from Hecate's lap, it was not such a huge step for Rufus.

'Hi,' she said, going straight past him towards the door. No shadow of curiosity, Rufus thought. It doesn't surprise her to find a strange man lurking downstairs on a Sunday morning.

'Hello, I'm Rufus.' He dodged round a carousel of feathered hoops, holding out his hand. 'Your mother will have told you about me, I expect...'

Then he forgot about such banalities in the face of the girl before him. He had been thinking of a seventeen year old as a skittish child, but to Rufus anyone taller than him ranked as an adult. And she was very tall, ethereally thin, with bloodless skin and the striking dark, long-nosed beauty of an Egyptian goddess. She reminded him of a coin-portrait he had seen of Cleopatra, that non-Egyptian, looking more like a sexy giraffe than a beauty queen.

'Sure.' She gave his hand a dismissive little smack by way of a handshake. 'I'm Tara. My *'mother'* will have told you about me, I expect.'

Rufus laughed bitterly, despite his nervousness.

'Actually no. She hasn't told me about anything.'

'Bloody typical. That's adults for you though, always bent on their own sweet pleasure.'

She smiled at him, but her deep-set eyes were cool and challenging. He looked away, embarrassed.

'You opening up today?' Tara asked.

His initial reaction was one of horror at the thought of actual involvement with this place, much less sole responsibility.

'Not on Sunday, surely?'

Tara shrugged and went to the door.

'There'll be a lot of people about.'

Rufus looked around hopelessly.

'People really buy this stuff?'

She followed his gaze, mystified, as if he could see something she could not.

'Sure. Why wouldn't they?'

He was desperate for her not to go and leave him alone in the shop.

'It's just I've no experience of this sort of thing. I had a regular bookshop in London, literature, classics, that sort of thing.'

The purple wings around her eyes rose in wry acknowledgement.

'Bit of a shock for you then.'

Rufus clutched gratefully at this potential empathy.

'It is, actually. I could do with some help ...'

Tara took a sharp step back and threw up her hands as a barrier, as if he had made a move to assault her.

'*Not* part of the deal. Having to share the flat was bad enough.'

Rufus felt this was a bit of a cheek as he'd been offered an empty flat in the first place. Nothing ever seemed to work to his agenda. Irritated, he raised his own hands in mockery of her gesture.

'Not part of the deal,' he said, as if the idea was unspeakably distasteful to him. 'I'm making my own arrangements on that score and won't be bothering you.'

She looked at him for the first time as if he might be worth some attention after all.

'OK. You keep out of the flat and maybe I'll give you a hand now and then - but not today.'

He was just about to say that he had no intention of working today anyway, but she was gone before he could do so, turning over the sign on the door to read OPEN as she went out.

After shutting up the shop, he went back to the pub to fetch his bag. He couldn't stay there indefinitely, but was

Mean Cottage even barely habitable? He thought back to the old woman's words. Was he prepared to rough it, now he'd been inside and got the measure of the place? Rufus, having encountered Tara, rather thought he was, and after asking directions, set off in the car for the nearest country supplies store.

Two hours later he was back at Mean Cottage, surrounded by a mountain of purchases, pretty pleased with himself and his resourcefulness. Once he'd made a cup of tea on the camping stove and arranged all the other essentials he'd bought, he sat back in the clammy old armchair by the fireplace and surveyed his kingdom. He firmly dismissed thoughts of Alison's disapproval at his primitive surroundings.

Here he was, in his own house, making it habitable, providing something for himself. He felt good.

'Settling in, are you?'

He'd left the front door open to let in the afternoon sun. Now he saw the old woman framed in the doorway, bobbing up again when he least wanted to see her. She'd wheeled her bike all the way down the path from the road without him seeing her. He would have to be more alert in future, or put a padlock on the gate.

She was peering round the door at his camping bed. A look he didn't like came into her eyes. In it was calculation mixed with mischievous glee.

'You took my advice then.'

'Not much choice really,' he said awkwardly. He didn't want to encourage these spontaneous visits, but she was the nearest thing to an acquaintance he had down here, now that Charlie had buggered off. He didn't count Tara, although the image of her wide mouth with its thin black outline kept popping into his head. He suppressed it deliberately now, in case this psychic old bat took hold of his thought and twisted it into something unsavoury.

But she didn't seem so interested in him today, her eyes wandering all over the room as if she was revisiting an old familiar scene.

'He'd be glad to see someone back in the old place,' she said at last. 'It's been empty a long time.'

So absorbed by his own situation in relation to the cottage, it had never even crossed Rufus' mind to be curious about the previous owner. Of course, she must know something about him if she was a long-term resident of Creech. But before he could open his mouth to frame the question, she was already turning her bike back down the path and on her way.

He decided to let it go for now, but the old woman paused as she reached the gate and called back to him.

'Seen the garden yet?'

But she then went on her way without waiting for an answer.

Rufus went through the house and out of the kitchen door. Directly behind the cottage were the overgrown traces of a large vegetable plot, a ramshackle shed and then the stream. To the right was a small orchard, with long grass between the unpruned apple trees, and beyond this he could just see an old brick wall, about eight foot high. The only possible place for a garden was behind that wall, but it seemed to run continuously. He went over, looking for a gate or something, but it ran for quite a way unbroken before he found a rounded opening, almost obscured by a huge swathe of ivy which concealed its strange circular shape. Stepping through Rufus realised that here were the remains of some sort of formal garden. Was it part of his property? He didn't remember anything in the original details and the wall was obviously a barrier. He'd have to check when his solicitor sent the papers through.

It didn't look like much anyway. The brick wall completely enclosed a rectangular space about the size of a tennis court. There were no other gates or openings that Rufus could see. In the centre was an empty circular basin, its stone greening with rank weeds. A wide band of paving surrounded this former pond with smaller paths radiating out to the edges of the garden. The intersecting beds, once planted with care, were now straggled with weeds. A sad state, he thought, for what must once have been a well-kept, carefully thought out design. On the wall at the far end was a wide niche with a slabbed stone bench. Through the trails of creeper escalating down the wall, he could just make out a curving pattern in the brick. Further sign of a guiding hand creating something to be enjoyed, maybe even loved. Perhaps the annoying old woman had known the former owners and seen it at its height. Surprising what a strong impression it had made on her, though. It was only a garden, after all, with nothing out of the ordinary that Rufus could see. And it would take a lot of work to restore whatever glory there'd been.

For the moment, Rufus thought, he'd concentrate on the vegetable plot and manage with the wooden seat outside the back door for his relaxation.

Well after midnight, he lay awake in the camp bed, missing Alison's physical presence as he still did each night, and restlessly wondering what the morrow would bring. He dreaded his first day as patron of The Craft Shop, feared slipping back into the nightmare world he was trying to inch his way out of, where everything seemed out of his control. But he comforted himself with the thought that however ghastly the shop turned out to be, he could come back here to a place of refuge. That was the only thing that seemed to be turning out better than he'd hoped. At least Mean Cottage was one place where no-one and nothing would disturb him. He turned over to a comfortable position and closed his weary eyes.

A blood-curdling howl close by outside made Rufus sit up in his makeshift bed and then stumble across to push back the shrivelled lace curtain from the side window, his heart thumping.

It was a moonlit night, but he could see nothing unusual in the small strip of grass or the elder thicket. Too stirred to go back to sleep, he padded out to the back door in bare feet and tugged it open just as the second piercing wail echoed into the night sky. He looked out, blinked and looked again.

Sitting in the middle of the vegetable garden, head thrown back to the sky in full ululation, was a huge blue dog.

Chapter 3

Whilst he was still struggling to take in the scene, the hound got up and in one fluid bound was out of the vegetable remains, lolloping away towards the brick wall. Rufus lost sight of it in the shadows. He noticed that the moonlight seemed strangely brighter beyond the wall and took a few hesitant steps in that direction before stopping. His reason was inclined to follow the unaccountable dog and see what it was up to in his garden, but not without proper shoes on and warmer clothes.

As he was struggling to push his sleepy muscles into the sleeves of a jersey in the house, another howl sounded and he rushed back out to find the dog firmly ensconced among the decaying sprouts again. It looked at him reproachfully, as if disappointed at his feebleness. It was pretty much the sort of look Alison might have given him.

'Alright, I'm coming,' he said crossly and stomped off in the wake of the blue dog as it streaked away.

The grass was long and laden with dew. Before he'd gone twenty yards, wet trouser legs were flapping against his cold skin and the damp had begun to filter through to his feet. The dog was no longer in sight, subsumed in darkness in the lee of the wall. Rufus walked into a bush and cursed as a phalanx of thorns pricked the length of his leg. He had no idea what he was walking on or through, but his legs felt heavy and unresponsive to his brain's commands.

Groping his way along the solid bricks, he thought that the entrance couldn't be far now. There was certainly a diaphanous edge of glowing silver just up ahead, although he couldn't imagine where it was coming from, in contrast with the subdued moonlit orchard behind him. He inched his way forward, fingers reaching out for the smoothly curved opening he'd found the day before. Then he stepped forward through the rounded entrance and stopped in amazement at the inconceivable transformation before him.

The garden was alive with light. For a painful moment when he was blinded by brightness, Rufus thought someone must have put up floodlights, but slowly, like a valley revealed as morning mist lifts, he saw that the garden's only source was moonlight. The dazzling effect was produced by strong shafts hitting the niche in the wall at the far end, where the round carving he had seen before was now a mirror, and bouncing back, zigzag, over the garden, flooding a silver pool in its centre. But he barely took this in, and registered the pearly plants now vibrantly filling their beds all around, before he was transfixed by the sight of three moving figures at the heart of the garden. Three figures in silver robes, dancing in unison around the water, arms raised freely above their heads. He strained to see them more clearly, to make out a face, an expression, anything to ground them into the real world he knew and was striving to retain. He had seen this wasteland of a garden only the day before. No effort of manpower could have produced the metamorphosis before him now - the mirror, the pond, the plants must be a mirage. But something obstructed his view of the dancers: he glimpsed at most a trailing sleeve, a flash of bare foot below the hem of a robe, and always the gentle swirling movements, but hard as he tried, Rufus could get no clear fix on the faces or figures of the dancers in his mind's eye. Deep inside his body, however, he felt the rhythm of their steps and the soft sweep of their limbs. It was like a resting place within him, warm and soothing.

In fact, he soon began to feel physically increasingly

heavy-lidded and somnolent. Desperate to make sense of what was before him, Rufus fought the waves of tiredness that threatened to engulf him, but he felt rooted to the spot. Tall stems of white flowers - hyssop, horehound and foxglove - swayed before his eyes, joining the dance, wafting out soft resonant music to lull his mind to rest and oblivion. But he had to stay awake, he had to find out what was happening...

He heard the sound of laughter, a high note of elation, as his eyes closed. Were they coming towards him? Rufus began to lose awareness of his surroundings, sinking down into a new slumber. On the verge of oblivion he thought he heard voices close to his ear, perhaps the touch of a hand on his arm. Then nothing.

He woke early in the morning and stretched, being careful not to fall out of the camp bed. It took a few moments to take in his surroundings and then he got up to light the little gas stove to boil water. It was not until he was dressed and stirring his coffee that he remembered what had happened in the night. Except that it couldn't have. His memory was elusive, preventing him from piecing together any narrative of his actions. A blue dog, silvery dancers and a moon garden. There was no way he could now believe in them. The fact that he woke up in his bed was enough to convince Rufus that he had dreamt it all. He was rather amazed at the powers of his usually prosaic imagination, but perhaps it was a mark of his over-stimulation in an extraordinary new life or some mysterious country phenomenon, like an overdose of verdure. Maybe all that stale incense in the shop had done his sensory perceptions some real damage. His mother would doubtless have nodded knowingly and said "something in the water" in the annoying way she had when she knew nothing whatever about anything outside her own narrow parameters, but liked to pretend she was omniscient.

He pushed aside the habitual irritation that still arose with thoughts of his mother, even all these years after her death, and wandered outside with his coffee. The sun was already well up and dew sparkled like diamonds on the rough grass. He sat down on the old bench by the back door and tried to concentrate on what he must do that day. Opening up the shop was obviously his priority, but he should also buy cleaning materials and paint to make a start on Mean Cottage in the evenings. If he could make it half-way decent inside himself, he might be able to afford a builder for the more serious problems like the roof. He'd also need to get his own things from London soon if he was really going to make the cottage his home.

An unfamiliar feeling which he recognised, with a little jolt of surprise, as a sort of contentment crept over Rufus as he sat in his garden, sipping coffee and making plans. Thinking about the future as if it had some possibilities and was worth doing was a novel experience: it was no longer an endless wodge of time to be filled remorselessly with artificial activity. No, he had something to do now and he was damn well going to enjoy it.

He smiled to himself and gazed about, savouring the clean early morning air and listening to the birds singing all around. He was disconcerted to discover that he could now discern a myriad of individual tunes when once the most he could have done was tell the sound of a cuckoo from a nightingale. He felt absurdly proud and self-satisfied for a moment. Then he spoilt it all by wishing he could share this new world with Alison.

Forcing himself back to his immediate surroundings, Rufus' eyes fell on a trail of trampled grass leading through the apple trees to the brick wall. If he hadn't been outside the night before, why did it look as if a whole group of people had made their way after the dog? That was another thing - the dog! Whatever had happened to the dog the night before? He had forgotten all about it after he saw the garden. Where could it have gone? This was ridiculous, Rufus had to remind himself, shuffling his ideas of real and unreal like a pack of cards. There had been no dog in the first place. But could he really have made such a mess of the grass when he first inspected the long-forsaken garden only a day before? He got up. He had to see for himself again now, to make absolutely sure.

It was just as he'd first seen it, of course, the weeds as invasive, the niche as overgrown and no water in the circle which had shone with molten silver in his dream. It must have been a dream, here was the proof. Rationally, he had always known it must be so, but a little trickle of disappointment ran through him nevertheless.

'What does this do?'

The woman at the counter was holding up a small striped brown stone she'd fished out of one of the baskets. She looked in her late fifties, skinny and falsely tanned, with hennaed hair sticking out in wisps from a multi-coloured headscarf. A huge pair of sunglasses masked most of her face, her words coursing their way through a thick orange slick of lipstick.

Rufus cleared his throat nervously, glancing up at the ceiling as if hoping to manifest Tara, who had been conspicuous by her absence this morning, although it was past eleven.

He'd survived a few days in the shop now, but so far trade had been undemanding, with customers who browsed and quietly chose their purchases, requiring little more from him than a bag for their aromatherapy oils or incense cones, the right change and a polite valediction.

Now suddenly he was faced with a raddled harpy in search of information. All he could do was hedge and pray for salvation.

'How do you mean 'do' exactly?'

The sunglasses pushed nearer to him.

'What does it *do*?' This last syllable came at him very slowly and clearly. 'What are its properties?'

Rufus tried to smile so that his next words could be taken in jest if they were, as he already feared, inappropriate.

'Well, it's a brown stone.'

'Excuse me?' The force of her disbelief at the paucity of his response was enough to shunt Rufus forwards into greater folly.

'Its use is mainly ornamental...' - he saw the orange mouth held open in stupefaction - 'or' - looking round frantically - 'in jewellery making,' he finished firmly, comparing the stone not unfavourably with some of the gaudy offerings on the counter stand.

The glasses were slowly raised to reveal a watery blue stare unsullied by the least trace of humour.

'Are you trying to be funny?'

Rufus felt himself reddening. The sheer ridiculousness of his tenure of the shop welled up inside him.

'Actually I was trying to be helpful, but if...'

'Who's in charge here?'

'I am.'

Tara stood in the corner of the shop, swathed in the customary black, pale and unsmiling.

'It's called tiger's eye,' she said. 'For mental clarity, will-power, that sort of thing. Very grounding.'

'Why couldn't that... that person have told me that? Don't you train your staff?'

Tara took the woman's arm and turned her away from

Rufus, talking softly as she did so. The woman swung round suddenly and stared at him, her face full of alarm and pity. Then she drew away from Tara, tossed the stone back into its basket and went out of the shop muttering to herself.

'What did you say to her?'

Tara shrugged and his eyes were drawn to the rise and fall of her narrow-boned chest in the tight black T-shirt.

She opened her eyes wide and batted the long eyelashes innocently. He noticed a myriad of tiny silver stars around her eyelids. The absence of the purple wings softened the intimidating aura of sophistication she had carried the day they met.

'Care in the community is *such* an important cause, don't you think?'

Rufus stifled a yelp of laughter as Tara disappeared into the back room. He followed and watched her put the kettle on.

'No school today?'

'School?' she said derisively. 'I'm not a child, you know.'

'I'm sorry...'

'Coffee?'

'Please. I didn't get any milk, sorry.' He couldn't seem to say anything to this extraordinary girl without an apology.

'I prefer black anyway,' she said, holding out a full mug to him.

Rufus determined to lighten up: only a minute ago they'd been sharing a joke.

'Why does that not surprise me, I wonder,' he said flippantly, looking pointedly at her outfit.

'You're full of personal comments,' she snapped back at once.

'No, well, yes, I suppose.' He was taken aback by her sudden changes of mood. 'Sorry, none of my business.'

'Right.'

He decided to change the subject quickly.

'Can you mind the shop for a bit later? I need to get some things for the place I'm living in, or camping out in to be more accurate.'

She looked mildly curious.

'What, like squatting?'

'No, like camping out in my own property.'

'Weird.'

'No, it's just that it needs some repairs and decorating before it'll be comfortable.'

'Joe does painting and making stuff, he could do with a bit of extra work.'

She sounded proud and possessive. Rufus hated Joe at once, whoever he was.

'Really, it's fine, I can do most of it myself.' He hoped to avoid having to employ someone for things he could do, albeit badly, himself.

'Who's Joe anyway?' He tried to sound casual.

'There you go with that personal crap again.'

'For goodness' sake, *you* brought him up, Tara, and if he's going to work in my house I think I'm entitled to know who he is at the very least. I should be asking for detailed references...'

'So you'll give him the work?'

'I didn't say that exactly...'

'Where do you live then?'

'Oh, miles from here. Right out of the way.'

'Where?'

'You won't know it, it's a tiny place called Creech.'

'You're kidding.'

'It's not such a bad place,' Rufus was quick to defend his new home.

Almost a grin appeared on Tara's face. The brief sight of a silver stud through her tongue made him wince with vicarious pain tinged with excitement.

'No, no. Joe lives there. In Creech. It'll be no problem for him to help you out.'

It's happening again, Rufus thought. The Creech syndrome. It was a community that seemed to run on co-incidence and oddities. Everything in that place had connections, threads that seemed to entwine him ever closer into its meshes. Where was the line, he wondered, between belonging and being trapped?

Time always seemed to drag in the afternoons, especially when bursts of summer rain kept the customers away. He assumed that bad weather meant good business for the shops centrally placed by the river: proper establishments like Neville King's bookshop, for example, Rufus thought bitterly. After a week without total disaster at The Craft Shop, Rufus was resigned to his fate, but no less furious with Charlie and the irresponsible Rita who had not cared enough about her business to talk him through it nor about her daughter to be in touch since leaving.

He attempted to juggle with three quartz spheres until, in dropping one, he noticed the tiny price label with its unbelievably massive total and put them all down carefully. His knee was beginning to ache again and he perched on a stool behind the counter, falling into a reverie as he watched the passers-by, huddled under umbrellas, making quickly for cafes or cars.

He thought about Tara and the weird fascination she held for him. Not a sexual attraction, he told himself quickly, although he was only too aware of her strange bloodless beauty, but more to do with the scary allure of the unknown. She was totally alien to anything in his previous experience of the female sex and he reckoned that was a form of magnetism in itself. He studied her savage unpredictability like a surfer reading the pattern of a wave, awaiting his moment to demonstrate a masterly control of the game. It would probably be a long time coming, he acknowledged ruefully.

Tara had agreed to mind the shop for an hour over lunch before going into college, but then expertly negotiated what she regarded as adequate financial recompense. He had not realised that she would expect a formal payment structure, and it was liable to reduce the day's takings to about £4 unless a large coach party of rich hippies were let loose in the town before five thirty. He had noticed the derisive looks given to the luridity of The Craft Shop by the more usual elderly trippers in search of fudge and tea towels.

He wondered how they would respond to Tara with her exotic looks and long flowing clothes. He loved the layers of black, from thinly pellucid sleeves ending in lacy fingerless gloves, to obscuringly dense floor-length skirts and hob-nailed boots. Alison had been so neat, so relentlessly orderly in her appearance. He sighed. Rufus himself was congenitally untidy. His wife bought him and insisted that he wore the smart clothes that within a few days on him were out of shape, torn or frayed. He wondered if the basset hound wore his school jacket and tie at home or even when they were in bed together. The image gave him a jolt of anguish. He would willingly have put on a dinner jacket and bow tie himself if it came with the opportunity of sleeping with Alison.

Rufus chided himself for his weakness at the same time as being overwhelmed with longing to hear her voice. He'd loved the comfort of being married, relished the sounds and smells of intimacy which he assumed had finally repelled Alison, at least those shared with him. Perhaps if he'd had his hair cut more often or worn after-shave, none of this would have happened, and he'd now be behind the counter of his own shop in Fulham, surrounded by objects of beloved familiarity, awaiting the last flurry of customers as workers hurried home. As things were, he was alone in Bruford accompanied only by crop circle postcards and the dreadful strains of sacred spring music which Tara had left playing on an endless loop.

He wondered what Alison would make of Tara, although he knew full well in his heart. His wife never had any time for the free-thinking individuals among her pupils. She liked hard-working, self-motivated students who never gave her any trouble and kept their teenage emotions reasonably in check. Rufus knew that she discouraged personal confidences at school in much the same way as she had done in their home, now he came to look back on the last few years. But he admired her strength and resolution even now. It had served him well enough in the years when they got along and the marriage might have turned into a true partnership.

There had been a time when they talked to each other, and laughed and shared things easily. Alison would once have seen the funny side of this place, he thought, looking round at the alternative junk he was supposed to be selling. Once he would have readily told her about buying the wrong house at auction without fearing the sort of tight-lipped reaction he'd get now - or would he? He hadn't even tried to talk to her since he moved to Mean Cottage, feeling he had nothing to say that wouldn't make him seem even more useless than she already thought him. For all he knew Alison could have been trying to contact him, although his mobile was rarely switched on these days.

Perhaps hope of reconciliation was a bit much, but she wouldn't have completely lost interest in him, surely? And wasn't she entitled, as his wife, to know where he was at least? I'll phone her tonight, Rufus thought, with a sudden spurt of masochistic pleasure.

He arrived back at Mean Cottage with a takeaway, parked off the road just past the house and walked back to the front gate. He hobbled down the path, pleased to be back on his own patch and looking forward to resting his knee.

As he neared the door, a young man, head shaved around one wild magenta tuft and with a bat's wing design in black liner encircling one eye, came round the corner of the house from the back.

Rufus' instinctive reaction was to put down his carrier bag and run, but the lad was right in front of him, wearing a grimace that might have worked its way up into a smile were it not for the impediment of two large cheek-studs.

'Rufus, right?'

Rufus tentatively shook the outstretched filthy hand.

'I'm Joe.'

With mingled relief and apprehension, Rufus greeted him and, accepting Tara's fait accompli, took him inside to look at the jobs that needed doing.

He soon discovered that Joe appeared to be an adolescent of few words beyond 'right' and 'yeah' which seemed to cover most situations. He was unphased by the broken stair-tread, and climbed carefully over it to inspect the two bedrooms above. Both were heavily wall-papered, with mouldering carpets on the floors and lovely views over the fields from their tiny windows. Joe pulled back a flap of carpet to reveal the wide elm boards underneath. A gentle smile completely at odds with his savage appearance came over his face when he saw them.

'Yeah, right,' he said softly, staring at the boards.

'Will these be alright on their own, do you think?' Rufus asked.

Joe nodded, still smiling.

'Yeah, right,' he said again, dropping the flap.

They went back downstairs to look at the kitchen.

'I could do with some proper cupboards and perhaps a couple of shelves in here. I'll be getting a cheap cooker and fridge at the weekend,' Rufus said.

'Right.'

'I don't suppose there's any chance of making a start before then?'

Joe looked startled.

'Depends.'

Silence.

Rufus waved his hand like the conductor of an orchestra, trying unsuccessfully to encourage further speech, but soon gave up the pantomime.

'Depends on what?'

A shrug.

'Is it the money? What do you charge per hour?'

Another shrug.

Joe mumbled something incoherent.

Rufus tried to fill in the missing gaps himself.

'You need money to get materials. That's fine. How much?'

Shrug, eyes sliding away.

Rufus took out his wallet and found thirty pounds in notes.

'This'll have to do for now, but I want the receipts. I'll pay you for your time at the end of the week, if that's OK and we can agree on an hourly rate.'

Joe took the money and plunged it into one of the huge pockets in his outsize scruffy jacket.

'Right.'

Rufus tried again.

'So, what would you charge?'

Shrug.

'You must have some idea.'

Joe was sidling away towards the door.

'Ask Tara, right.'

That was not at all the answer that Rufus wanted, having experienced Tara's business acumen at first hand, but he let it pass. He'd rather have a monosyllabic mohican who was visibly moved by elm floorboards than some chirpy conman. He'd already decided to take a chance on Joe, so there was no going back. With only momentary reluctance, he handed over the back door key and watched Joe slouch off down the path like a young offender just released from community service.

Rufus put off calling Alison for a few days as his nerve failed him each time he sat down to do it. When he eventually plucked up the courage, it was every bit as bad as he'd feared.

'Hello, it's me,' he said. 'Just thought I'd let you know where I am.'

Rufus was horrified to find his hand was shaking as he held the phone. Alison's non-committal response didn't exactly inspire him with confidence, but he ploughed on in the brightest tone he could manage.

'Well, I'm not in London any more.'

She obviously hadn't tried to make contact with him in the last few weeks, if she didn't know that. Probably hadn't even given him a thought.

'That's right,' he replied to a pedestrian enquiry. 'Yes, the cottage is pretty good really, though there's a lot of work to be done. Stream all round, vegetable garden...'

He paused for her incredulous interruption.

'Thought I'd get stuck into it myself actually,' he said defensively.

Feigned laughter came down the line.

He jumped in again quickly before the sarcastic

comment that he suspected would follow.

'I know I didn't do much at home,' - a lump came into Rufus' throat at this unexpected image of their little terraced house - 'but you only wanted pots and decking, which was hardly real gardening, was it?'

He heard the whinge of tired old arguments in his voice, hated himself and determined to change the subject.

'Look, how are things with you?' And the bloody basset hound, he thought bitterly. The bastard was probably sitting there in the background smirking at this very moment. The thought made Rufus hot with anger and violent urges...

'I'm glad to hear that,' he said humbly and insincerely.

It was not to be a long conversation. They were going out. The sound of that 'we' meaning Alison and someone other than him made tears start in Rufus' eyes.

He cut his losses with as much dignity as he could muster.

'Take care of yourself then. Bye.'

She had shown barely a flicker of interest in how he was doing. It was as if six years of marriage had meant nothing whatsoever, had dissolved without a trace of attachment between them. How had it happened? He'd asked himself this over and over again, analysing, regurgitating, searching for the key, the seminal moment when an apparently workable and steady relationship began its fatal tail-spin. But he knew that the whole thing was a good deal more insidious than that.

It had taken a couple of years of marriage for Alison to start jibing at him for his ineptitude. It was always done with her light, high laugh, a source of amusement to them both, the sort of licensed cruelty that intimacy offers so readily, should either partner in the relationship feel like taking it up. It stopped being a private joke when she treated others to accounts of his lacklustre performance at this and that. There was nothing sexual in her gently persistent innuendoes, but the implications were there for those who expected to find them after looking at Alison's attractive face and then at Rufus. Something more than Rufus' penis shrivelled at becoming the butt of his wife's humour, although he continued to smile dutifully and praise her competence in contrast to his own uselessness. Nevertheless a secret smart of humiliation began to fester in his heart.

He should have railed against the unfairness of it all and withstood her sarcastic surprise at his spirit. But the fact was - and he acknowledged it readily now - that, although he liked to think of himself as easy-going, he was often just lazy, and far too inclined to go along with others for an easy ride. The subtle nuances of these things creep up on us, he thought. Looking back he could see how over time he'd begun to act up to the image of him she'd created. Trivial actions like locking his keys inside the car, spilling things in front of guests and forgetting to carry out some of the numerous commissions she gave him were almost deliberate. It seemed in a perverse way to make his life easier, to give him a well-defined role. His behaviour reinforced her interpretation of their relationship and so it became the fabric of their daily lives. As time went on, the lines between reality and pretence became blurred and he *was* lax and negligent, his character apparently reformed to fit the circumstances of their marriage. It was a form of homage, a manifestation of his love for Alison, doing what she had so artfully decreed. And for that loyalty, he'd paid the price of dismissal, like an abused servant put out of his master's home.

Rufus got into the camp-bed feeling wretched and lay awake for hours, brooding on Alison's coldness and the chain of alienation that had brought them to this paltry ending. He fell asleep eventually, longing to be woken by a howling blue dog and mystic dancers in the moon garden. Instead he dreamt of a woman in a floaty dress with beautiful long russet hair and eyes the colour of a summer sky. She was coming towards him down a grassy slope, her arms outstretched in welcome. The complete antithesis of Alison all round, he thought, breaking the spell and waking abruptly.

It was a small indulgence to lie for a while in the morning light, desperately trying to revive the impression of that lovely face. His newfound capacity to conjure these compelling images in sleep was really rather impressive, Rufus felt, and not something to be worried about at all. It was perfectly natural that he should be having harmless escapist fantasies after all he'd been through.

Still, reality dictated more pressing engagements, like opening the shop. Reluctantly he got out of bed, blundering past bags and boxes of possessions on the floor, telling himself firmly to put aside all thoughts of his dream woman in the long dress. Then he stumbled into the kitchen and found her standing by the sink.

Chapter 4

Well, it was a pretty close thing - blue eyes but with a hint of green, the hair a little shorter, but he wasn't going to quibble about minor details.

At the sight of him she smiled just as she had done in his dream, high cheekbones rising to push out very fine lines at the corners of her eyes.

'Hello,' squeaked Rufus, with the pitch of a counter-tenor.

'Hello. I didn't mean to scare you.'

She was wiping her hands on an old tea towel. Last night's dirty washing up was now cleanly stacked on the draining board. The whole room, small and inadequate though it was, looked miraculously improved as if touched by a good fairy. And what else could she be, Rufus thought? There was no *reason*, no rational explanation why such a vision should be performing his domestic chores. He stood with his mouth unappealingly open whilst these thoughts ran through his head.

'I've really startled you, haven't I?' She smiled again, sending flurried ripples down his spine. 'I'm Lily, Joe's mother.'

Joe's mother!

This set Rufus' mouth flapping like a goldfish. How could a goddess, obviously sent from heaven as a reward for all his suffering, be the flesh and blood mother of a bald, punctured and verbally challenged juvenile like Joe. Even if Rufus could begin to accept the concept of her earthly womanhood - not so disappointing after all, now he began to think about it - she didn't look more than twenty. Elementary mathematics suggested that a mother must always be at least twice as old as her child - so that made Joe about ten and therefore very big for his age but with not quite so limited a vocabulary after all.

Lily looked at him quizzically as he gawped silently.

'And I'm a lot older than I look,' she said, seeking a reaction by dipping her head towards him so that crinkly chestnut waves fell forward to frame her face and halcyon eyes looked up (marginally) into his.

The shock of this proximity was too much for Rufus. He couldn't think of any suitably worshipful offering for her except his current mantra, absurd though it was in the circumstances.

'I'm sorry,' he said.

Rufus was still trembling as he drove into Bruford to open the shop.

Lily had come to drop off Joe's tools and just thought she'd lend a hand by doing a bit of clearing up without disturbing anyone. Excruciatingly embarrassed, Rufus realised that she must have looked in on him as he lay, probably snoring like a pig, in a grubby T-shirt on his rickety camp bed. Sensing his tongue-tied confusion at her presence (without knowing the true cause of it), she'd gone off quickly, leaving Rufus leaning on the doorjamb, feebly sniffing the air for a lingering note of her floral perfume.

Now he was driving along like a zombie, an unwashed wreck, mentally ill-prepared for the day ahead, buffeted by emotions he'd forgotten had a place in the world and completely thrown off course by his brief encounter with a dream.

The old woman was standing at the gate of Mean Cottage. Although she stood very straight, her whole attention apparently fixed on the façade, in fact her eyes were closed, her hands held slightly away from the body with fingers loosely spread. She had walked up the lane from her own house as soon as Rufus went off to work that morning, feeling it was time to explore the altered atmosphere since his arrival three weeks ago. She was taking in new energies on the air around her and assessing her instinct in favour of the newcomer. On a superficial count, he seemed an unnatural inhabitant: a city-dweller, doubtless driven mostly by getting and keeping, unresponsive to surroundings and impervious to local customs. There'd been a few like that in the village over the years, buying up old houses to despoil, driving down at weekends laden with boxes of food from city shops. She didn't care about them - Creech had a way of dealing with people and none had stayed long - but she had a fiercely protective perspective on the cottage, which made Rufus' case rather different.

She sensed who he was at their first meeting on the bridge and had given him a hard time as a matter of course, challenging his fitness for the duty of care the cottage deserved; but there was something about him that made her inclined to take him seriously, something beyond the disheartened eyes and susceptible manner.

She opened her own eyes and traced the carving on the gate with one finger, satisfied with the changes she divined. Then she gave the austere grey stone house a smile of collusion and went on her way towards the village.

When Rufus reached the shop, the front door was wide open and he assumed Tara must have forced herself out of bed early. There was no sign of her, however, and when he saw the till was also open and, more alarmingly, empty, Rufus began to panic.

He'd got as far as stammering 'S-s-shit' a few times and doing a peculiar little jig with his feet when he remembered that he'd taken the money to the bank the day before and left the float locked away in the back room. Also, from a quick glance around the shop it was clear that nothing had been taken. He didn't know whether to be relieved or sorry. An enforced ending to his stint as an incense mogul might have been a blessing in disguise.

A customer put paid to these speculations, and to his distaste Rufus was soon occupied with wrapping up one of the dreaded figurines with overdeveloped organs for a perfectly ordinary looking middle-aged woman who obviously saw nothing extraordinary in her choice of knick-knack. The temptation to ask her what she wanted it for was strong, but he felt there was no possible answer that wouldn't make him laugh rudely.

When she'd gone, he wandered over to the books and picked out one at random, hoping for some distraction from his thoughts of Lily. The Goddess Without and Within. He read the title slowly, as if acquiring a new language skill. What the hell did it mean? Some feminist claptrap about God being a woman probably. What a load of bollocks! He was about to put it back on the shelf when he stopped himself. If he really had to spend a year in this shop - and the thought, even as it formed, appalled him - then he'd better get some idea of what he was really up against. He began to flick through the pages.

'This deity is neither remote, nor wholly benign. We see contradictory forces at work in the wider world - love, anger, desire, greed, altruism, etc. - just as we must acknowledge the play of varying inclinations within ourselves. Ripples of all these emotions permeate the atmosphere in which we live. We need to tap into the *positive* energies through communication with the goddess, the primeval and quintessential being of the universe.'

It really is bollocks, he thought with some relief and read on with a superior little smile playing on his lips.

'...connecting with the power that lies within us all brings a real, meaningful ability to change the course of our lives. We can even, with practice, direct and focus these hidden energies to achieve a desired outcome in particular situations...'

Rufus gave a hollow laugh. If only. There were a few people on Rufus' nasty happenings list. Charlie most of all at the moment, closely followed by Rita, whom he'd never even met. And as for Alison...

A paper bag was thrust under his nose.

'I got you a chocolate croissant,' Tara said. 'And you forgot to leave the till open last night.'

'I what?'

'So people can see there's no money in it.'

'Is that necessary in a place like this?'

She laughed without mirth at his innocence.

'Bruford's full of shit, like everywhere else,' she said scornfully. 'What are you reading?'

'Oh, just some nonsense about using your internal power to make all your wishes come true.'

She snatched the book out of his hand and glanced down the page.

'Looks good to me.'

'But it's all crap - it doesn't mean anything.'

She gave him a hostile look.

'How do you know? Have you tried it?'

'Don't be daft. There's no such thing as magic and curses and all that rubbish!'

She glared at him in silence.

'Come on, you don't mean *you* believe in this?' he asked. 'Some unseen, indefinable power mysteriously wafting about in the ether?'

'People with closed minds must have said that about electricity once.'

'That's not the same thing at all. It's a scientific fact.' He strode across the room and flicked on the lights. 'There, I can see it. It's real. Cause and effect. Can you show me a physical manifestation of your mysterious powers?'

'I can actually. Karen Taylor.'

'Who's she?'

'Some stupid cow at college who was after Joe last year.'

'Sorry, you've lost me.'

'I hexed her.'

'You WHAT?'

'Put a curse on her.'

Rufus was appalled and intrigued.

'Whatever do you mean?'

'She broke her leg on the ski-ing trip.'

An unpleasant smile of triumphant satisfaction at the memory hardened Tara's thin features.

Rufus was horrified by her vehemence.

'That sounds kind of nasty and vicious to me.'

She shrugged carelessly.

'She's OK now,' she said.

'And it had nothing to do with whatever you did. Hundreds of people break their legs ski-ing every week.'

She flashed a spark of pure loathing at him.

'Why you think you're so fucking superior, I can't begin to imagine.'

With that she went upstairs, banging the door so violently that books leapt off the shelves.

Bloody adolescents, he said to himself as he stomped back behind the counter, but, in fact, Rufus found himself smarting at Tara's displeasure and regretful of his own dismissive attitude. She was only a kid after all, and although he didn't have much direct experience of them, everyone knew kids had mad ideas and fantasies about their love lives. A bit like adults really.

Minutes later he caught himself in a daydream about Lily, imagining them dancing together, lightly in each other's arms, her beautiful hair pillowing his face as they twirled across a meadow filled with summer flowers. It was the sort of image that usually made him switch channels on TV or doze off in the cinema. He shook his head, amazed that he should be embroiled in reveries of another woman he'd met briefly once, when he still loved Alison and hoped she'd come to her senses about the basset hound. A chance meeting was hardly anything to weigh in the balance against years of marriage, but he couldn't help the fomenting feeling that something had happened inside him that morning when he saw Lily standing in his kitchen.

Joe saw the old woman go as he came round the side of the house with a bag of rotting plaster from the bathroom wall and a mouldy shower curtain which he tossed onto the ever-growing pile of rubbish. Anything that could be salvaged or re-used he was placing carefully in another pile near the wood-store.

He took his tasks seriously, still not quite believing his luck that Rufus seemed content to entrust the improvements at Mean Cottage to him. He'd done plenty of painting and decorating jobs to earn money in the past, but this was real craft, making things work properly, bringing the place to life. Even making the simplest shelves for the kitchen had given him enormous satisfaction. He'd loved wood all his life, from his earliest forays into the New Forest with his father, who at that time was working on huge collages of branches and greenery. He was fascinated by the variety of textures - light, dense, rigid, whippy - and their pliant predilection to be fashioned into simple or ornate forms. Not an academic star at school, Joe had spent most of his time in the woodwork department - actually a shed - skiving other lessons to continue his carving or planing and sanding, totally absorbed in the silent rhythmic disciplines of the craft. The teacher had responded to this rare devotion to an old-fashioned skill and taught his strange, inarticulate pupil all he knew, whilst unbeknown to Joe, passionately protecting him from the strictures of other staff on grounds of exceptional natural ability. When others were making ash-trays and later salad bowls, Joe produced intricate boxes and small pieces of furniture, beautifully made, meticulous in execution.

Now, in the cottage, Joe lovingly touched the oak beams and their lintel partners above the windows, all the history of the building subsumed into the fabric under his finger-tips. It was the first time he'd been left alone in such an old house and he felt the pull of the past despite his own youth. It was the building of the house that interested him primarily and he longed to study the whole structure piece by piece to glean details of earlier methods and materials. Rufus, however, was more concerned with having a comfortable shower each morning, and, remembering this, Joe went willingly back to work in the less wholesome atmosphere of the lean-to, his mind occupied with plans to make a simple wooden settle as a practical expression of his gratitude for the chance he'd been given.

Looking around the shop for purposeful distraction from day-dreaming about Lily, Rufus suddenly noticed at the end of the counter a display box he hadn't bothered to examine before. Its banner read The Perfect Pagan Present and it contained a mixed collection of small square hardbacks in three rows. The top book on the first was called 'Circle Casting: how to create a sacred space', but it was the second that had caught his eye.

Unable to resist his curiosity, he reached out for 'A Little Book of Curses' with its striking red and black cover. All that hexing stuff *was* nonsense. He remembered from his dismal Latin lessons the lead tablets found at Bath inscribed with savage sentiments like "May Gallus' sperm rot" and "Let all Corinna's teeth fall out." Surely human society had evolved a little bit from then?

He had just opened the book at random to a page entitled "Make Your Boss Suffer" when he heard Tara's footsteps rushing down the stairs. She had kept up a cold silence since their recent difference of opinion and Rufus was anxious to re-establish peace between them. He thrust the book into his jacket pocket and tried to lean nonchalantly against the counter with a friendly expression on his face. It was a waste of effort. She simply brushed past him and out into the street without the least glimmer of recognition of his presence.

It was all too much, Rufus thought as he drove back to Mean Cottage. Fantasies of wreaking revenge on enemies and anyone who slighted you in everyday life might be the refuge of the weak and feeble, but there were times when they became alarmingly attractive and all one's notions of courtesy and good behaviour flew out of the window.

He had hated cruelty and injustice since childhood and the savage bickering of his parents which usually ended with one or the other turning on him as an easier target. In the last year of increasingly painful verbal tussles with Alison he'd become adept at parrying blows from her sharper, crueller wit but his own lunges with intent to draw blood were lamentably few. He lacked the killer instinct, the even temporary indifference to another's pain when roused by anger. Too sensitive for your own good, his mother used to say to him. You should give as good as you get, then they'll think twice. It was true enough, but he disliked the notion of using attack as an instinctive defence, of hitting out at others to protect yourself. If someone criticised him or made fun of him he was inclined to take it to heart and assume the worst about himself. People like Charlie couldn't give a toss about the good opinion of others, but, Rufus reluctantly had to admit, it did seem to matter a great deal to him.

He was pleased to get back to the cottage. His knee was hurting and he was looking forward to a large intake of alcohol for medicinal purposes. The late afternoon sun cast strong shadows across the straggly front lawn and the house looked calmly welcoming in the mellow light. It was actually quite appealing after the frustrating sort of day he'd had to get home to some peace and quiet - no-one to be polite to, no-one with expectations or demands to be satisfied. He gave a deep sigh of contentment as he went in.

The first thing he heard was voices in the kitchen.

After a fleeting moment of annoyance, he remembered that Joe was supposed to be working here and, when he realised the other voice was a woman's, Rufus' heart leapt at the prospect of seeing Lily again.

Joe was sitting at a makeshift table of breeze-blocks and a plank with a mug in his hand. He leapt up nervously when he saw Rufus as if ashamed at being caught slacking. The other person in the small room was the old woman, who was tinkering with the portable stove.

'Sit down and drink your tea,' she commanded Joe. 'You're a good worker and any fool can see that.' She waved the kettle dismissively in Rufus' direction as she spoke. Joe slunk back to his seat, one eye on Rufus for his reaction.

A glance round the room showed Rufus the extent of Joe's diligence. The old sink was now flanked by worktops with cupboards below and a couple of shelves above. Even the rough plastered walls looked cleaner and the window frame had been stripped of its flaking paint.

'It's fantastic,' Rufus said, twirling round to admire everything. 'Looks like a proper kitchen already. I don't know how you've managed to get so much done in the time. Well done, Joe.'

Joe's silent head hung low over his mug but Rufus thought he could detect a slight flush of pleasure around the nearest cheek stud. Then he turned to the old woman.

'And have you been helping?' he asked as facetiously as he dared.

A suspiciously sweet smile was all he got in reply, as she held out a steaming mug to him. The smell almost knocked him over backwards.

'What is it?'

'Tea.'

'Made of what?'

'Try it.'

It was the last thing he wanted to do. His stomach heaved as the smell wafted up into his nostrils, but he didn't want to offend this infuriating woman whom he found unaccountably scary. Swallowing hard, he blew quickly onto the dark liquid and took a tentative sip.

He held the hot liquid in his mouth for a second, conscious of Joe's anxious glance and the old woman's amused stare. Then he dashed over to the sink to spit it out and douse his mouth with cold water. As he gargled noisily he thought that he was going to have to find some way of keeping her out of his house. She'd either drive him mad or poison him before she was finished at this rate.

When he straightened up and turned back to the room, Joe was still at the table engrossed in picking at a splinter of wood in front of him. The old woman was

68

winding a long green silk scarf around her neck.

'Are you trying to get rid of me already?' he asked, not entirely in jest.

She gave a dismissive bark of laughter.

'If I was,' she said, 'you wouldn't still be here.'

Rufus didn't like the particular relish with which she said this, but his discomfort only seemed to amuse her more and she gave him an almost affectionate clap on the back as she passed him by the door.

'But that will actually do you some good,' she said, pointing at the teapot, 'so try to drink some.'

She went out with an affectionate nod to Joe.

Rufus limped over to the table and sat down.

'What is it with that woman that I always feel in the wrong?'

He was really speaking to himself, and was surprised to get a response from Joe.

'That's just her way.'

'Do you know her well?' Rufus was suddenly curious about the old woman's background.

'Everyone knows Cate. She's been in the village for ever.'

'And does she follow every newcomer around or have I been singled out for special attention?'

Joe contorted his face with the effort of thinking about this.

'I don't think it's you,' he said and then - apparently in a hurry to change the subject - 'what's wrong with your knee?'

'Oh, I twisted it badly a few days ago. Fell over when I was drunk actually,' Rufus added, assuming a jocular man to man tone.

Joe lowered his eyes.

'Sad,' he said and went back to drinking his tea.

After a meal and several large scotches to get over the disappointment of not seeing Lily again, Rufus felt better. The only way he knew of getting through bad patches was to make concrete plans and then carry them out religiously. One thing he really had to do was get his things from London. Despite his shaky start in Creech, Rufus knew he was not going back to the city. He'd try to stick it out at the shop and when Rita came back he'd - well, he didn't have the faintest idea what he'd do, but it was a long way off and he'd worry about it later. The odd bit of furniture, like a bed for instance, would greatly improve the comfort of Mean Cottage. There were a few things waiting in a friend's garage in Maida Vale, including some quite valuable antique pieces he'd bought long before he met Alison. They'd look pretty good in his new home he reckoned, once it was all cleaned up. He imagined his old yew chair with a comfortable cushion by the fireplace. As soon as his knee was better he'd make a start on some decoration and put his own mark on the place. It was time for some exertion and positive effort. He reached for his mobile phone.

'Hello, David. It's Rufus.'

'Rufus! Good to hear from you. How's it all going?'

This was surprisingly hearty for David, who was habitually saturnine. Rufus felt a twinge of uneasiness.

'I'm fine, settling in well. You and Jane?'

'Absolutely fine. No problems at all.'

Now Rufus knew there was something wrong.

'I was just thinking about the furniture and getting it down here as soon as possible now things are sorting themselves out at this end. I expect you'll be glad to have your garage back!'

'Oh, there's no hurry on that score, no hurry at all, except, well, the thing is... in fact...'

'In fact what? Are you alright, David?'

'Yes, yes, it's just that, you see, I don't quite know how to... Ah, right, handing you over to Jane now. Hope it all goes well. Bye, Rufus.'

'Jane?'

He'd known Jane since university, far longer than he'd known Alison or any of his other friends except Charlie. She was loyal, direct and totally trustworthy.

'Hi, Roo. What my bumbling, inarticulate husband was trying to say is that thanks to him we've already got our garage back. Alison came round here last week, apparently to pick up some small thing you'd taken by mistake.'

Rufus grabbed wildly at the bottle of scotch.

'And?'

'And David gave her the garage key and went out, leaving her to it. And she's taken most of it. All the good bits anyway.'

'My oak dining table?'

'Certainly. And that lovely yew chair from your old study.'

'Shit.'

'As you say. But she always was a prize bitch, Roo, though you refused to see it for all those years. You're well rid of her.'

But not my furniture, Rufus thought dejectedly, as he listened to Jane warming to her theme of Alison's perfidy at some length. He was soothed by the fierceness of her attack and wondered not just how he would have managed without all her support in the terrible weeks after his wife walked out, but also how different his life would have been with such a staunch partner.

'You're not going to let her get away with it, are you?'

'Well, I don't know quite what I can do...'

Rufus imagined trying to physically wrest his possessions from his resolute wife and the basset hound

71

and did not fancy his chances.

'For God's sake, you can't just lie down and let her walk all over you!' Jane yelled.

Rufus held the phone away from his ear and looked around the room while she ranted on. He stretched out a hand to pick something up from the camp bed where it had fallen. Something he'd forgotten all about. A ridiculous idea leapt into his head. It made him think that all his rational faculties, of which he'd once been rather proud, were being steadily undermined, if not actually eroded, by the influences of his new life. On the other hand, it would certainly be more satisfying than the crush of Alison's heel on his head as he lay prostrate before her.

He tuned back in to what Jane was saying.

'...why you never stood up to her, I can't imagine. She's just an emotional bully who won't stop till she's got your balls on a stick. Where's it going to end if you let her get away with this?'

'Don't worry,' Rufus said, 'I've no intention of doing so.'

Jane stopped her tirade abruptly at his decisive tone.

'Well, I'm delighted to hear it. What are you going to do?'

'Something rather unusual,' said Rufus, looking down with a smile at the little red and black book in his hand.

Chapter 5

He was ashamed of his folly in the morning, but soon forgot about it during the next week as the town got busier and busier with daily coach parties and families on holiday. Suddenly the shop seemed busy throughout the day and he had little time on his hands to dwell on Alison's treachery or his yearning for Lily, for that matter. Tara's hostility thawed suddenly without explanation and she was in an alarmingly sunny mood, relaxed with Rufus and ruthlessly charming to clients. He barely recognised her with a constant smile on her face.

'How's Joe doing at your place?' she asked in a brief lull.

'Great. He's made the kitchen look like one. The bathroom, however, is a greater challenge.'

'He'll do it. He does everything well.'

Rufus reddened slightly and looked away from her glowing eyes. She and Joe had obviously reached some new height of pleasurable experience and Rufus very much did not want to know what it was, especially as thoughts of sex only brought striking images of Joe's mother into his mind.

'Yes, he's very talented. Does he get that from his mother?'

'Not exactly. She's a healer.'

'A what? You mean, like a doctor?'

'Absolutely nothing like a doctor. They just stuff you with anti-biotics to get rid of your symptoms. Lily treats the whole person, you know, mind, body and spirit. Even you must have heard of holistic medicine?'

'Of course I have.' He was stung by her sarcasm and at the same time foolishly disappointed to find the object of his new-found desires was what, only a couple of weeks ago, he would have called a crank.

Tara thought for a moment.

'But then I suppose in a way you could say that Joe's healing your house,' she said.

Rufus considered the image for a moment, then looked at Tara with renewed admiration.

'Yes, that's a good way to put it. I like that.'

They smiled at each other, restored to harmony.

'What about Joe's father?' Rufus asked casually.

'Oh, Joe's dad's an artist, a really brilliant one. But he went off with a ballerina when Joe was ten, so he hasn't been around for ever.'

Secretly thrilled by this news that Lily had been abandoned by Joe's father, Rufus asked if Joe still saw him.

'Not very often. He lives in Scotland in some kind of artistic community. Joe's been up there once, but he didn't like it much.'

Rufus looked at Tara with concern in his face.

'I suppose it must be hard, you know, a single parent family,' he said, as empathetically as he could manage about something he'd never even considered before.

Tara glared at him fiercely.

'There you go getting personal again.'

'What?' Rufus was horrified at the swiftness of this volte-face. 'I was only wondering...'

'Just because my dear mother has swanned off with your slimy mate...'

'What are you talking about? I was just curious about Joe!'

'Joe?' She sounded confused for a second.

An old lady was approaching the till, laden with enough smudge sticks to envelop the whole of Bruford in a thick haze for a week.

'But Joe's got a perfectly good step-dad,' Tara said, as she turned a beaming smile on the customer.

She wasn't so happy when Rufus had gone out later and she sat on the stool behind the counter, chewing her nails and thinking with subdued fury about her own father. She had thought for a minute that Rufus was trying to patronise her with sympathy in a clumsy sort of way, but on reflection she realised it was possible he didn't even know about that scum-bag loser and his serial entanglements with women. Rita had been an early link in the chain and he had already moved in with someone else by the time Tara was born. Tara followed her mother's lead in never mentioning him, although there was plenty of external evidence of his existence in the fact that Tara had a litter of assorted half-siblings to endure when she'd been at school. Her lips tightened in anger as she remembered the humiliation of it. She'd have nothing to do with a single one of them and turned her back on the bastard himself on the very rare occasions their paths crossed in Huddlebridge where he lived now with wife number four - and counting. But it was weird sometimes, to know well enough who your father was and yet not know anything about him. But then, it wasn't as if he'd ever shown the slightest interest in her either.

Although she always feigned weariness with her mother's frequent tirades against the entire clan of males, Tara secretly feared that she might in fact be right. Why, in that case, Rita continued to take up with one tosser after another, she wasn't sure, unless it was just for the sex. It wasn't what she wanted for herself, but Joe was different, of course, and Tara was beginning to think maybe Rufus wasn't so bad. That was as far as it went, though. She wasn't going to go soft over a couple of exceptions to the general rule of dickheads.

Rufus sat on a bench by the river to eat the sandwich he'd bought for lunch. When Joe finished the kitchen would be time enough to get properly organized about food and stop wasting his money at Buns in the Oven.

He couldn't stop thinking about the existence of Joe's step-father - and Lily's husband, presumably. It would have been extraordinary if such a woman were single, of course, but Lily carried with her an air of freedom and Rufus had just thought of her as unattached.

A large blob of egg fell onto his knee and he began to dab at it ineffectually with a handkerchief.

It reminded him, ruefully, that she wouldn't have looked twice in his direction in any case.

'Well, if it isn't my rival bookseller!'

To his horror Rufus looked up at Neville King looming over him. He lost control of his baguette which sprayed bits of egg and bacon around like machine gun fire as he stood up too quickly.

'No, don't get up on my account.'

King held up a long-fingered hand and then sat down at the other end of the bench, stretching out his crossed legs. Sitting down again, Rufus glanced out of the corner of his eye at the spotted bow-tie and well-tailored linen jacket and then at a line of pink neck above the collar. The man looked extraordinarily clean, he thought, as if he'd just stepped out of a hot bath or been polished with one of those attachments from the carwash. Rufus was suddenly conscious in contrast that his reluctance to spend any time at all in his mouldy little bathroom at Mean Cottage might be starting to affect his own personal hygiene.

'And how is business down at the sharp end?'

There was an unpleasant smirk on King's face.

'Good,' said Rufus firmly. 'We've been run off our feet

this morning. I'm glad to get out for a rest.'

'That little tart helping you out, is she?' The words were deliberately suggestive.

Rufus kept his temper in check with effort.

'Tara's certainly been a great help'.

Neville King rested his neck on the back of the seat and squinted up at the fiery sun.

'I'll bet she has,' he said with a silly half-laugh. 'They say her mother's a witch, you know - she's certainly been up to a few tricks in her time, but whether they were magic or not, I couldn't say from personal experience.'

Rufus suppressed an instinctive defence of Rita, whom he'd never met, after all, and of whom he had hardly formed a much higher opinion than that of this obnoxious creep. He remained silent, ramming the baguette into his mouth and chewed furiously in his anxiety to finish and get away.

'So you're into all this alternative stuff yourself, I suppose?' King went on.

It sounded more like a sneer than a question.

'No, not really,' he said, whilst wishing totally irrationally that he was, and had the knowledge and experience to defend something, anything, from this particular opponent. 'It has positives and negatives like everything else, I should think.'

It was a half-hearted attempt that seemed to please King no end.

'Ah, a man who likes to sit on the fence! Or is this New Man speak for the Age of Aquarius? How is it that any sane person...'

As King began to expound his derogatory views on alternative religion, Rufus concentrated on finishing his lunch and watching the coots on the river. He'd heard it all before - in fact it was exactly the sort of thing he'd have expressed himself, this blind confidence of intellectual superiority in the face of something based on instinct. It was only hearing his own prejudices and ignorance from the mouth of the objectionable Mr King that made Rufus realise what an arrogant prick he must have sounded to Tara when they quarrelled about elemental forces and electricity. He sighed. How could he start a new life with the same old ideas still firmly engrained, dependent as they usually were on received wisdom and without a spark of his own experience or understanding? Perhaps it was time to find things out for himself.

A direct gibe broke into his gloomy thoughts as King turned to face him.

'And tell me, will you be deputising for Rita at the goddess festival this year?'

Rufus nearly choked on the last of his sandwich.

'The what?'

'Oh, it's an important part of town culture now. Every year women come from all over the world to worship the goddess and every year the town turns out to laugh themselves silly at the sight of them. I can just picture you with your thyrsus in the leading wagon...'

Rufus' fear of the reality of this image prompted him to anger although he fought to keep his tone neutral.

'I don't think symbols of the god Dionysus would be very suitable at a goddess ritual, do you?' he said. 'Except in the sense that his worship in Greece was a reaction against the old patriarchal religious structures - perhaps that's what you meant?' Rufus looked innocently at his adversary. It wasn't difficult to play this empty academic game, spouting meaningless words he'd read in a book somewhere. It was nothing like the deep, visceral reaction he had experienced in his dream about the moon garden. The memory of that powerful feeling of connection with something elemental flashed back through him now, but he had no time to assimilate it.

King got to his feet, scowling at Rufus' challenge.

'I only meant you'll look pretty stupid,' he said and stalked off along the riverbank.

Rufus sat on, pleased that he had felt able to give a stirring response under extreme provocation. Once he would have laughed meekly at a joke against himself - he'd had plenty of early practice as the butt of his mother's wit - but he was starting to feel tired of justifying his existence in the face of others' needs and creeping about, side-stepping their bad moods. His parents were always so absorbed in their private struggle that he often wondered why they'd bothered to have him at all. His mother had hinted once, in a particularly foul mood, that it had been a mistake and by the time she found out it was too late to do anything about it. His father said little to him at any time and ignored or was openly exasperated by any overtures Rufus had made as a child or an adult, but it was the venom of his mother's tongue that Rufus always feared. He grew up with a strong sense of peripheral existence and the need to keep on the right side of other people.

The last few years with Alison had been full of delicate evasions and extracted apologies on his part. It was only now that he realised the extent of his compromises and how unhappy it had made him. One thing was forming into a hard certainty inside him - it was a role he wouldn't play again.

He mulled over Alison's latest perfidy, which had wounded him deeply. The loss of his furniture was something he would have felt powerless to deal with a few weeks ago, but now he knew a sudden determination not to put up with it. She knew damn well what those pieces meant to him and still thought nothing of stealing them. That was the level of respect she had for his feelings now, was it?

No longer feeling like eating, he threw the heel of bread into the water and let the ducks compete for it. He would phone Alison later and if she wanted a fight, he'd give her one.

Joe was still working away on his transformation of the bathroom.

'No-one to make your tea today then?' said Rufus thankfully as he put the kettle on.

'Cate was here earlier. She left something for you on the table,' Joe called out.

It was a bottle, its contents murky through the brown glass.

'What's in it?' Rufus held the bottle at arm's length as if it was a hand grenade about to go off.

Joe stuck his head round the door.

'Some sort of tonic, I think. She noticed you limping yesterday.'

'There's nothing wrong with me,' said Rufus, wincing as he spun round to pour water into the mugs.

'My mum's on your case, too.'

'On my case?'

'About your knee.' He looked at his watch. 'She'll be here soon.'

Rufus tried to conceal his glee by fussing with the tea.

'That's very kind of her, but I'm sure it'll soon pass with a bit of rest. I haven't had much chance to sit down today, unfortunately,' he said.

Joe just shrugged and disappeared into the bathroom with his mug.

Rufus sat in silence, imagining that the whole room throbbed to the rapid thump of his heart at the thought of Lily's arrival, perhaps her cool hand on his skin...

She arrived with a light tap on the back door and a

ravishing smile for Rufus, who stood up too quickly in greeting and fell forwards into her as his tired knee gave way. Lily caught his arms and they did a little caper together before she could manoeuvre him back onto the kitchen chair. Rufus fumed with frustration.

'It's no better, then?' Lily asked.

'I don't want to make a fuss,' he replied. Neither do I want to make a fool of myself in front of this wonderful woman, he thought miserably, even if she has got some hulking great husband.

'I've brought something that will help, but you need to put the leg up. What about a lower chair? In the other room?'

She went through to the living room with him and settled Rufus comfortably in the old armchair before unpacking her hessian bag.

'It's really very good of you,' he said awkwardly. 'I'm not used to being looked after.' It was true. Any whiff of illness as a child had been taken as a sign of malingering and Alison's brusqueness when he had a severe bout of flu had disabused him of notions of the comfort to be had from kindly nursing. The gentleness with which Lily was propping up his foot on a cushion and carefully pushing up his trouser leg brought a lump to his throat, not from the sexual desire he had expected to feel at her touch, but simple childish longing for this type of loving care. She looked up at him at that instant with such kindness in her bright eyes that Rufus felt she had understood his thoughts.

'Now, I'm going to rub some of this cream in. You just take it easy.'

It wasn't difficult. Rufus closed his eyes and relaxed his back muscles into the cushion behind him. His mind was gloriously filled with the sense of her nearness and the gentle pressure of her fingers, delicately massaging a cool embrocation into his swollen knee. Everything else was gone - Alison, Neville King, the ridiculous shop - he was alone with Lily in a roseate universe, drifting inside a huge pink bubble above fields, woods and streams, innocently naked and weightless, free to roll over and over...

'That should do it, but you must rest. Sit like this with your leg up this evening. Next time I collect Joe we'll have another go, OK?'

'Yes, thank you. It's really kind of you to take so much trouble.'

'No problem. I'm so grateful to you for giving Joe a chance to work here. He's been much happier the last few days.'

'It was Tara's idea,' he said. 'I wouldn't dare deny that young lady anything.'

They both laughed.

'I haven't sorted out Joe's wages yet...' Rufus began, but Lily brushed the detail aside with a little wave of her hand.

'The money's not important,' she said. 'He'll be glad of whatever you give him. But the opportunity to do something he cares about will have an enormous effect. And the fact you've just left everything to him and trusted his knowledge and judgement is worth more than any price you put on his labour. I can't tell you how much that's meant to him.'

'That's just down to my own ignorance, I'm afraid.' Rufus wanted to be honest. 'I haven't really got a clue about home improvements, but I saw the look on Joe's face when he saw the old boards upstairs.'

'Exactly.' Lily leaned forward and put a hand on his wrist. 'You saw something in Joe, not his appearance or his clothes but his essence, his true self, and you honoured it. There's no greater gift you can give another human being.'

Rufus shifted uneasily. He didn't feel he deserved this amount of praise for giving the kid a few quid in return for labour, but the idea itself appealed to him.

'Do you really believe that?' he asked almost shyly.

'Of course. The even harder thing is to honour ourselves though. And that's something we have to find out before we can truly give to others. I learnt that lesson a long time ago, but it was painful. It's so easy to convince ourselves that as long as we are trying to make others happy we are doing the right thing. But it's not, not without paying ourselves an equal regard. It meant the end of a relationship in my case. What about you?'

'Me?' He was startled.

She laughed lightly, but there was a serious note in her question.

'Do you honour your own desires?'

If only he had the opportunity, thought Rufus, remembering the pink bubble and the freedom of their flesh. But he knew that she was stirring a deeper feeling than that superficial, laddish reaction. It was a fair question in his present situation.

'I don't really know what they are these days. Life seems to have changed so radically in the last few months. My wife left me for someone else and I gave up my business to get away from London. I've just been struggling to keep my head above water really. Thinking about what I actually want has never been much of a priority.'

Rufus was amazed to find he wasn't embarrassed to say this to Lily. Something in the quality of her attention made him feel safe and unexposed. There was no judgement, no appraisal in her face, but only a sympathetic interest in his situation and his feelings - the greatest luxury imaginable, it seemed to him. He hadn't looked directly at her as he spoke and now risked raising his eyes to meet hers. They held each other's glance for a moment.

'Perhaps the time has come now,' she said quietly. 'What could be more important?'

Rufus thought about Lily's words long after she and Joe had left. He sat in the armchair, his knee, so pleasantly painless since Lily's healing touch, comfortably supported on a footstool, and a large glass of whisky in his hand. She was right, of course, but it took courage to put aside layers of conditioning about selfishness and notions of bad behaviour to stand up for one's own well-being against the demands of others. He had tiptoed around his parents throughout his childhood and tried to be considerate to Alison's needs in their marriage. The fact that he had failed in the latter case now seemed less important than the fact that he'd done his best, often at the cost of his own wishes and inclinations.

And now, in the matter of his furniture, she was treating him with such total disregard that Rufus' innate sense of fair play, coupled with Lily's promptings about honouring his own desires, threatened to lay waste at last his adherence to concepts of what was due to the woman he had loved and respected as his wife.

He suddenly heard the muffled squeak of his mobile phone and realised after a frantic look around the room that he must be sitting on it. Squirming from side to side, he extricated it with difficulty and flicked on the call, registering Alison's number on the display as he did so.

'Not disturbing you, am I?'

She didn't sound as if she cared particularly one way or the other.

'No, it's fine. I was going to call you later. About my furniture.'

The underlying aggression in his voice must have surprised her, as she faltered for a moment.

'I...'

'Yes? You what?' He was quite determined not to let her off the hook.

'I was going to talk to you about it,' she said evenly, 'but then we were round at Jane's to get my things and it seemed pointless to make another trip...'

'Hold on. There wouldn't have been any need for another trip. You could just have taken your stuff and left mine alone!' Even she can't argue with the logic of that, he thought with satisfaction. Far from being his usual inarticulate self, thanks to the whisky and thoughts of Lily's understanding face, he felt positively lucid.

Alison certainly seemed taken aback by his forcefulness.

'But the furniture was getting damp in that garage, Rufus, and it's not as if you've anywhere to put it, is it?'

'You know I've bought a place here!'

'Yes, but you can't put good things in some grotty hovel. Brian says...'

Brian the bloody basset hound!

'Fuck Brian! This is absolutely NOTHING to do with him!' Rufus yelled. 'And this cottage, far from being a grotty hovel, is a beautiful, ancient dwelling place, well on the way to full renovation and feeling a great deal more like a proper home than I've known before.'

He knew that he had shocked her by this uncharacteristic outburst and the thought gave him nothing but pleasure.

Her voice when it came was tight and sour.

'Well, I think you've made all that pretty clear, so there's nothing much left to say, is there?'

If she was hurt, good, it was about time he made some dent in her emotional armour. Rufus steeled himself to carry on as he'd begun.

'No, except that I shall expect you to organise a van and get my furniture delivered here within the next seven days.'

There was a moment's silence. He thought he heard her

swallow hard at this belligerence, but Alison was only gathering her resources.

'You can whistle for your precious furniture!' she hissed and cut the connection.

Rufus got up to fetch the whisky bottle and found himself staggering into the kitchen. Perhaps he had had enough to drink, but the adrenalin of his confrontation with Alison was draining away already, only to be replaced by anxiety at the thought of the battle to come. He poured another large slug and drank it straight down. It made his eyes water but did nothing to restore his spirits. Then he noticed the bottle the old woman had left. Surely she wouldn't try to poison him so obviously? He unscrewed the top gingerly and sniffed the contents. The smell was not bad at all, nothing like the obnoxious tea she had given him before. In fact, in his sozzled state, he found the fruity tones quite attractive and took a tentative sip, licked his lips and then tipped his head back to gurgle down some more.

He stumbled back into the sitting room, still clutching the brown bottle. No, he wasn't going to let Alison get away with it. Not this time.

There on the table was the little book of curses with its black and red cover. He sat down and opened it. His head was feeling woozy and light as he turned to the page he wanted, which he read through once with some difficulty. After another couple of swigs, he tried again. On this second attempt the words seemed to metamorphose into strange dancing symbols as if he was trying to follow the patterns in a kaleidoscope.

A sudden hot, melting sensation in his stomach and a wave of nausea passed through him with a single shiver and a large hiccup. After that he began to feel marvellous: strength and vigour swept over him. He got up and strode about the room maniacally, seeking an outlet for the energy coursing through his veins. Even his knee felt strong enough for a marathon.

Waving the bottle around, he began to list Alison's crimes under his breath and then more loudly until he was shouting to compete with the noise coming from the garden...

Rufus stopped suddenly and stood still, listening through the wild pounding of blood in his ears. It came again almost at once, the long-drawn thin wail of an abandoned beast. He ripped back the flimsy curtain and there in the vegetable patch was the unmistakable outline of the same blue dog.

This time Rufus hurried outside without hesitation, fuelled by alcohol and the old woman's mysterious potion, full of excitement, curses still ringing inside his head. The dog had disappeared, but Rufus went straight through the orchard to the brick wall. He stepped through the rounded entrance, prepared for dancing figures in the moonlight, prepared for anything, but all he saw was the decaying garden, barely visible in the dim grey light. Frustrated, he looked up at the sky and the dark cloud trailing across the surface of the moon.

'Come on, Moon,' he entreated. 'I need you to throw light on a very important subject.' He giggled at his own wit, carelessly slurping from the bottle so that liquid dribbled down his chin.

As if in obedience to his will, the cloud sped past and the garden suddenly flooded with a sweep of silver.

He flung down the bottle and waved his arms around like a delighted baby as the moonbeam soared from mirror to pond, and the silvered plants rose up, stretching themselves towards a new source of life.

Rufus began to lumber across the stone slabs in ungainly imitation of the dancers he had seen before, muttering the words of the curse to himself and laughing.

When his clumsy pirouettes brought him to the radiant circle at the centre of the garden he stopped and gazed upwards at the moon as it seemed to hang there, huge in the sky, for his benefit alone.

He wagged a finger in the air.

'My wife,' he said sadly, 'my wife has treated me very, very badly. She left me, she took away my home and everything and now, now she's stolen my furniture! But that's a bridge too far!'

Rufus threw his arms up high above his head.

'I'm going to get her back for that! Revenge! Revenge!'

A sense of power surged through him. Not wanting to stop now he was in the pleasurable swing of things, he gave an idle wave of his hand in the direction of Creech.

'And a plague on all your houses,' he yelled finally.

Chapter 6

Rufus woke the next morning with a blinding headache. It was all he could do to get out of the camp bed, limp to the bathroom and splash cold water on his throbbing temples. He couldn't remember anything beyond drinking that wretched tonic; presumably it had reacted badly with all the alcohol and he'd passed out.

He struggled to dress, make coffee and then get himself out to the car. The vibration of the engine sent juddering waves of pain circling round his head as he made for Bruford and he needed sunglasses to protect his eyes even so early in the morning.

He was relying on Tara to cover the afternoon in the shop as he had to buy furniture and appliances for the cottage. A bed was top priority now that Joe had fixed the staircase. Rufus wondered vaguely why Joe hadn't turned up that morning, as Lily usually dropped him off outside before 8.30. He couldn't face anything going wrong on that score, now that the house was beginning to take shape so well. Still, Tara certainly wouldn't be slow to tell him if there was any problem.

She didn't appear downstairs until after 11, looking even paler than usual without the eye-liner and black lipstick.

'Joe's ill,' she said. 'Can you give me a lift over to Creech to see him?'

'After work, sure. What's the matter with him?'

'No, now. I want to see him.'

'No, not now, Tara. What about the shop, customers, that sort of thing, you know?'

She tossed her head at the insignificance of his priorities and then seemed to notice him properly for the first time.

'You look pretty terrible yourself. Perhaps we should just close up for the day?'

It was ridiculously tempting. All Rufus wanted was to be horizontal and close his eyes.

'Definitely not,' he said.

'But he's ill. He might need stuff.'

'I'm sure his mother is quite capable of looking after Joe,' Rufus said firmly, remembering the touch of Lily's hands as she massaged his knee.

'She's ill, too,' Tara said.

'What?'

Rufus was startled into betraying a greater anxiety than was prudent.

Tara looked at him closely.

'Yeah, must be a bug or something,' she said with a knowing little smile which infuriated him. 'You could always go over and hold her hand if it's Lily you're worried about.'

'Nonsense.' He tried to make a joke of it. 'Not in my interests for Joe to be ill, is it? I want the house finished!'

She said nothing, just went on looking at him.

'Oh, for God's sake,' he snapped, 'you're supposed to be looking after things this afternoon, remember?'

Tara screwed up her face in an effort of concentration.

'OK. Here's the deal. You go out now and get your stuff this morning, then shut for half an hour at lunch time and take me to Joe's.'

'I suppose I could.'

'You'll get to see Lily then too.'

'Shut up, Tara,' Rufus said.

Lily lived in a semi-detached brick cottage at the far end of Creech. Hanging baskets of petunias and a bamboo wind-chime decorated the porch and bright curtains hung at the two downstairs windows.

When she came to the door, Lily did look dreadful, amazing though that seemed for someone so beautiful, Rufus thought. All the vibrant colours of her skin, hair and eyes were faded by the lacklustre tones of malaise. He wanted to throw his arms round her and make her better somehow.

'Hello. I'm sorry you're not well,' he said.

Tara pushed past him and after briefly laying a sympathetic hand on Lily's arm, ran up the stairs to see Joe.

Lily grimaced.

'I'm nothing like as bad as Joe. He's had a rotten night.'

She stayed in the doorway and did not ask him in.

'What do you think it is?' Rufus asked.

'I've no idea, but it's pretty virulent. Half the village have gone down sick this morning. I've been out twice with remedies already.'

'You poor thing. Someone should be looking after you,' he said longingly.

She smiled at his concern.

'Thanks, Rufus, but I'll be fine. Now Tara's here I can stop running up and down stairs with things for Joe for a bit at least.'

'Can I do anything for you?'

He was looking for an excuse to stay, but Lily shook her head.

'No, you get on, but thanks for the offer. I appreciate it.'

A phone began ringing in the hall behind her.

'That'll be another sufferer, I expect. I'd better go.'

She must have noticed his desolation.

'See you soon, Rufus.' She leaned forward quickly and kissed his cheek. 'And thanks.'

Cate had spent a disturbed night, full of unsettling dreams. She remained in a state of apprehension as she got up and looked from her upstairs window over a restless sea of willow, stirred by the sharp breeze under a swirl of grey clouds. It was not at all the weather she had been expecting that morning, and she hurried to dress and get outside. Then she knew at once that something was wrong. The air was full of messages, heavy with a burden of agitated thoughts and distressed feelings. She wondered what on earth had happened to cause this commotion. She could envisage one explanation, if Rufus had made the discoveries she had been waiting for. She shook her head vexatiously. He was far from ready and, in the wrong frame of mind, might have unleashed all sorts of ill-disciplined powers. But was she to interfere, to involve herself in his tribulations and save him from whatever folly he might indulge in? Cate folded her arms across her chest, hands tucked tightly under her armpits, and walked slowly around the garden, her mind reluctant for change and disruption in her own life. A bird began to chirp vociferously in the laurel bush beside her. She stopped her pacing to listen for a moment and then sighed resignedly as her thoughts crystallized. It was not a role she would have chosen, but she would do what was necessary. She might owe nothing to Rufus, but there was someone else who did have claims on her with regard to the cottage and its occupants.

Rufus stopped in the centre of the village to buy some lunch.

It was the first time he'd braved the locals since his ominous visit to The Green Man and he had a good look round for loose dogs before crossing the road, but there was only a man pushing a wheelbarrow full of dead rabbits to nod a greeting. The general store had a freshly painted jaunty red and white façade and the sparkling clean window revealed a lavish display of pasta, jars of olives, pesto and small bottles of truffle oil all artfully arranged around a selection of woven baskets.

He pushed open the door, entered the empty shop and stopped in surprise. He had the strangest feeling that he had been transported in that one step from Creech to a bijou delicatessen on Chiswick High Road.

Swags of dried hops and plastic ivy adorned the rustic wooden counter and upper shelves. Wooden trugs and half barrels all over the floor were filled with red-skinned potatoes, mounds of lentils and one extraordinary extravagant structure of fennel. In a large cool display unit Rufus noticed at a single glance Roquefort, buffalo mozzarella, parma ham and several types of Polish sausage. Inching forward to investigate further, he nearly knocked over a baker's basket packed with olive bread, ciabatta and fresh croissants. It was all startlingly familiar to him, but he couldn't help wondering how the residents of Creech felt about it. He couldn't imagine that old woman, Cate, buying kumquats or tapenade here.

'Good morning!'

A woman's voice hailed him from the ether. Rufus jumped about a foot in the air and looked round wildly for its source.

A head was appearing slowly from beneath the counter, a head topped with a mop of black and silver curls, shortly followed by a long, sausage-shaped body draped with a gleaming white apron with thick red stripes. The face was highly coloured - to the extent that Rufus wondered if its owner had already had a glass or two that day - with mottled patches of lighter skin around her eyes and forehead. She had a large nose and a large mouth which stretched into a smile to reveal large, strong teeth.

'Good morning,' he said, somewhat dazed by her peculiar appearance.

'Sorry' - she gave a hearty laugh - 'I was hiding.'

He resisted the temptation to ask her why.

'What can I get you?' This time her words were accompanied by a winsome smile and fluttering eyelids.

A instant irritation at her exaggerated mannerisms rose in Rufus.

'Just a sandwich, if you have any,' he said brusquely.

'I can make you up today's special. It's gorgonzola and watercress on walnut bread.'

It was about the last filling he'd have chosen for himself but he did not want to prolong the transaction. He had seen her cast a glance at his left hand to check for a wedding ring (which he had never worn) and now she was eyeing him avidly as if he might prove the answer to a prayer.

'Fine.' He turned his back on her and pretended to be interested in the labelling of adzuki beans while he waited.

'Do you come here often?' She laughed gaily as if this was a tremendously amusing joke. 'I mean, I haven't seen you in Creech before.'

He watched her big red hands wrapping his sandwich in greaseproof paper.

'No, I've just moved down here.'

He was reluctant to say more.

'From London? Please let it be from London!'

As she spoke she clasped her hands together across her bosom and raised her eyes heavenwards.

'Yes, as it happens.' Rufus was embarrassed by her performance and wished he'd never come in.

'Thank God for that! An oasis of sanity beckons!'

She strode round the counter to present him with his package and held out a red, beefy hand.

'Jacinta Jacobs. I'm delighted to meet you.'

She gave a brief glance over his shoulder, tensed from head to foot and then scuttled back behind the counter where she crouched down out of sight.

'Say I'm not here,' she hissed in a stage whisper.

He turned to see what had frightened her. Cate was passing the door of the shop. He smiled to think that someone was more scared of the old woman than he was.

'It's OK. She's not coming in,' he said, although he had not liked the glint in those fierce grey eyes when Cate saw him inside.

Before Rufus emerged exhausted from the shop ten minutes later, he felt he had already known Jacinta for rather too long. She told him that her husband had left her, but paid dearly for his desertion financially by setting her up in this shop. Where she assumed - Rufus assumed - that all you did with a shop was put things you liked in it. In reality she was terrified of the locals, lived alone in the flat above and would be more than happy to offer him dinner any night he chose or every night for that matter as she was never doing anything else. She clearly regarded Rufus as a heaven sent potential toy boy.

Rufus regarded her as a rather stupid woman who had made a dreadful mistake in leaving the safety of SW7 and who must be avoided at all costs.

A perverse little voice in his head could not refrain from pointing out that she was merely another refugee from the metropolis, out on a limb in a new strange life and in need of a little company, just as he was. But he refused to acknowledge any parallels with his own situation and returned to the car with his headache revived and a grim determination never to set foot in the village shop again.

As he fumbled with his car keys, he felt a nudge on the seat of his trousers and swung round in fear of an assault by Jacinta to find a goat trying to rummage in his back pocket. It was a handsome animal, with a strong head

95

striped like a badger and two stubby horns. The goat sniffed up at the greaseproof paper packet Rufus was holding high in one hand, but seemed less interested in this than in rubbing itself fondly against any part of Rufus' body it could reach. When he tried to push the amorous neck of the goat away with his other hand, its little yellow eyes looked up at him in sad reproach.

An elderly man wearing what looked like a white judge's wig came along the pavement with three big dogs at his heels. Rufus recognised them at once and decided this was not the time to remonstrate with their master for past misdemeanours. He instinctively tried to manoeuvre himself as far as possible from the dogs, behind the protective barrier of car and goat. The goat turned to glare at these rivals for Rufus' attention. Rufus recoiled nervously as the old man stepped into the road to get a better view of the tussle with the goat, but his panting dogs showed no interest in the proceedings whatsoever, and not a flicker of recognition of their former prey. Rufus wondered fleetingly if he had imagined the earlier incident, until he remembered having to buy a new jacket.

'Bloody nuisance, goats,' the old man was saying. 'Can give you a nasty bite if you're not careful. Give me a dog any day.'

He then made off smartly up the alley, dogs closely to heel, as the goat seemed inclined to take offence at that remark.

With the distraction, Rufus finally managed to put a couple of inches of air between himself and his admirer, squeezed into the car and pulled the door to quickly. He looked back in the mirror as he drove off. Jacinta Jacobs was outside her shop waving a lavish farewell and the goat was standing in the middle of the road miserably watching the receding car.

Jacinta was thinking that perhaps things were looking up in Creech. Rufus was a bit younger than her - well, alright, a lot younger - but he was charming and very presentable compared to the farm workers and young tykes who seemed to make up most of the population. How she hated it here! How she loathed the slow progress of each working day, trying to be pleasant, to make polite remarks, when all she longed to do was run upstairs and hide.

It was astonishing how marginalized one could be in a small place like this, where no-one was interested in what went on beyond the borders of the village. She had been shocked to find that many inhabitants of Creech had been no further than Huddlebridge - a good thirty miles - and NEVER as far as London. It was beyond belief that such people existed. But someone to talk to properly, someone who knew her own world, even geographically, would make such a difference to the quality of her life. And Rufus *was* different and really rather nice-looking in a cuddly sort of way...

Rufus thought he might as well go home to Mean Cottage to have his lunch and then go back to open the shop for the afternoon.

He flung open the back door intending to eat his sandwich outside on the bench overlooking the vegetable garden. Someone had beaten him to it. The old woman was comfortably installed, head back against the wall, eyes closed on the warmth of the sun, cigarette smoking away between her fingers.

'You're back early,' she said without moving a muscle. 'Not sick, are you?'

'No, I'm fine. Just looking for a bit of peace and quiet in my own home,' Rufus said pointedly.

She opened her eyes and gave him a steady gaze.

'Then I'll leave you to it.'

She got up, picked up the basket from the bench beside her and stepped past him.

'I'm glad this seems to have done the trick.'

Rufus turned round to see her holding up an empty brown bottle. He looked quickly at the kitchen door - had she been inside the house? Surely not - Joe wasn't there to let her in and the door had been locked when he came through.

'Where did you get that?'

'Over there.' She pointed in the direction of the moon garden.

Rufus rubbed the palm of his hand hard across his forehead. Had he gone outside last night? It was possible, he supposed.

'And I found that too.' Cate pointed at something she'd left on the bench. He recognised the black and red cover at once. Discomfort washed over him and he wondered whether to risk denying all knowledge of the book.

'You should be more careful,' she said levelly. 'A lot of people in the village are sick today.'

Rufus guffawed hollowly.

'What's that got to do with me?' he said. 'And may I ask why exactly you've been traipsing around my garden in my absence?'

She took a step closer and fixed him with her steely grey glare.

'You've a lot to learn,' she said thoughtfully. 'But anything's possible.' She looked him up and down. 'The house seems to like you. But until you know what you're doing, be more careful about what you ask for. Those sort of powers carry a lot of responsibility.'

'I haven't got a clue what you're talking about.' Rufus felt his dignity receding fast in the face of her insouciance.

She was very close now. He caught a faint scent of sandalwood mingled with tobacco. He could see that his protests made no impression on her whatsoever.

'You were out there last night, Rufus,' she said softly. 'You called down the moon and your words were empowered. Be careful of the consequences, I say.'

'That's ridiculous.' Rufus laughed. He needed to break the spell of her proximity and the seriousness of her expression. 'I had too much to drink and I let off steam about my dear wife who ruined my old life and is now doing all she can to spoil the new one. Such as it is.' His voice wobbled slightly on the last words. 'Even if you *could* harm people with spells and mumbo-jumbo, I didn't say anything about anyone else...' A cruel flash of memory made him stop. His foolish rider to the curse on Alison came back to him. His hesitation was as bad as an admission and he saw the recognition in Cate's eyes. But it was impossible. He wasn't going to be made to feel responsible for a bug going round the village. It was absurd, like some new and extreme form of emotional blackmail to make him feel sorry and culpable and small.

Cate took him by the arm.

'Sit down, Rufus,' she said gently.

They sat side by side on the bench. Rufus's stomach was churning with confusion and the remnants of his hangover. He dropped his head towards his knees and tried to breathe deeply. This woman had done nothing but irritate him since he arrived in Creech with her mind-reading and toxic potions, but suddenly he was confused to find himself glad of her presence. It felt calm and supportive, with no sense of accusation which had been entirely in his own mind, the product of childhood patterns he had never been able to lose. He had to stop jumping to these defensive conclusions...

Cate's voice broke into his thoughts.

'The garden has a history of moon worship, you know. Hundreds of years ago, where the stone basin is now, there was a tree sacred to the moon.'

'Is that where the moon dog used to lift its leg?' Rufus asked innocently.

She stared at him fiercely, her eyes narrowed.

'I'm sorry,' he said quickly. 'You weren't joking, were you?'

She went on as if he had never interrupted.

'It is said that witches danced there for the silver goddess. Those who were favoured enough to be able to see them would have their wishes granted.'

Rufus smiled.

'So you think I'm specially favoured?'

If so, it will be the first time in my life, he thought.

'*Have* you seen them?'

Her eyes were close to his and he felt their almost hypnotic power. It seemed impossible to lie to her, to avoid further discussion of this ridiculously fanciful topic by denying his nocturnal experiences as he would like to have done.

The grey eyes bored into him, ferreting out the truth.

'Only once,' he said sulkily.

'*Only* once!' she repeated with a soft laugh. 'You are honoured indeed.'

'But why?' he burst out, suddenly desperate for a tangible explanation. 'Why me? What have I done to deserve anything, if you say it's such an honour?'

She shook her head with a wry smile.

'I really can't say, but something has drawn you here, to this place of transformation.' She lifted a hand and stirred the air around her head with a light, caressing movement. 'Yes, there are omens of change,' she said quietly, to herself rather than to Rufus.

'But I didn't see any figures last night.' He could not

bring himself to say the word witches. 'They were only there the first time. Yesterday it was just that incredible light and the plants were sort of moving about, but there was no-one in the garden except me.'

'Indeed?' She smiled as if at a private joke and then was suddenly brisk. 'Now, to work. Can you tell me what you said?'

Rufus sighed miserably, wishing he'd forgotten.

'Something like "a plague on all their houses", just something stupid like that. I never thought...' It seemed pointless to go on.

Cate patted his hand in reassurance.

'I see. Well, that's not too much to worry about. I'll need to get home now, though. I've some things to see to.'

'OK.' He tried to smile at her in gratitude. 'But I still can't believe that I could make people sick with drunken ranting.'

'You weren't alone in that garden. You had help.'

'Did I?' Rufus immediately enjoyed a mental image of a conjuror's glamorous assistant in tights and a sequined basque. 'I don't remember that.'

It was Cate's turn to smile at him as a teacher might to some worthy but tremendously dim pupil.

'Never mind. Let's leave it at that for the moment. Unless... unless you can remember what you said about your wife?'

'Oh, you know, revenge, that sort of thing.'

'Nothing really specific? You didn't wish her dead, for example?'

'Good heavens, no!' He furrowed his brow and ransacked his tired brain for the exact memory. 'She's stolen some of my furniture and I said I'd get it back somehow.'

'That doesn't sound so bad. Anything else?'

'No, I'm pretty sure that was it. But...' he was worried that she'd go without a resolution of what was most

101

confusing him - 'how can it be real? The moon garden, curses, all of it. It's so completely unbelievable!'

'And yet, you do believe it, don't you?' she said benignly.

'But how...?'

She pulled out a roll-up and took her time lighting it, as if considering her answer.

'If your head aches, your body feels the pain.'

'That's true,' Rufus said feelingly.

'Your eyes take in images which your brain records and stores as memories,' she went on.

Rufus nodded eagerly, pleased that he could follow this.

'Do you accept these things because they are "scientifically proven"?' she asked, turning the full force of her attention on him.

Rufus hesitated, torn between yes and no. He wanted to give the right answer, but couldn't immediately work out which it was.

'Yes,' he said finally, deciding to stand up for the rational principles he always clung to when confused and uncertain.

'I see.'

When she said nothing else, but went on smoking contentedly, raising her face to the sun, he realised he must have got it wrong and thought again.

'No,' he said after a while. 'I believe those things because I have personal experience of them.'

He was rewarded by a swift glance of more positive appraisal than he'd seen from Cate before.

'So if science told you those things were impossible, you'd perhaps think scientists still had a lot to learn.'

'I suppose I would,' he said hesitantly. 'So the moral of the story is...?'

She gave an almost imperceptible shrug.

'Your spirit knows its own realities, and they are no less valid. Forget mechanics, allow yourself to feel what's real,

102

simply, without complications or rationalities, just instinctive, gut-reaction. Learn to trust yourself.' She stood up and smiled at him. 'Try it and you'll discover there's knowledge and understanding without scientific proof. Now, I must be on my way. And, Rufus...'

He looked up.

'Yes?'

'I wouldn't think about going back to the shop today. Lie down and rest, listen to music, think positive thoughts - just take it easy. Alright?'

She squeezed his shoulder and took the path round the corner of the house.

With only a few seconds' hesitation, Rufus decided to take her advice. He went back inside, settled down in the armchair with his feet up and was asleep before he had a chance to consider all that had happened.

The next few days were pleasantly busy for Rufus and he willingly put all demanding thoughts about his bizarre encounters aside.

Joe, pale but restored, returned to work on Mean Cottage, and all the things Rufus had ordered were safely delivered and installed. He had a cooker and a fridge, a sofa-bed downstairs and comfortable beds upstairs in the two bedrooms. Tara came over at the weekend and did a day's cleaning and painting. He had been hesitant about this arrangement, especially as it involved him parting with forty pounds, but she had proved surprisingly thorough and effective. She and Joe carried the old furniture outside and beat, dusted and polished until it vied in appearance with his newer things.

When Lily came round with some old curtains, Rufus spent a happy couple of hours in her company, draping the windows and then drinking tea companionably in the garden. He plucked up courage to ask about Joe's father and heard, from Lily's own lips, what Tara had already told him. In response to his tentative question about her current partner, she just smiled and said only that he wasn't around at the moment. Rufus at once imagined a huge tough fellow working away from home on an oil-rig in the North Sea or a fishing boat off Iceland and hoped that months would elapse before he was allowed any sort of leave.

At the door when she left, he stumbled endlessly over asking if he could take her out for a meal to thank her for all her help. She listened to his broken sentences with her customary smile and then leaned forward to put an end to his babbling by kissing him fleetingly on the lips. When he opened his eyes in wonder a moment later, she was still smiling.

'You're a very sweet guy, Rufus. I'd love to,' she said.

When Lily had gone, he felt a deep sense of happiness as well as the more superficial excitement of anticipation.

He was quite at home in the house now, nourished by its undemanding, peaceful and restorative space. He liked to wander around the large main room, much as he done on his first visit, but now touching his own things and arranging everything to please himself. It was a far cry from the flat he'd lived in before meeting Alison. That had been his only experience of living on his own and, ill at ease with himself and his surroundings, he could not imagine why anyone would ever choose to live alone. Now he felt quite differently, and in some strange way he thought it was due to Cate rather than his yearning for Lily or the edgy camaraderie he had forged with Tara at the shop.

He began to wonder for the first time who had owned the house before him and how it came to be sold off at auction. Cate would surely know the whole history of the place, not just the wacky bits of old wives' tales, but facts about real people who'd lived here. He decided to ask her next time they met.

Cate seemed altogether inextricably bound up with Mean Cottage and her belated acceptance of him as its owner had somehow settled things with the heart and soul of the house. He surprised himself with this thought, and even more with the next, which was that he wondered when she would be coming to see him again. She had not been around since the day of the plague, as he had come to think of it, and he was beginning to wonder if he had unwittingly done or said something then to put her off.

Rufus smiled to himself - "think positive thoughts" had been her last injunction! It was something he always found difficult when it came to other people's opinions of him, and assuming he was in the wrong was as natural as breathing. Perhaps that was why he'd been drawn to Alison, a critical and demanding woman like his mother, although with the redeeming gifts of intelligence and, unlikely though it now seemed, a sense of humour. He must have been grateful for very little in those days when he first met Alison.

She came into the bookshop in Fulham one day late in August and they began talking about the books she wanted. She told him that she had just moved up to London to start a new job at a private school in Chelsea and had found a room in a shared flat not far away. Rufus was impressed by her strong, confident manner and the fact that she lingered to talk to him beyond what was necessary for her purchases.

She knew no-one else in London and it was natural that she should drop in again and before long they were going out for meals or to the cinema and Rufus found himself one of a pair. He enjoyed the luxury of a working day on his own in the shop, knowing for certain that she would phone just after six and that he would have company and stimulation and a real life of his own at last. They managed an uncomfortable sex life in his single bed in the flat above the shop or an anxious one in her room with her flat-mates watching television just beyond the thin walls.

When her lease was up, it seemed natural that they should look for a place to live together and somewhere along the line - Rufus never *was* quite sure where - they decided they may as well get married. As Alison pointed out, they'd be sure of a lot of presents that way, which would help towards furnishing their new home.

It had all seemed so full of hope, that early period of marriage in their snug little terraced house near Turnham Green. Rufus had happily envisaged the secure progress of their lives - deeper companionship, children, a bigger house, grandchildren one day in the far future: all the things he'd never imagined having for himself as he sat day after day in the bookshop, too shy to do more than admire from afar the few attractive women who came within his very limited orbit or as he endured horrendously tongue-tied blind dates with totally unappealing friends of Charlie's girlfriend of the moment.

Rufus' smug sense of security and well-being had begun to wear off after a couple of years. Alison was more and more involved with the school, bent on promotion and determined to make herself indispensable there. As well as a heavy teaching commitment, she produced plays, ran theatre trips, organized poetry readings and generally ran the rest of her colleagues ragged in the effort of keeping up with her. She made it clear that children were out of the question until she had achieved all she wanted to outside the home. He never saw any sign of interest in them from her anyway. Every evening was about work and the tedious trivia of the school day; as they shared less and less between them, Rufus found himself increasingly the whipping-boy for every petty frustration and reverse she suffered at work. Eventually Alison was, inevitably, made head of department on the incumbent's retirement.

And after that, thought Rufus, I didn't stand a chance. I just clung on to the idea of Alison as she was in the early years and tried to ignore every sign to the contrary of her real character. It's what people do, it's how they survive, how empty, rotten marriages go on and on and on. And I'd never have had the courage to face up to the truth of it and break away, so I suppose I should to be grateful to her for that at least.

It didn't seem half so sad a story now as he sat at leisure outside Mean Cottage, enjoying a glass of wine and the evening sunshine as it streaked low across the vegetable garden. He had just begun to wonder idly about the whereabouts of the blue dog again when he heard a loud knock at the front door. Surprised, as anyone he knew in Creech simply came straight round the back these days, he went through to open the door.

It was Alison.

He had never seen her look so hot and dishevelled. There were dark circles under her eyes and her face was haggard.

He opened his mouth to speak but she was too quick for him.

'Rufus,' she said, 'I'm so sorry. I've been a bloody fool, haven't I? I don't know what I was thinking about with Brian. That bloody bastard!' Her tired eyes flared briefly. 'I don't know how I let it go on so long. But don't worry. I'll make it up to you, Rufus. I promise I will. Everything's going to be alright from now on.' She pushed past him. 'Just get my things from the car, would you?'

Chapter 7

Rufus was too astonished to do more than obey her.

It was partly shock and partly habit, of course, he thought as he went out to the Peugeot which was parked on the verge, almost blocking his car in. He was rather glad of the time to assess his own reaction to her appearance.

On first finding Alison on his doorstep, looking more vulnerable and dejected than he had ever seen her, he had felt sorry for her. The novelty of that feeling took a few moments to wear off, by which time the tone of her voice had switched from distress to a familiar sharper note which suggested that she was well on the way to recovery now that she had a new situation to command.

As he trudged back inside with two weighty holdalls, the thought of her presence in Mean Cottage made Rufus feel decidedly uncomfortable.

Alison was sitting in his armchair in the sitting room, looking around her with the critical expression he knew so well.

'So this is where you've been hiding.'

He laughed nervously.

'Hardly hiding. It's where I live.'

'Yes, but it's not much of a place, is it? No wonder they called it Mean Cottage!'

Rufus conveniently forgot this had been his own initial reaction and mentally apologised to the house for his wife's insensitivity.

'Would you like a drink?'

He fetched her a glass of wine and brought his in from the bench. He did not want to invite Alison outside into the garden, which was his own domain, reserved for personal reveries. He looked across at his wife, her sleek hair restored to neatness and those sharp eyes flashing around the room, taking everything in. He suppressed a sudden dart of nostalgic affection and tried to look at her as if she was a character in a play instead. He needed to observe her without any impingement on his own identity. Something had emerged in the last few weeks, something in him, that she knew nothing of: he realised happily that it might be a source of new power in their inevitable struggle of wills.

'Perhaps you'd like to tell me why you've come?' he said.

She was clearly surprised by the neutrality of his tone.

'I'd have thought that was obvious. Brian and I had an awful row and he said things about me... well, we're finished and I can see now that it would never have worked.'

She smiled at him as if this was a complete and satisfactory explanation.

'And?'

'And what?' A keener edge to her voice.

'I'm sorry to hear about you and Brian, although I always thought he was a total tosser, but I don't see why you've come all this way. Couldn't someone from school have put you up?'

'Rufus! You're my husband, for goodness sake!'

He was starting to feel a little nervous now. Her very presence in the house, his safe haven, was beginning to undermine his confidence. Perhaps it was natural that she should come running back to him in the circumstances: he didn't know what was expected of deserted husbands at a time like this. Even now, a cowardly part of him was tempted to cave in and submit to whatever she wanted, but he was astonished to discover an equally strong desire that she should go away and leave him alone. A short while ago he'd have given anything to have Alison here. Now he was confused and disorientated. What exactly was she after, chasing all the way down here to find him?

'Like you were my wife when you ran off and left me?'

He intended this as a comment not an accusation.

'Look, Rufus.' She put down her glass and came over to sit beside him. He felt an involuntary thrill of anticipation, in the knowledge that her desire could still sway him, but she made no move to touch him and her eyes slid away from his. 'I realise your pride's been hurt,' she went on, 'and I'm sorry. Truly. But there's no point being bitter about it. Perhaps I should just sleep on the sofa tonight and then we can take things from there in the morning.'

He was both disappointed and relieved. Some deep emotional stratum still responded automatically to Alison, but he was beginning to resist this damaging proclivity with a strong impulse to defend his new independence.

Battered by conflicting emotions like a tree in a storm, he wanted to shout NO! and order her to leave his house immediately, but he saw the weariness in her eyes and suddenly understood that it was *her* pride that had been hurt, firstly by the ruckus with Brian and then by his own apparent lack of enthusiasm for her appearance. Perhaps beneath the confident façade, Alison was running scared.

'OK,' he said reasonably. 'But you take my room. I'll stay down here. I haven't even worked out how to open up the sofabed yet!'

She was already on her feet, picking up one of the bags.

'Can I get you anything else first - are you hungry?' Rufus asked.

She shook her head.

'No, I'll just have a quick wash and then bed. It's been quite a day. You do have an inside bathroom, I suppose?'

110

After a fitful night, Rufus was awake before seven the next morning and leapt out of bed, remembering at once that Alison was overhead. He did not want her to find him still in bed or even in a vulnerable state of undress. But there was no sound from upstairs and after a brisk wash and shave, he took the coward's way out and fled, leaving a note saying he had things to sort out with work and he'd be back as soon as he could. Much as he hated the thought of Alison roaming freely around his territory, he also knew that he needed space for his own thoughts and maybe someone else to talk things over with. He thought of phoning Jane in London, but rejected the idea almost at once. He had started a new life here and he needed to find the answers to his problems on this territory.

An hour later he was sitting in a café, empty breakfast plate and coffee cup in front of him, staring out at the workers of Bruford on their way to shops and offices. He had decided to persuade - or more likely bribe - Tara to do another long stint at the shop and then go back to Creech in search of Cate. He felt she was the only person he could ask for advice about his current situation. Cate wouldn't plague him for explanations, but he felt she would listen. He thought briefly about going to Lily's, but talking about his wife wasn't something he wanted to do with the woman he was falling in love with. Shit! Thinking about Lily reminded him that Joe would be turning up at Mean Cottage any moment... He looked at his watch. Too late, he'd already be there, probably grouting tiles in the bathroom when Alison came down for a shower. He wondered what Alison would make of Joe. Joe, he thought, would simply grunt and get on with his work, without surprise or curiosity. Alison's reaction would be more interesting.

Tara did not respond well to Rufus hammering on the door of the flat until she got out of bed.

'What the fuck do you want?'

She looked about twelve without makeup. He now found this appearance more startling than her usual persona.

'I need you to look after the shop today.'

'No! For Christ's sake, Rufus, I've got a life even if you haven't.'

She began to close the door in his face.

'That's the trouble actually. My past life has just turned up and I have to deal with it.'

Her eyes widened with a flicker of interest.

'What's going on?'

'My wife, or ex-wife, I suppose, is at the cottage. I've got to go back.'

Tara looked almost animated.

'Charlie said your wife's a tight-assed cow.'

'Did he?' Rufus could imagine it without difficulty. 'Well, he shouldn't be so free with his opinions given his track record.'

'If that's a reference to my mother...'

'No! Of course it isn't, Tara, I've never even met her, so just simmer down and help me out here, OK?'

'Can't you bring this *wife*' - she managed to make the word sound slightly disgusting - 'into the shop?'

'No, I bloody can't! Sorry. I really don't think that's such a good idea.'

'Why, what's wrong with the shop?'

She was bristling again.

Where shall I start, Rufus was about to say when he stopped to consider this instinctive response for a split second. It was the sort of thing Alison would certainly say if she got anywhere near. But there was nothing wrong

112

with the shop when you looked at it squarely. Rufus had seen over the last few weeks that it provided many things that people seemed to want and paid a fair price for. It made a steady but not excessive profit, which was more than many small businesses these days. Who was he to criticise it? And besides, Rufus realised with a flood of incredulity, he quite liked the place.

'Nothing at all. But we've got things to talk about in private and then she'll be going back to London. I just need a bit of time, that's all. Please?'

'OK, I s'pose.'

'Thanks, Tara.' He impulsively grabbed her shoulders and gave her a quick kiss on the cheek before hurrying away.

She followed him to the top of the stairs.

'But you...'

'I know, I'll have to pay you,' he called back over his shoulder.

'No, I was going to say - you won't take her back, will you?' she said to herself as the door slammed.

Tara stomped about the flat, eating cereal, dragging on an assortment of dark clothes and putting on her make-up. Just as she was beginning to like Rufus, he treated her as if she was a little kid after more pocket money. She drew a small dagger and crimson blood drops down one side of her face defiantly. People were always misjudging her like that, it was so unfair. All she'd been thinking of was Rufus himself, not wanting him to be hurt, and he jumped to the immediate conclusion that she only cared about money. Why couldn't anyone stop and look at her properly, listen attentively and think over what she had to say? Was it so much to ask? From what she had seen, Tara reckoned adults were just as demanding and thoughtless as they always accused teenagers of being. She was grown-up now anyway and - she smiled provocatively at herself in the mirror - if she wanted to close up later and go off somewhere with Joe or back to bed or both, she'd damn well f-ing do it.

Three Ways Cottage was a small square house with a low thatched roof, set on a T-junction of two lanes as its name suggested. A wooden fence separated it from the narrow road and two huge yew trees overshadowed it from behind. Rufus pushed open the gate and paused by the open front door. On the lintel stone he could just make out the date 1794. A strange spiral symbol carved on a circle of thin wood hung from a metal spike over his head. He was looking at it when a voice called from inside the house.

'Come in, Rufus.'

He stepped into a large ground floor room with stairs straight ahead, a sitting area on one side and the kitchen on the other. Cate was cutting up vegetables at an old pine table and motioned him to sit down opposite.

For a few minutes he sat in anticipatory silence, watching the smooth motion of her wrist slicing the knife through a huge mound of carrots and then an assortment of herbs from the garden chopped briskly with an ancient mezzaluna which she took down from a wire rack above the old-fashioned stove.

'Tell me about it.'

She was watching him, taking in the slumped shoulders and tension in his face.

He shrugged wearily.

'Alison - my wife - turned up on the doorstep yesterday evening.'

'Ah.' She pushed back a stray strand of grey hair from her forehead. 'So there *was* more to your antics the other night.'

114

Rufus shook his head in irritation - he didn't want to get drawn into all that stuff again now. The urgent reality of his situation was more important.

'Nothing to do with that at all,' he said firmly. 'She's quarrelled with the basset hound - that's Brian, he looks like one - and has decided to come back to me by the look of things.'

'You don't know?'

As she spoke she put a ceramic saucer on the table near his elbow and after rummaging in a low cupboard near the stove she placed on it a tiny purple cone. Rufus watched her strike a match and set the cone alight. A pungent waft of smoke made his eyes water.

'We didn't really talk last night,' he said. 'This morning I left her a note saying I'd be back later and went into Bruford to sort the shop out. I just don't know what to do.'

Cate said nothing for a while, just carried on with her cooking as if he wasn't there. Rufus had expected something more from her - attention, sympathy, advice - anything but this belittling silence and stinking smoke.

He stood up moodily, thinking he may as well go back to Mean Cottage, where at least Alison was unlikely to be lost for words for any length of time, but his legs felt suddenly woozy and he sat down again quickly.

'If you've come here expecting me to give you instant solutions to your problems, it's better if you do go now, Rufus.'

Cate's stern voice unnerved him.

'I'm sorry,' he said, disconcerted at her quick understanding, 'but I could do with a bit of help. One order from Alison and I'm afraid I'll jump to it and obey, even if it means going back into something I don't want. Haven't you got any potions that instil unflinching resolution or something?'

She smiled at that, then wiped her hands on a cloth and

came over to him, drawing another chair up close so they were sitting with their knees touching. He felt no embarrassment at this physical contact, nor when her wrinkled hands took hold of his wrists and she raised her eyes to meet his. Smoke drifted hazily between them, but he sensed himself being drawn into her sphere, as if a powerful magnet tugged at his will. To his surprise, he had no impulse to resist it and rested quite secure in their connection.

'You must think back,' she said, speaking in a slow, measured voice, 'and remember exactly what you said in the garden under the moon.'

'I can't...'

He tried and failed to tear his gaze away. Cate waved a hand in front of his face abruptly and his eyes snapped shut immediately, his mind spiralled downwards, melting and dissolving in the face of a fiery heat inside his head. He felt a tremor of excitement and then the cool breath of the night sky over the moon garden, but all he could see was the white face of the moon and all he could hear was his own voice, its tenor sharp and clear against a background of total silence, repeating his foolish curses. Then the sky darkened and he was floating away, watching the moon diminish to a pinprick of light and finally vanish altogether in a violet haze of smoke.

He opened his eyes to see Cate a little apart from him, rolling one of her thin cigarettes and chuckling to herself.

'What's so funny?' he asked defensively.

She shrugged.

'What you said explains your current predicament well enough.'

'But when I said "I'm going to get her back for that" I meant pay her back, for taking my furniture, not "get her back" as in into my life.'

'Interesting that you chose the words you did then.'

'But it's just another figure of speech! I wasn't thinking about the form of words. My intention was perfectly clear!'

'Exactly.'

'What do you mean?'

'On the surface you wanted your furniture back. On another more important level you needed to sort things out with your wife, to come to some conclusions. It seems clear to me that you've created the opportunity.'

'But I could just have gone to London to talk to her anytime!'

She shook her head.

'It has to be here, on your own ground. It's about you, Rufus. All this is about you and who you are and what you want. You have choices to make. The only advice I can give you is don't think about it at all.'

Rufus was astonished.

'That's hardly the most practical suggestion when Alison's sitting there waiting for me!'

Cate looked at him with amusement.

'The old tradition was that the moon garden - or grove as it was then - was a place that discovered or denied true love. Don't think, Rufus. Just look inside yourself and feel.'

He drove a little way up the road and then pulled over into the mouth of a green lane wandering off between the high hedgerows. His breathing had been rapid and shallow all morning and he tried now to steady his treacherous digestive system to enable him to clear his head.

His first, apparently totally irrelevant thought was how much he liked the scenery around Creech. Just being surrounded by greenery and gently flowing water had done wonders for the day to day quality of his life. He was

117

aware of the elements, the natural energies at work all around him, as he sat in the garden on long summer evenings, or pottered around the vegetable plot, watching ducks on the stream. All this had given him a kind of undemanding contentment, and a quiet appreciation of things he would have dismissed cursorily in the city. The gentle rhythm of this sort of life suited him surprisingly well and he now realised he could never go back to London or even be happy living in the centre of a nice little town like Bruford, which he liked well enough as a place to work.

The fact that this was his first input to an analysis of his situation was instructive. It was based entirely on pleasing himself as a sentient individual being, to arrange his life as he wanted, with simple pleasures and few expectations. For Rufus, so used to performing to the tempo of others, this was an intoxicating form of freedom and one he was not inclined to relinquish.

For too long he had assumed he needed Alison's direction, but the new confidence of controlling his own life - and not making such a bad job of it - made him now regard his situation from a very different point of view. He also remembered with a sudden bodily twinge of excitement how much he was looking forward to his evening out with Lily.

What life would be like in a cold, damp winter in Creech at the mercy of Jacinta Jacobs or when Rita returned and he had no means of livelihood, Rufus chose not to consider. He would manage somehow because it would be a choice he had made for himself, not something he felt he *should* or *ought* to do as a duty to other people.

He leaned forward and rested his forehead on clasped hands on the steering wheel. He could no longer avoid the image of Alison.

For all those weeks after their separation when he had

slept on the sofa at Jane and David's and then during the first unfortunate days of his arrival in Creech, he had clung on to his notions of love for Alison. He had not for a moment looked again at his feelings to redefine them in the light of events. Faithful and loving by nature, he had *assumed* he still loved her, and without challenging this basic idea had indulged himself only in a few angry thoughts about her betrayal. He had never tried to visualize himself in a post-Alison light. The future he daydreamed about, if he was brutally honest, was precisely what had come to pass now - that she and Brian would split up and she'd come back to him. He had imagined both that she suddenly realised she couldn't live without him (very much first choice) and that she came back simply because he was still on offer. The fading hopes of either of these scenarios being realised had determined his move to the country, to take himself off the scene. Jane had advised him strongly to do so, from the point of view that he'd be much better off away from Alison, and he had pretended to share her motives, but in fact he had hoped, deep in his heart, that Alison would miss him and value him more for his independent stance in moving to Creech.

And now, ironically, he did actually feel independent of her and not minded to resurrect what had ultimately been for him an unsatisfactory relationship. There was a moment the previous evening when he had nearly put his arms round her in reassurance, and who knew what might have led on from there, but there was something incongruous in the sight of Alison in Mean Cottage that had stopped him. She did not sit happily in the house, quite literally, and it was that simple fact that had opened Rufus' eyes to the true and very new state of his feelings for her. What had Cate just said about true love? The moon garden was a place where it was 'discovered or denied'? Well, what love had existed in him for Alison was gone,

119

evaporated into the salubrious country air. Bleakly Rufus raised his face to this reality. It was a cold, hard shock, but it was the truth. How could he possibly tell Alison that?

Rufus' visit had stirred Cate's thoughts to the extent she could no longer concentrate on her work in the kitchen. Taking a basket from behind the door, she wrapped a light scarf around her neck and set off slowly down the lane, picking elderflowers from the hedgerow methodically with long fingers, as her mind stayed firmly fixed on Rufus' plight. It was a serious test for him and there was no telling if he would yet have the strength to withstand a force such as she sensed Alison's must be.

But she was probably worrying unnecessarily. The bond he had formed with the cottage was strong and that alone should give him courage enough. It was a form of relationship between occupiers and houses, after all - she did not like the word "owners," reckoning the spirit of the earth remained eternally free, whatever ravages it suffered at the hands of man - and she sensed that Rufus had a great sense of loyalty towards those things he cared for.

Perhaps it was time to tell him more about the history of the place and how the garden came to be created there. Whether or not she would talk to him about Adam remained to be seen. There were some things too important to be lightly shared.

As he walked up the path at Mean Cottage, Rufus couldn't help hoping for a fleeting moment that he'd got it all wrong. What if he went in and found a gentler, more appreciative Alison waiting for him with a loving smile and a solicitous concern for his happiness? Let's wait and see, he told himself and stepped inside the back door.

Joe stuck his head out of the bathroom door and looked

wordlessly at Rufus, his usually placid face full of nervous disquiet. Rufus put a reassuring hand on his shoulder and then went into the living room.

Alison was sitting in the armchair reading a book. Her mobile phone and personal organiser lay on the low table beside her. She looked as neat and punctilious as ever, he thought. What appeared to be a major crisis has simmered down into the merest pinprick in her emotional defences.

Please let her say something kind, he begged inwardly, some pleasantry about the cottage or even the weather. Anything at all that was non-censorious and benevolent.

'Do you think it's wise to give a house key to someone like that?'

She didn't even bother to look up fully from her book to say this.

Rufus' anger flared up as he thought of Lily's generous spirit and her son's devoted care of Mean Cottage, but he concealed it for the moment with an incredulous laugh.

'Someone like what?'

'Like that... punk in the bathroom.'

'His name's Joe. He's very hard-working and amazingly skilful with anything involving wood or painting. I wish I was half as talented as him and I'm very grateful to have him working in my house.'

'Oh, come on, Rufus. Is this some kind of care in the community, your pet project for the quality of rural life?'

My God, she's enjoying this, Rufus suddenly realised. It's me or Brian or her inadequate colleagues she's longing to take out all her rage and frustration on, but Joe's an easier target, so he'll do just as well. It's not just mean, it's positively dishonest.

He stood with his back to the mantelpiece and faced her.

'Alison, I don't know why you thought it was a good

idea to come here yesterday. I don't really want to know because it doesn't matter. I'm not interested in you or our relationship - whatever that was - any more and I just wish we could have had a sensible talk about it without you being a prize bitch about Joe, who's a friend and important to me.'

Her eyes narrowed.

'Is that how it is? I'd never have thought it of you, Rufus, but it might explain your lack of interest in that department when we were married.'

She folded her arms, eyes gleaming with self-satisfaction and the joy of battle.

How fruitless this all is, Rufus thought. He had felt angrier with her earlier judgment of Joe's character by his appearance than he did about her aspersions on his own sexuality. It was another hollow game, where victory was its own reward and the cost was never counted. He didn't want to play.

'You're quite wrong, Alison' he said calmly. 'Not that it's any business of yours, but it's Joe's mother I'm in love with.'

For a second he saw her hesitate, weigh up his sincerity and then falter.

'I see.' She sounded suddenly deflated. 'Then I suppose there's no point talking about our marriage after all.'

He shook his head.

'I'm sorry.' His voice was firm and authoritative. 'We'll have to see about a divorce eventually, when you've had a chance to sort yourself out properly.'

She nodded silently, looking down into her lap, all the fight gone out of her. He wondered if she had ever seriously considered coming back to him.

'Where are you going to stay?' he asked more gently.

'Oh, I phoned the school earlier. There's a house mother's flat free for the summer. It'll give me plenty of time to find somewhere of my own.' Her chin came up suddenly. 'I didn't much fancy staying in this place anyway.'

'It suits me very well,' he couldn't help himself saying.

She looked very hard at him, as if considering.

'Yes, I can see that it does,' she conceded finally. 'God knows why.'

'I think God-dess might be more appropriate actually.'

He was amazed that he had said this at all, let alone out loud and to Alison of all people. It was a relief that she misunderstood him so easily.

'Spare me the details, Rufus, please,' she said, glancing in the direction of the bathroom. Her manner became brisk and business-like. 'I'll get my things ready now. It's a ridiculously long drive back to civilization.'

When Alison had gone and Rufus discovered that Joe had also slipped away, he sat alone outside in the garden until the sky grew overcast and the air was chilly. It was perfectly natural to be sad at this loss of so great a part of his life, but he was also curiously depressed. Had those years been completely futile and devoid of meaning, to end like this with mutual misunderstanding and the absence even of basic friendship? Had it all been one huge waste of time and effort? He feared that now he would remember Alison at her worst, the harsh side of her he had dwelt on exclusively since the balance of his feelings shifted. Presumably we performed this cruel metamorphosis on people we'd once loved to make it easier to accept the loss, he thought sadly.

The effort of the last twenty-four hours had stripped away Rufus' habitual layers of protection and support, leaving him enervated and low in spirits. He wanted something he couldn't name, but knew it was neither food nor drink nor company.

He got up and wandered through the orchard towards the brick wall, tracing its ivied length to the rounded hole. Catching his foot on a loose stone, he stumbled, feeling a familiar wrench in his knee as he did so and made an undignified jarring entry to the moon garden.

He limped along the overgrown paths, surrounded by parched, decaying plants. Even the weeds that thrive on neglect seemed browner and the stone circle in the centre was bare and dank. He touched the stark wall which he had twice seen as a refulgent mirror and looked up miserably at the lowering grey sky, which promised nothing but rain and where not a chink of hopeful brightness appeared.

Rufus took the hint and went back slowly to the house. There was no more magic here for him.

Chapter 8

'Cool coat,' Joe said as he came in at the back door and saw Rufus preparing to go to work.

Rufus looked down at the old mac he'd decided to chuck in the car when he saw the colour of the morning sky.

'Really?' He was surprised, but there was no reason why Joe's penchant for charity shop clothes should not stretch to shapeless gaberdine, given his usual attire. 'I've had it for about twenty years.'

'Oh.' Joe looked surprised. 'I didn't know they lived that long.'

Rufus was puzzled.

'Well, if you look after them and take them to the cleaners about once a decade,' he said.

'Is that all?'

'Well, I suppose a regular going over with a clothes brush would help.'

Seeing the bewildered expression on Joe's face, Rufus decided to get off this strange subject once and for all.

'How's your mum?' he asked.

Joe pointed to the garden.

'She's out there with the goat.'

'What goat?'

Joe stared at Rufus as if his brain had finally gone.

'The one we've just been talking about, yeah?'

'I'm sorry. You're not making a lot of sense, Joe.'

'It's eating your vegetables.'

Rufus went to the kitchen window and groaned.

Lily was standing amongst the staked beans feeding lettuce to the goat he had encountered in the High Street.

'He's lovely, Rufus. How long have you had him?' she called.

'It's not mine,' Rufus answered crossly. 'I had the

dubious pleasure of making its acquaintance for the first time in the village the other day. I've no idea what it's doing here.'

As soon as the goat caught sight of him, it skipped over to the door at once, drawing thick black lips back in a grotesque parody of a joyful greeting.

Rufus tried to fend off the playful prodding muzzle. After the stresses of the previous day, an amorous cloven-footed sparring partner was the last thing he felt he could cope with.

'He seems very fond of you,' Lily said, coming over to join them.

Rufus hid his irritation in the face of her serene smile.

'Lucky me! I've no idea how it found its way down here. Aren't they usually tethered or something? Ow!'

The goat trod on his foot in an effort to get closer.

Rufus hopped clear, and turned away swearing under his breath.

Lily tried to position herself between Rufus and the goat, but it swung its body round sharply in a tight circle to resist her intervention and its rear end gave Rufus a hard enough whack to knock him into the spiky embrace of a pyracantha.

He struggled to regain his balance, speechless with indignity.

Lily took his arm, barely able to conceal her amusement.

'Come on. I'll escort you to your car and protect you from any further assault.'

He forced himself to laugh.

'I had an excellent goat curry in Shepherd's Bush once.'

'It'll be OK,' she said, squeezing his arm. 'It'll probably just wander off again when it's ready.'

She shut the garden gate neatly in the face of Rufus' tormentor, who was tripping after them, and they departed in their separate cars to a chorus of frustrated bleating.

It was market day and the shop was surprisingly quiet. Locals came into town early when they could still park and went straight home with their fish and vegetables, while the tourists lingered most of the morning around the striped stalls, spending their money on chutney and miniature paintings of the abbey.

Rufus spent his time checking stock and phoning orders to suppliers. He put up a poster someone had left about the dreaded Goddess festival, which seemed to be going ahead without Rita's input, but mercifully no-one had seriously suggested he might like to participate in her stead.

There was silence overhead. Tara had stuck a Do Not Disturb notice on the door to the stairs. Under the gothic lettering was a Runic symbol. Rufus was rather proud of recognising this from his own clumsy attempts to play three of a kind with a bag of runes during one particularly boring afternoon.

It was a relief to him to be quiet after the trauma of Alison's appearance and his reluctant acquisition of a goat. The light on his horizon was an arrangement to meet Lily that evening. He had bought a local paper and scanned the advertisements for a suitable venue for their meal. The thought of being alone with her made him shiver with both pleasure and anxiety. He wondered what they would talk about and what might happen at the end of the evening. Some blot on his anticipation, some presentiment he couldn't define niggled away at his brain. He thrust negative thoughts aside. First he was amazed that she'd agreed so readily to go out with him and now he was worrying about the outcome in advance. It was time to grow up and - what was that expression he'd seen so often since browsing in the books at the shop - trust the universe. Didn't he have reason to believe all this nonsense about getting what you wish for?

As Rufus was on the phone to a scented candle producer, the bell jangled to alert him to a customer's arrival. It was a young man, with greasy shoulder-length hair, rampant acne and an astonishingly clean pair of shoes.

Rufus' shop-keeper's antennae twitched at once. He knew the signs from bitter experience in his own shop in Fulham: here was someone longing to confess or confide, to involve another in their personal fantasies. They would engage the poor sucker stuck behind the counter in fruitless conversation for the best part of an hour and often leave without buying anything.

He half-turned away to finish his call, watching the young man surreptitiously. He was looking at the books, running a stubby finger along their spines, casting regular sidelong glances in Rufus' direction.

There was no escape. As soon as Rufus put down the phone, the young man sidled over to the counter, a book in his hand and a disturbing zealot's gleam in his eye.

'Hi.'

An American accent.

Rufus hoped to head him off with formality.

'Can I help you?'

'My name's Guy.' Rufus could not ignore the outstretched hand, but he shook it unenthusiastically and without words of welcoming encouragement. Not that it made the slightest bit of difference.

'I'm over here for a bit of re-search.' Guy leaned intimately cross the counter. 'I'm studying the Craft,' he said in a loud, clear voice.

Which one, Rufus wondered facetiously: needlework, origami, spun sugar?

'Well, you've come to the right place,' Rufus said with total insincerity. 'This is The Craft Shop.' He spoke in capital letters, spreading an expansive hand around the shop.

'Yeah' - Guy didn't actually seem much interested in the shop - 'I've been reading on the net. Seems like there's a lotta paths to the power. I'm kinda attracted to Druids, but' - this was confidential Guy again - 'men only, you know. I'm not so keen on that, if you get my drift. What do you reckon to shamanism - is that a bit more earthy?'

Rufus was inclined to give him directions to the nearest mental hospital (or vice versa), but he pretended to consider the question seriously for form's sake, dredging his schoolboy memories for some gruesome Tacitean detail.

'It really depends on your attitude to shrunken heads, I suppose,' he said at last.

'Hey, are you into all that pagan sacrifice stuff?' (Don't tempt me, Rufus thought). Guy's eyes were alive with interest. 'Does it still go on round here? I heard there was a coven operating near Bruford.'

'Have you tried the Tourist Office?' he said brightly.

'Excuse me?'

'I'm sure you'll find they have details of nocturnal gatherings and' - this was a flash of inspiration - 'I believe the bookshop by the bridge, you can't miss it, it says Neville King on the door, has a wide range of books on special "esoterica".' He drew the word out salaciously and then dropped his voice and leaned forward. 'Just tell him what you're interested in. King is a local man, he knows what goes on, if you understand me.' He made a pretence of looking at his watch. 'You'll need to hurry, though, he closes at five.'

Guy seemed very excited. 'Sure. I'll get down there right

now. I'll just get this.' He handed over the book he'd been clutching.

Rufus scrutinised the cover and tried to conceal a smile.

'It's for a friend back home.' Guy said quickly. 'Hey, thanks for the information about the coven and all that.'

'You're very welcome, Guy.'

He began laughing as soon as the door had closed and went over to take another copy of the book Guy had bought from the shelf. He flicked to the title page.

'What's so funny?'

Tara had slipped into the shop without him hearing, in full goth make-up, with a black bandana forcing her dark hair up into an array of mad tufts.

'Sex spells: when all else fails, get a mate by magic,' he read out.

'Hope it works for you, Rufus.'

She moved over to the counter.

'It's not mine,' he spluttered. 'Some jerk just bought a copy.'

'I know. I heard you talking to him. But how did you know about the coven? And Neville King?'

'What are you talking about?' Rufus asked.

'You told that man to go and see Neville King if he wanted to know about the coven.'

'Yes, but I was joking. I just wanted to get rid of him and I don't have a very high opinion of Mr King,' Rufus said, thinking that Tara wouldn't have either if she knew what King had said about Rita.

'He had a thing about my mother, you know, a couple of years ago.'

'Neville King did?' Rufus was incredulous.

'Yeh, it was spooky. He used to hang about outside the shop to get a glimpse and then started following her everywhere to find out what she was doing. He's one sad bastard.'

Tara opened the till, took out a £20 note and stuffed it down the front of her T-shirt. She paused at the door.

'That's how he knows about the coven,' she said.

'*What!*' Rufus screeched, to stop her leaving without finishing this alarming conversation.

'From following Rita,' she said patiently.

'Tara, I don't understand. I'm old and tired and feeble, so just give me a break and explain in words of one syllable.'

'You *must* know,' she said, as if he was being deliberately obtuse. 'My mother's a witch.'

Of course he must have known. Neville King had sneered about it and Rufus was sitting day after day in her premises called The Craft Shop, a name he soon learnt was synonymous with modern day witchcraft, surrounded by books on spells and metal cauldrons. But he had never acknowledged these things for what they were, never bothered to distinguish between them and the more common sales of incense, crystals and candles, never really considered that some of the people he served might be directly involved in magical practice, whatever that was. Despite his browsing among the goddess literature on the shelves, he'd avoided anything with magic or witchcraft in the title. Except - he gulped at the sudden realisation - he'd actually taken home and tried to use a book of curses! But that was different - it had been a joke, a way of releasing his feelings about Alison's behaviour, influenced by too much alcohol and worse, if he counted Cate's tonic. It was true that the moon garden was an extraordinary place, somehow mysteriously enlivened by a quirk of light refraction. He didn't pretend to understand all that, but, at this distance, he was more inclined to dismiss the veracity of what Cate had almost persuaded him to accept - that he had brought about a chain of events by exercising his will. A ridiculous concept, and yet, in a funny kind of way, it *had* worked.

Rufus forgot about witches and wondered if he could manage the same sort of thing for his date with Lily.

The goat was tied to a stout metal peg on the side lawn. He heard a noise coming from the woodstore and went over to find Cate re-arranging piles of old deckchairs and garden utensils. He no longer felt the least surprise to see her on his property.

'What are you doing?' he asked, peering over her shoulder.

'Making room for the goat. Joe sorted out his chain, but they need shelter too, you know.'

'It's not my goat, Cate,' he pointed out reasonably. 'I'm not responsible for it.'

She stood up, one hand in the small of her back, to give her tired muscles a good stretch.

'He seems happy enough here,' she said. 'And he's a bright, curious soul. Goats can be good company when you live alone. The last person to live here had several. He used this shed for them.'

Rufus forgot the goat for a moment in his curiosity about the previous history of Mean Cottage.

'How long ago was that? That someone lived here?' he asked.

Cate brushed a hand over her thick loops of hair.

'It's more than ten years since Adam Hunt died.'

'And no-one's been near it since?'

'I've kept my eye on it,' Cate replied dryly, 'but no, the house was left to his sister, in Lincolnshire. She had a stroke soon after and was never well enough to deal with it. When she died last year, her executors put it in the auction.'

'Where I found it by mistake,' said Rufus with a grin,

secretly marvelling again at his good fortune. He felt the force of her grey eyes immediately and for a pleasant change knew at once what she was thinking. 'I suppose you're going to tell me it was all ordained,' he said provocatively.

Cate turned away to avoid conceding the point.

'He seems keen enough to stay,' she said, nodding her head in the goat's direction.

It was trying, as far as the limited length of chain would allow, to climb a grassy hump to get a better view of what they were doing.

Rufus looked at the jutting horns and mad yellow eyes.

'I really think I've got enough on my plate at the moment,' he said.

Cate raised her eyebrows in amusement.

'I wasn't suggesting that you eat him.'

They both laughed, and Rufus began to relent.

'I suppose he can stay for the moment, but there must be someone in the village who knows where he comes from. Could you ask around a bit?'

'We'll see,' Cate replied noncommittally.

'Well, at least tell me how to look after him. Would you like a quick cup of tea? I have to go out later.'

She seemed to be waiting for him to continue with an explanation. Rufus shuffled his feet uneasily.

'I'm taking Joe's mum out for dinner, to thank her for all her help, you know.'

'Are you taking Joe as well?' Cate asked, eyes wide with innocence.

Rufus refused to be drawn.

'Did you want the tea?' he said.

When they were sitting at the kitchen table, he remembered what they'd been talking about before he got distracted by the goat.

'Did you know him well, the chap who lived here before

me?'

He noticed a brief flash of an emotion he did not recognise cross Cate's face before she answered.

'He was my nearest neighbour for many years.'

'And?'

She glanced up sharply as if he had been impertinent.

'I mean, what was he like?' Rufus said quickly. 'Apart from keeping goats.'

Cate sipped her tea thoughtfully.

'He always had a dog,' she said.

'How did you feel about that?' Lily asked.

Rufus had just finished relating Tara's startling pronouncement about her mother. They were sitting at a quiet table in The Old Bridge, a restaurant on the other side of Bruford, where they'd talked easily throughout the meal about buying houses and moving to new areas and now, over dessert, were feeling comfortable and at ease,

'Well, I've never even met Rita, but - witchcraft? It's crazy, isn't it?'

'Why?' Lily's head was tilted to one side, her clear eyes watchful.

Rufus gave up on his treacle pudding.

'Oh, I don't know,' he said vaguely, waving his spoon in the air. 'Broomsticks, black cloaks, pointy hats, that sort of thing. How can anyone take it seriously?'

In truth, he was having trouble concentrating on anything except Lily's stunning appearance. She was wearing a long emerald dress, close fitting from her breast to her hips and then swirling in full folds almost to the floor. Its colour emphasised the green of her aquamarine eyes and the russet tints in her hair. A large ruby pendant hung around her neck. Never had Rufus been so fully aware of the subtle nuances of shade and hue since meeting Lily. He wanted to study her intently, to identify every little shift and shadow of light on her soft face...

She was laughing at him gently now.

'You're a few hundred years out of date. Modern witches look like anyone else, like you or me!'

'Aren't men wizards?'

'In general or are we still on magic?' She was teasing him.

'Ha, ha. But what does a witch do, for goodness sake? Apart from flit around the night sky with a bat on her shoulder, I mean.'

She sat forward, leaning her folded arms on the table.

'Seriously? There's a long tradition of wise women - or men - especially in rural communities. The Church villainised them precisely because people relied on them for advice or midwifery or herbal preparations to cure illness.'

'Or to get the better of their enemies,' said Rufus, feeling ashamed as he remembered his own performance of that ilk.

'Naturally,' Lily said. 'They didn't make the same distinctions between physical and emotional well-being then that the development of science brought in later.'

She took a delicate bite of the chocolate confection in front of her.

'So modern witches are a combination of doctors and agony-aunts?' He laughed as he spoke.

She hesitated, then held out another piece of cake to him on her fork and the intimacy of the gesture as their heads came close together made his skin spark like a lighted charcoal disc.

'Something like that.'

Although she was still smiling, Rufus felt he'd said something foolish. 'Sorry. You must excuse my ignorance. This kind of thing is all new to me.' Nervously, he tried to change tack. 'I suppose you must know Rita quite well, with Tara and Joe being so involved - did you meet my mate Charlie before they went off?'

'Charlie, no. It was a bit sudden for that. But Rita's been a good friend for years. We've got a lot in common.'

Her eyes were fixed on his, but he looked away and picked up his wine glass.

He didn't want to risk any more banal remarks about single parents after the way he'd upset Tara with them. He desperately did *not* want to put a foot wrong this evening, but there was something indefinable in Lily's manner that made him wary.

'What would Charlie think about teaming up with a witch?' Lily asked.

Rufus laughed.

'He probably wouldn't even notice or, if it was forced on his attention, he'd deal with it by making some crude remark.'

She raised her eyebrows.

'Such as?'

'Oh, I don't know. "It must be my magic wand she's after" - something like that.'

To his amazement, she laughed.

He was very unused to amusing people intentionally. He laughed too, but tension was creeping over him as he thought that soon they must leave the safe predictability of the restaurant.

Everything about Lily, from her beautiful rippling hair to her graceful movements and ready smile spoke to him of one without self-constraints. She had an aura of freedom and ease with herself that left him all at sea and only too aware of his own clumsiness and naivety in comparison.

'I expect they're having quite a time,' he said.

'Do you envy them? Travelling free in the wide world?'

Rufus shook his head at once.

'No, I'd much rather stick around in one place. I like to know where I am when I wake up in the morning - I mean, know it in my heart, if you see what I mean.'

Lily leaned back in her chair.

'No craving for adventure, then?'

He thought about that.

'Adventures are relative,' he said. 'By my standards, coming to Creech and working in the shop has all the qualifications for an adventure - new people and places, unexpected situations, mysterious goings-on...'

'Rufus! You not trying to tell me your house is haunted?'

He realised she was joking, poking fun at him. And didn't mind, for once, what had caused him to suffer so often in his life. But her flippancy also stopped him from going on to what he'd been about to say - about his experiences in the moon garden. That would be a real exposure to ridicule that he couldn't risk. Part of him felt sad to acknowledge that: he wanted to tell her everything, to pour it all out like a spring bursting from its high rocky source, but something held him back.

'Only a few plates whizzing round and the occasional rattling of chains - nothing to get too excited about.'

She seemed satisfied with that answer.

It wasn't so important, after all. Plenty of people had partners they didn't confide absolutely everything in. His own experience with Alison had taught him that and he was probably being quite unrealistic to imagine it was possible at all. But he remembered Charlie's answer when he asked him why he'd never settled down with any of his numerous conquests. 'I'm always keeping something back,' he'd said. 'If I didn't, I'd know I was in trouble.' Rufus badly wanted to be in that sort of trouble and that was probably, he reflected sadly, why he never would be.

He paid the bill, ordering himself to snap out of this maudlin mood before he made a fool of himself by falling on his knees and begging Lily to come and live with him and be his love.

The sky was still light as they came out of the restaurant and wandered through an arch of honeysuckle and jasmine, powerfully fragrant in the warm air, to the old stone bridge spanning the river.

A long silence stretched between them as they leant on the wall. Away from the routine and structure of the meal, Rufus felt on edge and inadequate. If only he could command the words that would enthral this woman who had established such a hold over him in so short a time.

'What weather we've been having,' he said eventually, in desperation.

'Mmm.' Lily stood back and stretched languorously. 'I love summer. Slow movements, quick passions, the sense that anything could happen at any moment.'

'I'm an autumn man myself,' said Rufus and then cursed his prosaic instincts. He should have acted on her words and swept her into his arms. Instead he rammed his hands into his pockets and shuffled awkwardly.

'It's still early. What would you like to do now?' he said finally.

'I'm sorry, Rufus, I have to go.'

It was like a bucket of cold water in his face.

'Oh, right. Joe need tucking in, does he?'

His fearful heart was beating fast against this little death of hope. He wanted to know why she was deserting him, but lacked the courage to ask outright.

'Something like that. I've really enjoyed this.'

The sweep of her hand took in the river, the restaurant and Rufus himself.

'Thank you, Rufus.'

Some of his disappointment died. He heard his name on her lips like a caress. There would be other nights. He hadn't failed, had he?

138

Lily stepped closer and put her arms around his neck, pulling him forward into a deep embrace. He clung to her for the duration of a long, slow kiss. It was Lily who finally drew back and smiled into his eyes.

'I must go,' she said. 'Come on,' and, grabbing his hand, she began to run back towards the car.

The dark and total silence outside Mean Cottage only emphasised Rufus' solitary frustration as he got out of the car. He was keyed up and beset by a contradictory riot of emotions. Lily had momentarily seemed so close to him and yet she turned away as easily as an insect leaves one flower for another. One moment he felt the rejection keenly, a quick regression to his sense of abandonment when Alison left; the next he berated himself for such over-reaction. She could not have kissed him like that in finality. There would be more between them, it was a promise for the future. There again, he was reading an awful lot into one kiss fuelled by wine and a romantic summer evening.

As he came up the path with all these thoughts whirling in his head, Rufus suddenly smelt cigarette smoke in the air. He thought at once of Cate and felt a rush of pleasure at the thought of confiding in her and lending validity to his feelings for Lily by speaking them aloud. Eagerly, he hurried round the corner of the house.

The dark figure sitting on his bench did not look like Cate, although there was something familiar in the outline. With no sense of danger, but cautiously, Rufus went forward.

'Hello, friend,' a voice said.

A voice Rufus knew only too well.

'What the hell are you doing here, Charlie?' he said.

Chapter 9

'I'm waiting for you.'

'You know what I mean!' Rufus snapped. 'What happened to Bondi Beach and the Taj Mahal? More importantly, what's happened to Rita?'

Charlie shrugged.

'As far as I know, she's tucked up at home in bed.'

'At home? As in, Bruford?'

A nod as the cigarette end went sailing into the vegetable patch.

'I dropped her off at the shop. Gentleman to the end, that's me. Look, can we go in and have a drink or something. It may have escaped your attention but it's dark out here and I've already had to fend off the attentions of a decidedly gay goat. You didn't tell me you were going into livestock.'

Reference to the goat made no impact on Rufus. All he could think of as he got out the whisky bottle and two glasses was, if Rita's back, where does that leave me?

'So, how've you been?' Charlie leant back comfortably on the sofa and put his feet up.

'Never mind me,' said Rufus shortly. 'Just tell me what's going on, will you?'

'What's to tell? We went, we came back. End of story.'

'Did something go wrong? Have you quarrelled?'

'It's no big deal, mate. Though if I'd known her little secret, I'd never have gone off with her in the first place.'

Oh God, thought Rufus, remembering his conversation with Lily, he's found out and obviously didn't take it very well.

'I mean,' Charlie went on, 'you'd think it was quite an important thing to tell someone, when you're planning to go round the world together.'

'Well, maybe she wasn't sure how you'd react,' Rufus said hesitantly. 'I mean, it's quite a thing to tell someone, isn't it?'

Charlie swung his legs round and sat up, staring at Rufus.

'Is it?' he said. 'You seem to know an awful lot about this, for someone who's never even met Rita, that is.'

'Oh, I only knew today. Tara told me. So, how did you find out?'

'How'd you think?' The expression on Charlie's face was one of amused curiosity.

Rufus looked down into his glass in some confusion.

'She must have done something, well, unusual, I suppose,' he mumbled.

Charlie gave a bark of laughter.

'I'll say. The guy in that restaurant didn't know what had hit him.'

Rufus looked up in horror.

'You mean she hexed him?'

'Rufus, old friend, what are you on? I think we should forget about me and have a little talk about you and what's happened to make you considerably crazier than you were when I left.'

'No, I'm fine. Very well, in fact.' He decided to ignore tonight's set-back with Lily. 'I've got rid of Alison finally.'

Charlie laughed again.

'I was under the impression she'd got rid of you, mate.'

'She wanted to come back and I told her to stuff it.' The whisky was beginning to have an effect on top of all the wine he'd drunk. He thought with satisfaction of the deserted Brian. 'I've no use for another dog's dinner.'

'Good for you!' Charlie whistled his approval. 'She always was a...'

'Tight-arsed cow,' Rufus finished for him. 'Tara told me what you'd said.'

'And was I wrong? How is young Tara anyway?'

'She's probably at Joe's.'

'Still the boyfriend then?'

'Most definitely. And my handyman. And the son of the woman I love. So what did Rita do to this chap in the restaurant?'

Charlie ignored this last question and grinned.

'So that's it. Alison over and done with, Joe's mother in the frame. What's she like?'

Rufus got up, slopping whisky from his glass.

'You keep away from Lily!' He wagged his finger in Charlie's direction.

'OK, OK, not so fierce. Calm down and give me that glass.'

Charlie refilled them both.

'Here's to you and Lily.'

They drank.

'So what did happen with Rita?'

Rufus listened through a fug of wine and whisky to Charlie's account of their initial jaunt to Amsterdam, where they seemed to eat endlessly in pine-floored cafes serving twenty types of salad.

'How was I to know that's all she ever eats?' Charlie demanded indignantly.

'But you must have known about her eating habits before you left?' Rufus managed to formulate this observation with some difficulty.

Charlie grinned.

'We didn't spend much time eating,' he said. 'I thought the salad stuff was just some diet.'

Most of the many women he'd known had eaten green leafy things in front of him, saving the chocolate and chips for the privacy of their own homes. Charlie himself never strayed far from steak and sausages.

'And you thought vegans were something from Star

Trek, I suppose?' Rufus gave a condescending little laugh that turned into a very large hiccup.

'Yeah, right.' Charlie ignored this intervention. 'So we went on to Berlin and she was like a fucking maniac. Tipped some guy's dinner over his head.'

'Why? What'd he do?'

'That mad cow doesn't need a reason. Just went for him out of nowhere because he was eating some sort of sweets.'

'Sweets?' Rufus struggled to focus his fuddled brain. 'What's she got against sweets?'

'My point exactly, mate. Perfectly harmless. It looked pretty good to me actually, on the plate, before she chucked the lot all over his shirt, yelling and screaming at him, all this crap about baby animals. I should have dumped her right there and then, fucking loony.'

Charlie gulped down the remains of his whisky and then fiddled with the empty glass in his usual restless fashion, his handsome face clouded by memories of Rita's bad behaviour.

Rufus mulled over his narrative in puzzled silence for a minute before a dim light flickered on inside his muzzy skull. Sweetbreads! It would be just like Charlie to take a vegan to a place where they ate veal at the next table and not have a clue why Rita was so upset. He wondered if it was worth trying to explain and quickly decided that his head hurt too much and any effort he made would not have the slightest effect on Charlie's innate insensitivity.

'What did you say?' he asked instead, refilling their glasses with generous measures.

'Not a lot, mate, she was raving.' Charlie took another deep swig. 'The guy was about to cut up rough, manager off to call the Gestapo for all I knew, so I dragged her away and we got on the first train out of there.'

'And came back here?'

Charlie shook his head.

'Krakow.'

Rufus spluttered a laugh.

'Poland was on your list of places to see, was it?'

Charlie grimaced.

'Too bloody hot to see anything there. We practically lived in some underground bar trying to keep cool and knocking back the ale. Amazing stuff!' His eyes lit up at the recollection. 'I could hardly stand after a couple of jars.'

'And Rita?' Rufus prompted.

'Oh, she can hold her own with the drink.'

'No, you fool. How did you get on together?'

'Not so well. She's got a savage temper when something pisses her off and it doesn't take much. Every time we ate, I was scared shitless of another violent tantrum, so we finally agreed in a civilised way to forget the whole thing and come back.'

Rufus considered this.

'For jet-setting world travellers, you didn't get very far, did you?' he said finally.

'That's another thing about Rita,' Charlie said with some indignation, 'she's scared of flying.'

Rufus began to laugh and once he started, found he couldn't stop. Charlie stared at him in amazement as he wheezed and shook in his chair.

'Bit of a drawback in her line, I'd have thought,' Rufus said when he could finally speak again.

In the morning Charlie left after breakfast. He'd brushed aside all Rufus' hung-over anxieties about the shop, telling him to sort it out with Rita or get himself a place of his own.

As if there was money for that! Rufus looked moodily at an estimate for roof and chimney repairs on the noticeboard he'd hung in the kitchen. It might have been possible with a steady income, but without one how could he commit that sort of amount? And what would he live on? Things were looking worse by the minute.

He didn't even bother to take his coffee outside, but sat brooding in the old armchair, his world shrunk to the confines of a dilapidated house.

Finally he stirred himself to get up and drive slowly into Bruford, dreading the day and not fancying his pathetic chances in the coming encounter with a plate-throwing harpy who could take or leave Charlie's charms.

The shop was closed and unchanged. He let himself in and then did not know what to do in the face of silence from upstairs. Rita was probably having a lie in after getting back late last night. Should he open up as usual, he asked himself, or slink off before she made an appearance? Finally reasoning that she probably didn't even know Charlie had been to see him, he decided to carry on as if nothing had happened, although the implications of his precarious situation whirled round and round in his befogged brain like a spinning top as he sat behind the counter.

As customers drifted in and out he felt increasingly miserable. Handing over an out of print book on tree lore he had managed to track down through previous London contacts for a very appreciative customer, a defensive pride swelled in Rufus at all he'd managed to achieve in such a short time in a milieu very much not his own. It was true that he didn't want to stay here among the goddess figurines and dream-catchers for ever, but he wasn't yet ready to be cast adrift either. All he wanted was a bit of time without change after all he'd been through in the last six months, a chance to settle, to spend time at Mean Cottage and especially to see Lily...

Loud footsteps thumped on the floor upstairs. He

quaked at the reverberating boards overhead and wondered if the formidable Rita wore hob-nailed boots as her daughter did. He imagined her pacing the flat above in huge Valkyrie strides... The stairs shook menacingly and Rufus realised he was about to come face to face with this fearsome figure. The door crashed back against the wall.

'Why are you looking at me like that?' Tara said angrily after a moment's silence.

'I...' Rufus hesitated. 'I thought you were your mother.'

'You really are losing it, Rufus,' Tara said, giving a loud withering sigh as she passed. 'You've never even met my mother.'

When she'd gone, Rufus crept up the stairs, listened carefully and then tentatively opened the door to the flat. He was looking straight into the living room, where articles of Tara's clothing and possibly Joe's were strewn about on furniture. Trying to assess whether the silence was that of an empty house, he tiptoed across to the kitchen which was surprisingly tidy, as if no-one ever ate anything in this household and then he checked the shower room. What he was looking for, Rufus had no idea, nor how he would recognise evidence of Rita's re-appearance. Surely Tara would have said something about her mother if she'd seen her?

Rufus wondered if he had the courage to go up the next flight of stairs to the two attic bedrooms. He decided he didn't. It was possible that Rita was still up there sleeping, without Tara knowing she was there. Instead, he slipped back down to the shop as quietly as he could, backing down the last two steps to pull the door gently behind him as if afraid of being caught out in his snooping.

He straightened up, turned and walked straight into Lily.

'Aaah!' he yelped, clutching a hand to his chest in shock.

She smiled indulgently, lovely as ever, with her hair waving wildly over a jade green linen jacket he hadn't seen before.

'Sorry,' she said, grinning. 'I didn't mean to frighten you.'

He was too embarrassed to prevaricate.

'I was looking for Rita,' he said.

'You won't find her up there. I should think she's well on her way by now.'

He didn't really take in what she'd said.

'No, she came back last night. Charlie came to see me. I think she must still be asleep and Tara doesn't seem to know about it.'

He wandered back over to the counter, fazed at seeing her again so soon, wanting to touch her, but suddenly shy of their recent intimacy.

Lily put down her bag and leaned across to him, taking him by the wrist and squeezing it. He realised that she understood his discomfort and was regarding it with amusement.

'Rita's gone off again, Rufus. That's what I've come to tell you about. It's probably better if Tara doesn't find out. Did you tell her?'

Rufus was now immensely puzzled.

'No, but I don't understand. Where's she gone and why shouldn't Tara know about it?'

She patted his hand kindly.

'She wanted a bit of time to herself. A few weeks with your friend Charlie seems to have taken its toll.'

Loyal instincts rose up in Rufus.

'I don't think he exactly enjoyed every minute with her either!'

He spoke more sharply than he'd intended, saw the

surprise and disappointment in Lily's eyes and wanted to kick himself.

'So where's she gone now?' He tried to sound interested, but Lily had released his hand and was already picking up her bag to go.

'To Glastonbury to see friends.'

He followed her plaintively towards the door.

'But why didn't she tell Tara what she was doing?'

'It was better just to go. Tara's not expecting her back for months.'

'But she's her daughter! I can't understand why Rita would come back to the flat and not even leave her a note or anything like that. Just sneaking in and out again without a word seems a bit heartless.'

'Rufus, in case you haven't noticed, Tara is an emotional teenage girl who's inclined to kick up about the smallest thing.'

'All the more reason why she needs her mother then, I'd have thought.' Again he wished the words unsaid as soon as he'd spoken.

'Would you now? And I'd completely forgotten you were such an expert on childcare. Next time I'll get Rita to consult you before she makes any decisions of her own.'

She gave him a tight-lipped smile and a little nod and left without another word.

The deepest gloom descended on Rufus. He closed the shop early and headed home to Mean Cottage to salve his wounds with an indecently large scotch and some peace and quiet.

Sitting on the bench outside the back door, he wondered sadly if he was doomed to social ineptitude for the rest of his life or if there was any chance of curing it like an illness with a course of tablets or an operation. The suddenness of the change, the swift reversal of his fortunes with Lily made him shudder in retrospect. One moment they were on the brink of a promising relationship, careful and tender with each other, whilst the next the goodwill was shattered by one small difference of opinion. Was he wrong in what he'd said about Rita and her apparent callousness towards Tara? Or was Lily's inference right - that he was totally ignorant about such things and should keep his crass notions to himself? Alison would certainly have agreed with her. It was the kind of thing she'd accused him of on many occasions, but was it true or merely formulaic? He couldn't help thinking it was the kind of thing women threw too easily at men...

Rufus closed his eyes and immediately heard an echo of Cate's words - 'don't think, just feel.' But feelings only brought him back to Lily and the physical closeness of the previous night. He went through it all again, the easy conversation, the laughter and then the pressure of her body against his as they kissed. He was really in a dream now, reliving the sensations one by one, the sight and scent and touch of her filling him with liquid warmth. Her lips were wet on his hand... Something here jarred. When had she kissed his hand? And was it such a pleasant sensation after all?

Rufus opened his eyes to find the goat nibbling his fingers affectionately.

Lily banged her front door shut.

Looking up from the kitchen table where he and Tara were drinking coffee, Joe read his mother's body language and decided it was time for a walk. Lily was rarely cross, but better left well alone on those few occasions. He wondered what had angered her to this extent as the kettle crashed against the sink.

'Are you OK, Lily?' Tara asked curiously. She too was

surprised by Lily's discomposure.

'I'm fine,' Lily said through gritted teeth.

Joe grabbed Tara's arm and hauled her off, trying to impart a sense of urgency through contorted facial expressions that only made her giggle.

'See you later,' Joe said as they left.

Lily didn't reply. She didn't drink her coffee either, but sat at the table staring into the mug, trying to simmer her anger with Rufus down into something salvageable. Looking at it from his point of view perhaps Rita's behaviour was odd, but it wasn't really any of his business and Lily hated people who interfered in others' lives. Rita was an old friend and had first claim to her loyalty, just as Rufus had stood up for Charlie. On reflection, Lily liked him even more for that and sighed at her own defensiveness. She would ring him later and make everything alright between them again. She was sure Rufus wouldn't bear a grudge.

She did try that evening, but there was no answer and when Joe came in very late he told her that Rufus had gone up to London for a few days, leaving him in charge of Mean Cottage and the goat, whilst a very reluctant Tara had agreed to look after the shop. Lily shrugged off her disappointment. After all, it wouldn't do to get too fond of Rufus.

Rufus was enjoying himself enormously. It had taken a couple of days to shake off his sombre mood, but now he felt relaxed and optimistic after a healthy dose of uncomplicated and affectionate friendship. It was such a pleasant change to be looked after and made to feel important, he thought, as he sat in the conservatory at the back of Jane and David's house, stuffed with excellent food and wine, telling them more about the Craft Shop, blending self-depreciatory accounts of his early misunderstandings with the many perplexing encounters he had had with customers. Tonight it was surprisingly effortless for Rufus, who had never considered himself much of a raconteur, and they were laughing merrily about the limitless gullibility of New Age seekers when Jane fixed him with a typically knowing stare.

'It's really given you a kick, hasn't it, Roo?'

'What?'

'The shop, the hairy sandal brigade - you're loving it!'

He gave a little smile.

'I wouldn't go as far as that...'

'If you could see the smirk on your face, you would. Don't you think so?' She appealed to her husband.

'Oh, I don't know. He always looks a bit like that.' David was grinning too.

Rufus was suddenly overwhelmed by it all. Here he was, full and happy, in the company of his oldest friends who were beaming their pleasure at his new found success. As long as he didn't think about Lily...

After David had gone off to bed pleading an early start the next day, Rufus and Jane stayed up talking.

'So have you met some interesting people, apart from Tara and the weird customers you seem to attract?'

'Lots. The village is full of eccentrics. The shop is run by a man-eating ex-Sloane and there's an old woman who talks to rivers and cures plagues with homemade potions.'

'I was thinking more of younger women.'

He looked at her in some confusion.

'What do you mean?'

'Come on, Roo. Someone's put a sparkle in your eye and given you the gumption to jettison Alison without a backward glance.'

He gave a mock frown.

'You don't think I'm capable of that all on my own

151

then?'

'Not really, no. A bit of a shove is usually necessary to get you started in the right direction.'

'What, like you persuading me to go and live in the country, I suppose?'

'Exactly so, my perspicacious friend. I'm glad you recognise the hand of a master. So who is she?'

Rufus sighed and told Jane all about Lily. It seemed surprisingly little when put into words, but she listened carefully, head on one side in the birdlike manner that suited her small, sharp features.

It was easy to talk to Jane. She had always been his confidante, sharing the pleasure and pain of his earliest girlfriends at college through a couple of ill-matched relationships when he first worked at the bookshop to his fateful meeting with Alison. Jane had always disliked Alison and thought her quite wrong - and not nearly good enough - for Rufus, but she had not wanted to hurt him and after one attempt to warn him of what he was letting himself in for, had kept her objections to herself and tried to be friendly to Alison, who had clearly reciprocated her dislike and made less effort to conceal it.

When he finished talking about Lily, he looked to Jane hopefully for encouragement and enthusiasm, but she only raised her eyebrows and gave a little shrug.

'I can see the physical attraction, Roo, from your description, no problem, but if she's already got a partner - away a lot or not - don't you think you're letting yourself in for a lot more misery?'

He had longed for the release and indulgence of talking to someone else about Lily and trying to embroider the small stitches of their acquaintance so far into a fabric of weight and substance. What he had forgotten temporarily was that Jane would see it all from quite a different point of view, despite her willingness to try to understand the nature of his feelings.

'But I can't look at it like that, can I?' he wailed. 'I can't ignore my feelings just because it might not work out, surely?'

Jane put her arm round him and let his head rest comfortingly on her shoulder for a minute.

'I can't help thinking it's too soon after Alison to fall headlong for someone else,' she said slowly. 'I can see that Lily must be a refreshing change after bitch of the year, but she's not free, and the very last thing you need is complications that will tie you up in emotional knots and ruin the new life you've struggled to get going! Apart from that, she's a mother with a family and I just don't see you slotting into a step-father to teenagers role.'

'But I like Joe,' Rufus said.

'Of course you do, idiot' - she flicked her fingers against his skull - 'but that's not the same thing at all. Have you really thought about this beyond the possibility of a brief affair?'

'Why can't I just have a brief affair if I want one?' he asked peevishly.

Jane smiled down at him affectionately.

'No reason at all. But you need to pick someone who's free, and, preferably, someone you're not about to fall in love with.'

'Jane! You mean I should be on the look out for a purely sexual encounter and to hell with romance!'

'I really think it would be the best thing in your case,' she said. 'For now.'

Under the eaves in her attic, Cate was rummaging in a cardboard box, finally pulling out a faded green folder of old papers. She took it over to the light of the tiny skylight window and flicked through the contents. As she did so, a photograph slipped out and fell to the floor face down. In pencil on the back was the faint date 1947. She crouched and settled her balance carefully before turning it over to regard the figure of a man leaning in the doorway of a cottage. Tall and lean, with a mass of black hair swept back from his broad face, strong brows and an aquiline nose, eyes screwed up against the glare of the sun, he stood entirely at his ease with one elbow resting on the door frame, the other arm hanging loosely at his side, a cigarette dangling from the fingers.

Old memories descended on Cate like a fall of snow. This must have been taken shortly after Adam arrived at the cottage. He appeared one day in the autumn of 1945 - when she herself was just fifteen - a tenant at first, although he bought the place later from the Marsdens whose three sons were all killed in the war and their mother went quite out of her wits with grief. Adam must have been a little over thirty then, maybe more. Her own life changed from the day of his arrival, when she stopped in the lane to watch him unloading boxes from a battered Austin and was invited in for tea, although the dark brew he gave her tasted of berries and the hedgerows before all else.

It was Adam, to whom nothing was strange, who recognised and taught her how to use her gifts, instead of concealing them as a stigma to be feared. She'd always been afraid to set herself apart, to give her parents worry or rouse the mockery of the other village children, although she knew that something made her solitary and happiest so. 'It's knowledge you were born with,' Adam used to say. 'You can no more turn away from it than stop the day from dawning.' Then he'd grin at her. 'You lucky sprout! I had to learn all mine from books.'

Forcing her thoughts away from him, Cate restored the photograph to the folder and continued to rifle through it, suppressing the temptation to linger over every scrap of paper. She ignored the few letters he had sent her, some sketches and notebooks, and went on until she was sure that everything she wanted was there. Then she made her way slowly back down the ladder, clutching the folder in her hand.

Rufus returned to Mean Cottage much cheered by his change of scene and supportive friends, but unmoved by Jane's advice. He was determined to see Lily and clear the air between them. He was not going to spoil something so important by misplaced loyalty to Charlie who had himself never shown the least consideration towards Rufus' feelings in all his schemes. He was also prompted by a sense of fairness. Rita was nothing to do with him, he'd never met her and was in no position to judge her actions. He also had no reason to suspect that Tara wasn't more than capable of looking after herself.

He felt the renewed pleasure of ownership as he set foot in the cottage again and was even pleased to see the goat, which all but tore its tethering peg from the ground in its delight at seeing him again. If I can inspire such affection in a dumb animal, he thought, who knows what I might not be capable of with women if I really put my mind to it.

But it's Lily I have to convince, he thought, because she's the one. She's definitely the one.

Chapter 10

Cate didn't seem to think so.

Rufus went along the lane to her cottage ostensibly to see if she had the fresh basil he needed for a dish to impress Lily, but he was also hoping for something else, some seal of approval, or just a sign of her continued interest in his progress as he hadn't seen her for a while.

As she showed him dozens of terracotta pots of all sizes, containing all manner of herbs grown from seed, Cate scrutinised him closely, but said nothing. When he felt the weight of her silence too much to bear in his new-found determined state, he broached the subject himself.

'I've asked Lily to lunch. You know, Joe's mother.'

'Yes, I know who you mean.' She picked out a lush basil specimen and handed it to him, rubbing one leaf between her fingers, to release the evocative Mediterranean scent.

'That's wonderful,' Rufus exclaimed. 'Can you really spare it?'

Cate gestured ironically at the rows and rows of pots around the outhouse shelves.

'But be careful how you use it,' she said.

'Lily's a vegetarian,' he said eagerly. 'I thought she'd like homemade pesto.'

'Indeed.' Cate's silver eyebrows lifted. 'You know its reputation then?'

For one wild moment he thought she was talking about Lily.

'I'm sorry... I...'

'The herb, Rufus.' She shook her head in mock exasperation, hiding a smile. 'The basil you're holding.'

Rufus extended the arm with the pot away from him warily.

'No, except its name comes from the Greek word for

king, I think, and Keats wrote that ghastly gothic poem about some maiden hiding her murdered lover's head in a pot of basil.'

Cate seemed singularly unimpressed with this academic knowledge.

'It has an ambivalent history,' she said, fixing her attention on the bright green of the leaves, 'even if you discount Culpepper's story that one of its more alarming effects was to breed a scorpion in a man's brain. It's been feared as the devil's herb and at other times used as a remedy against witches, but its greatest potency has always been in love.'

'Which is your excuse for growing it, then?' he asked flippantly.

Her eyes narrowed, flustering him at once.

'Sorry,' he said quickly. 'I think I'll opt for love potion in the circumstances.'

'I hope you've chosen wisely.'

From her tone it was clear Cate thought he hadn't, and again he had the distinct impression she was talking about Lily rather than the basil.

Lily arrived for lunch at Mean Cottage looking more desirable than ever. Rufus had felt awkwardly tentative on the phone when he invited her, but now as she kissed him on the cheek in greeting, he was relieved beyond measure that there was no trace of embarrassment between them. He was determined to keep off all potentially controversial subjects and immediately showed her round the house with shy pride so she could admire all Joe's handiwork and his own attempts at decorative touches here and there. Her appreciation reinforced his pleasure in the surroundings he now regarded easily as home and security.

They went into the garden to eat at a green plastic

table Rufus had hurriedly purchased for the occasion, together with copious amounts of Chablis which were now filling the fridge.

His pesto took pride of place with the fresh pasta and parmesan he had braved the village shop and Jacinta Jacobs' innuendoes to purchase. Rufus also took great care with the salads he made from his own lettuces and spinach, marvelling at how well everything grew here. Almost from the day of his arrival produce had sprung up in the vegetable patch and packets of seeds he'd planted himself in hastily dug, shallow beds had produced phalanxes of brightly coloured flowers. Only the moon garden remained apparently barren, except in his fevered imagination. He was intending to show Lily round there later and perhaps confide in her about his peculiar nocturnal experiences. He took comfort from the thought that, numbering witches among her closest friends, she would hardly be likely to laugh him to scorn.

The good weather, almost unbroken over the last few weeks, was still going strong. The air hung hot and heavy in their faces as they sat back after their meal and smiled at one another with silent pleasure at the successful renewal of their friendship. Nothing had been said about their difference of opinion and in overcoming that minor but significant obstacle, Rufus thought that they had moved on now to a new degree of intimacy. There was nothing in Lily's behaviour to so much as hint at coupledom with someone else and when they were together, the unreal concept of her alleged partner went out of Rufus' head altogether. She was there for *him* and reality was the growing bond between them.

'I want to show you something,' he said at last, when the moment seemed right, bravely getting up and holding out his hand. When she responded at once, he felt a strong rush of confidence in the rightness of it all.

They strolled over towards the brick wall, Lily lacing her arm through his so he felt the warmth of her fingers on his wrist.

When they reached the entrance, however, Rufus felt suddenly strangely nervous at sharing these secrets with Lily. He vaguely grasped that it was a revelation of surprising importance, without being able to analyse the significance of anything that had happened there. And yet he had talked about it to Cate, who seemed to understand - surely Lily should be an even safer bet?

He took her hand to lead her through the round hole in the bricks, half-hoping that some miracle would have wrought a daylight transformation of the moon garden, so she could see what an extraordinary place it was.

There was a short silence as Lily looked around at the straggly weeds and brown withered stalks of his surprise.

'What a lovely garden,' she said eventually. 'It's a pity it's been so neglected.' She turned to him, smiling. 'You could make this into a show place with a bit of hard work!'

'I'm no gardener,' he said modestly, although her words echoed one of his own fantasies about the place.

'Come on, what about those wonderful vegetables? You mustn't play down your talents, Rufus.'

He wanted to kiss her then and took one step forward, but she moved past him, almost deliberately, he thought, as if the time was not right.

He followed her towards the centre of the garden, but as soon as she set foot on the stone path, she faltered. When he came up behind her, she had a hand to her forehead and colour was draining from her face.

He put his arm round her for support and she leant into his shoulder gratefully.

'I'm sorry. I feel a bit sick.'

'You'd better sit down...'

He made to lead her to the ledge around the pond.

'No, let's go back to the house. I need to get out of the sun for a bit.'

They went back slowly. He saw that at first her eyes were half-closed and her lips moved as if forming unspoken words. When they reached the shade at the side of house, she was better and he placed a chair for her carefully before hurrying inside to fetch cold water and paracetamol.

She shook her head at the sight of these.

'Thanks, but I don't use that kind of thing. Could you get my bag?'

She took two tiny pills from a brown phial and put them under her tongue, then smiled reassuringly at Rufus' anxious face.

'I'm alright, really. There's nothing to worry about.'

'Perhaps it was something you ate?'

'No! For goodness' sake, it's nothing to do with your lovely food. Stop looking so guilty!'

'Sorry.' He smiled foolishly, loving her more than ever, but sensing that an opportunity had been lost and that the day was somehow over before it had really begun.

Tara was sitting cross-legged on the floor in the flat, hands over her face. Joe shifted uneasily on the sofa above her, not knowing what to say or do without provoking another eruption of emotion. He was already exhausted with the struggle, but he badly wanted to say something that would make her feel better.

'Hey, maybe you're imagining it. How long is it since you've been in there?'

She whipped her hands away and turned on him savagely.

'If that's the best you can do, you can just fuck off, Joe! I *know* she's been in here, taken things from her room and

160

gone again without a bloody word.' A gulp for breath turned into a long single sob. 'She's supposed to be my mother, to care about me...'

'Come on,' he tried to get hold of her arms, only to be struck a forceful blow in the chest as she repelled him. It hurt and he withdrew, leaning back against the sofa in moroseful silence whilst Tara coiled her long limbs into a tight ball of anger and misery at his feet.

They stayed like that for what seemed like hours while the light outside began to fade. But when he tried to rouse her again with the gentlest of touches, Tara leapt up and ran up the stairs into her room, slamming the door behind her. Joe sighed and got up, then changed his mind, and settled down again on the sofa.

After Lily had gone, Rufus threw off his sticky shirt and began some agitated weeding in the vegetable garden, ignoring the goat's plaintive overtures. He wrestled and hustled intruders out of the carrot fronds with hot frustration, mulling over and over how uncannily he was constantly prevented from greater intimacy with Lily by adverse circumstances. Or was it that? She had left him after their meal at the restaurant, she had walked off when they quarrelled, and she had been ill today, preferring to go home rather than stay and be looked after by him. It was really more her own decisions than chance which were keeping them apart, he decided. But why? Was she not interested in him or not ready for a closer relationship? He had to admit to himself that he hadn't a clue how she really felt about him. It was something he was going to have to talk to her about...

'You *have* done well in so short a time!'

Rufus raised his throbbing head to see Dennis Braithwaite, standing at the corner of the house, watching him with eager interest.

'Hello,' he said wearily. 'I'm not ready to sell yet if that's what you were wondering.' What was the estate agent equivalent of an ambulance chaser, he wondered.

'My dear boy, no indeed. I can see that you are busy bonding with your soil.' Dennis hopped about, his little bald head bobbing from side to side in appreciative pecks. 'So productive! I just dropped in as I was passing to see how it's all going. Your front door was open so I had the slightest peak inside - a positive transformation, if I may say so.'

'I've had help,' said Rufus shortly.

'And the natives?'

'Sorry?'

'Are they friendly? Have you been made welcome in Creech?'

'I haven't had much time for socialising actually, with work and this place to organise.'

Rufus was wiping his dirty hands on a handkerchief and making for the kitchen in search of a cold drink.

'Of course you haven't. But I'm here to change all that.'

Rufus stopped, startled.

'A pleasant invitation, I hope,' Dennis prattled on. 'To dinner, in the village, Sunday evening, very select gathering. Chance to meet some decent chaps and chapesses.'

'Well, I don't know.' All Rufus' good intentions about embracing any opportunities that offered in his new life slipped away at the thought of a few hours conviviality with a bevy of parasites who fed on the blood of innocent house purchasers.

'Oh, go on,' said Dennis playfully. 'You won't regret it. Jacinta's a great cook.'

Rufus' heart sank even further. He was just about to open his mouth and fabricate any excuse he could think of, like he'd be too busy breathing on Saturday to go out

162

anywhere, but Dennis was too quick for him, skipping off as merrily as he'd come.

'Lovely. I'll come by and collect you. Just before eight. Right ho. Must dash...'

All I can hope, Rufus thought, is that one of us will be run over by a tractor before the weekend.

In the early years Adam had often been away from Creech, sometimes for weeks at a time, Cate remembered. The house was too far out for anyone in the village to take much interest in his comings and goings, although when he dropped into The Green Man for an occasional pint, there was usually a bit of good-natured speculation about what he got up to on his own at Mean Cottage. The only person who saw torches lit at night or candelabra burning outside on a still June evening was Cate, often out herself after her parents were fast asleep by ten o'clock in their early country way.

When they were friends and knew to trust each other without thought, she joined him naturally in simple rituals, in honouring nature, the seasons, the genius loci with words and gifts. He taught her many things - from herbal lore to the making of figures from corn stalks discarded at harvest, from deep meditation to the language of runes, etching the lines onto pebbles they gathered from the stream bed. The singular faculties she had internalised all her young life were gradually drawn out into open expression, her intuition focused into a practical understanding of the power to effect change by will. When she tried to thank him for all these lessons, he only shook his head, smiling ruefully, and said 'There's knowing how to and then there's doing it, sprout. At the point you're taking off, I'm held fast to the earth.'

For the last thirty years of his life, Adam settled entirely in Creech, filling his time with the garden, the

163

animals and, more and more as his physical powers declined, with writing. He had a great hunger for knowledge, the sort of book-learning that Cate had never known nor set much store by, squirrelling away scraps of information, gleaned from his researches, to piece together like a patchwork quilt.

Cate remembered clearly the day that Adam started writing about the legend of the moon garden. He had always eschewed the modern biro and notepad methods for his work, preferring to buy reams of hand-made paper from the mill on the Huele near Bruford and to dip his pen into a glass bottle of black ink. The discrete fastidiousness of these anachronisms always amused Cate, as she watched him working at the davenport - that same one that now stood in the corner of her own living room - his great thatch of hair, white as an egret in old age, flopping down over his forehead as he bent over the paper.

Cate held those same sheets now in her hands, and although she'd never had a lot of time for reading and knew the story well enough, she opened her ears to Adam's voice, echoing down the years, unable to resist a longing to feel his presence near her after ten years of absence. She closed her eyes and still the words went on, a strong spirit palpable in the room around her as the pages slipped to the floor.

Rufus was now resigned to the presence of the goat he had reluctantly named Gordon. No-one had responded to his notice in the village and there was no word of any animal missing. A call to the local rescue centre for help ended in Rufus promising to consider taking another goat to partner his new pet. But one was quite enough, he said firmly to Gordon, who was noisily engaged in hoovering up fallen green apples. Any more and the lush grass around the cottage would become an endangered species.

He was just leading Gordon for the night towards his shelter in the ramshackle old woodshed by the stream, when a whirlwind flew round the corner of the house and hurled itself on Rufus, yelling incoherently and thumping his shoulders with clenched fists.

As Gordon began to dance his outrage at this over-intimate interloper, Joe came quickly across the grass and tried manfully to wrench Tara away from Rufus, who had now lost his balance in the melee and was literally on his knees. He got up to see Tara's angry face, streaked with a dark flush, only inches from his own, with all Joe's efforts barely keeping her arms pinned behind her.

Breathing heavily at the force of this assault and the exertion of getting the goat to calm down, Rufus eyed her wildly.

'What the fuck are you playing at?' he shouted.

'You *knew*,' she shrieked, 'you *knew* she'd come back and you didn't tell me.'

Rufus felt guilty the instant he realised what her tirade was about.

'Tara, wait, just be quiet for a minute, will you?'

'You *knew*! I bet you both thought it was very funny, tricking me like that. Then saying you thought I was her, just out of nothing, but I never suspected even then, and all the time you'd seen her... I trusted you, you f...'

'Tara,' Joe launched in quickly. 'We should go. This is not a good idea.'

'No, I don't think you should,' Rufus said quietly. He felt unbearably sad at the strength of Tara's passion and her face, vulnerable and childlike still tilting towards him in the dusk. 'Come on, let's go inside and talk about it.'

Joe disappeared on pretence of checking some of his work as soon as he could see Tara was beyond the violent stage. She and Rufus sat side by side on his old sofa. He looked at her with tender concern as she stared rigidly straight ahead, her face tight with misery.

'Tara, I haven't seen your mother. Ever. She did come back, but I only knew from Charlie and when I got to the shop and she wasn't in evidence, I didn't know what to think. You went sweeping out before I could explain why I'd thought you were her and then...'

He stopped suddenly, realising too late where this was going.

She looked right at him then, eyes gleaming with hostility.

'And then you just decided not to bother, I suppose.'

He winced at the savage tone of her sarcasm and was stung to his own defence.

'No, not at all. *I* thought you should have been told. Of course I did. Shit, she's your mother!'

She glared at him steadily whilst taking this in.

'If *you* thought I should be told, who didn't?' Her voice was smaller now, more fearful of his answer.

Rufus was torn between two loyalties, but he knew he had to be honest with the exposed frailties of the girl in front of him.

'Lily,' he said gently. Tara's eyes widened in shock.

'Lily! What's it got to do with her?'

Rufus tried, ineffectually, to explain without diminishing Tara as he felt her mother and Lily had done in their decision. He could see from the storm brewing on her face that he had failed miserably.

Joe came nervously into the room at the sound of Tara's voice rising again to a thin screech. When she saw him, she turned on him furiously.

'Your mother's an interfering old bitch, Joe! I don't want to see her ever again.'

Then she threw herself on Rufus' shoulder in a fit of savage weeping.

As soon as her initial spasm of fury was over, Tara withdrew awkwardly from Rufus and wandered restlessly about the room. He took it as a good sign that she did not at once rush out after Joe, who had taken himself off somewhere after a miserable glance at Rufus over the top of Tara's dark head. When Rufus went to make them both some coffee, she followed him into the kitchen and sat down silently at the table.

'This is nothing to do with Joe, you know,' he said gently, placing a mug in front of her.

'I know that,' she snapped and then sighed deeply with a great heave of her shoulders. 'Sorry.'

'It's OK. And I can understand why you're so upset, even though if it was my mother I'd have been delighted to avoid seeing her.'

A flash of surprised curiosity lit Tara's face.

'Don't you get on with her?'

'Didn't,' said Rufus, 'when she was alive, but we're not talking about me now. This is about you and it's important.'

She nodded gloomily.

'It's Lily that really pisses me off,' she said. 'I never thought she'd treat me like a little kid. When I'm over there, we really talk about stuff, like we're on the same wave length, it makes me feel like women together and all that...'

Her words trailed off into a large sniff.

Rufus thought of how Lily had dismissively described Tara. It had surprised him that she regarded her son's lover as nothing more than a kid whose emotions were not to be taken too seriously. But perhaps he was doing just that now, when there really was nothing to get upset about.

'I'm sure she thought it was the best thing for you.'

'Exactly. That's what I'm saying, other people deciding what's best for me. As if I didn't have any thoughts, no brain, some dim skinny kid.'

'I've never thought of you like that,' Rufus said with feeling. 'I find you quite scary actually.'

He saw at once that this quick spontaneous truth had pleased her.

'I like you, Rufus,' she said in response and he felt suddenly proud and foolishly worthy. He had become very fond of Tara. Her moods and waves of emotion were what he expected as the language and communication channels of the teenage years. He did not think he'd be scared of them again after tonight.

'And Lily's not so bad,' he said coaxingly. He was ashamed to realise that he wanted to ensure Tara's approval for Lily so he himself could think unreservedly well of her again.

Tara's dark, deep eyes, their unfathomable quality so unlike the crystal clarity of Lily's, hardened.

'She just proves my point about so-called adults,' she said scathingly. 'They just do whatever they like and then go off on one when others do the same. Who is she to be judging me? At least I don't sleep around!'

'Tara!'

She leapt up from the sofa, scything through the hard-won atmosphere of complicity.

'It's true! You only don't see it because you're sniffing round her so hard yourself!'

She ran out of the room and he heard the back door slam seconds later. Not only was his attempt at diplomacy a miserable failure, but now he had more problems of his own to worry about.

He lay restlessly awake for hours and then slept deeply, his fears woven into strange dreams of being pygmy-sized in a field of hay about to be cropped, paralysed by the noise of the approaching blades. He woke abruptly, sweaty and uncomfortable, to see from the window a summer mist hanging around the willows along the stream.

Rufus went out into the early morning garden and walked slowly around, going over and over in his mind the sequence of worrying events of yesterday. He had been rejected by Lily again, he was estranged from Tara, and he had the dubious pleasure of an evening with Jacinta Jacobs to look forward to. And, despite the elusive Rita's new disappearance, he no longer felt secure in his position at the shop. She might well turn up again next week and he'd have no work to keep him occupied and very little money to survive on. He could always try to sell Mean Cottage, now that it was so much more habitable thanks to Joe's remarkable skills. Turning to look at the uneven outline of his house, the thought of breaking the connection he had made aroused such strong feelings that Rufus realised he didn't want to think of making another new start. Here was where he wanted to be. He would find other work and he would do his best to form a lasting relationship with Lily, but whatever happened on those fronts, here was where he stayed. A long bleat from Gordon echoed through the quiet morning air. After all, there was a goat to look after.

As he washed up the breakfast things he was still in the same positive frame of mind. He heard Lily's car draw up and prayed that she wouldn't just drop Joe off, but come in to see him. He was also anxious to ask Joe about Tara. To his delight the engine died and doors slammed.

Rufus stepped out of the back door and called a greeting to Joe's shambolic figure as he rounded the corner of the house. The words died on his lips, however, as he saw the second person. Male, dark, unkempt and dressed in black leather - anyone less like Lily was hard to imagine.

'Hello,' said Rufus lamely.

Joe mumbled a greeting and went on into the house. The other man stepped forward and held out his hand, a vulpine grin on his thin, unshaven face. He reminded Rufus of an illustration of a werewolf he'd once seen in a book of Latin stories.

'Rufus, hi - Lily's told me all about you.'

Rufus' heart sank still further. Somehow he didn't like the thought of what Lily might have said about him to this man. He shook the outstretched hand without enthusiasm.

'I'm Ged,' the other said and looked keenly at Rufus. 'I see she hasn't told you a lot about me. I'm Joe's step-dad.'

'I thought you were away,' Rufus blurted out, aware as he spoke of the stupidity of the remark.

'I've been away, but now I'm back.' He grinned easily, flashing the sharp teeth, but Rufus felt a harder underlying force at work. From whatever Lily had said, this Ged had deduced that Rufus was in love with her and now he was warning him off. That's why he'd brought Joe over and bothered to come in. He probably couldn't resist a look and a jibe at Lily's hapless suitor.

Rufus tried to rally himself.

'Joe's done some fantastic work here. Come in and have a look.'

It was a luke warm offer made out of loyalty to Joe. He really didn't want Ged setting so much as a toenail inside Mean Cottage.

'Can't stop, sorry. Got things to do.' He bared his teeth again and turned away. 'See you.'

Rufus watched him go and waited until the car had moved away before he went inside. He felt in some way diminished by the encounter and wanted to get himself together before talking to Joe.

He found him putting up a shelf in the bathroom. Rufus squeezed in despite the fact there was barely floor space for Joe and his large canvas tool bag.

'So it's good your step-dad's back then.'

'Yeah.'

Rufus did not discern much excitement in Joe's tone. He watched him work in silence for a few moments.

'Do you get on alright?' he said casually.

'Yeah.'

'I expect your mum's pleased too.'

A shrug. Rufus felt a stab of hope.

'Does he often go away?'

A nod. It was clear that Joe just wanted to get on with his work and Rufus gave it up. Getting detailed information out of him would require the skills of a medieval inquisitor, even though Rufus would like to have asked him where Ged got such a silly name from.

But there was something not quite right, Rufus was sure. The mysterious and predatory Ged coming and going - probably with the full moon, he thought facetiously - did not seem like a permanent fixture in Lily's life. She certainly didn't behave as if he was, which puzzled Rufus even more. He couldn't wait to see her again and make his own judgement of her pleasure at the return of the wanderer.

Chapter 11

Tara remained cool and aloof with Rufus when they met in the shop. She did not offer to help out at lunch times, nor hang around the counter chatting to him on her way in or out. Much of the time all he knew of her was the bass thump of music from overhead. It made Rufus very sad to think she had judged him so harshly when he had been on her side all along. Try as he might he could not think Lily had been right to keep secrets from Tara. As for Rita, Rufus was pretty sure he wouldn't like her very much at all when they finally met.

He went on running the shop as well as he could and in the evenings concentrated on improving the cottage. He decided there was no point in not getting the roof fixed, as it would increase the value and his chances of selling if it came to that financially. The work would take a week and then another to clean up the dust and debris, but at least the decoration could then begin in earnest.

There was no sign of Lily. Ged had got Joe an old motorbike from somewhere so he was not reliant on lifts to get to Mean Cottage any more. All Rufus had to look forward to at the end of the depressing first week of her absence was an evening with Jacinta Jacobs and Dennis Braithwaite.

Jacinta spent hours getting ready, but it was the meal that had taken most of her efforts, she reflected ruefully, looking at her flushed face and neck in the mirror. The black dress and Hermes scarf were designed to give her a little confidence, although she could see from Rufus' own casual sartorial habits that he was unlikely to be impressed by them. She made a few experimentally alluring faces at herself. Or, let's be realistic, by me, she thought with a deep sigh, and wished for the hundredth time that day that she was younger or braver or just less downright scared of everything.

When Geoffrey found someone else and ended their marriage, it was a shock to realise just how much she'd relied on him to deal with life on her behalf over the years. Shielded from practical problems by wealth and kept from close female friendships by chronic shyness, there was little in her life beyond cooking and arranging the elegant dinner tables she loved. This was the only way she knew to make her mark and the jolly hostess routine had somehow got tagged onto it as a required extra, concealing her social terrors beneath a fulsome front of house act.

Jacinta had never given much thought to filling her time in any other way, and here, in the barren wasteland of Creech, away from the shops and restaurants of her beloved Knightsbridge, she was brought up sharply against the inadequacy of her grounding at every turn. And if Geoffrey had put her aside so easily after all those years, who else was ever going to give her a second glance? Rufus Keene was the only appealing chap she'd laid eyes on in weeks, but he'd shown no interest in her whatsoever, despite her attempts to join him in merry conversation whenever he came into the shop.

The fragrant scent emanating from the kitchen summoned her from the bedroom. Pull yourself together, she said sternly to herself. He'll enjoy the food anyway.

Rufus was collected by Dennis, who was wearing a dark suit with a silk cravat and driving a silver Mercedes. Quite a contrast with the bike and cycle shorts, Rufus thought, struggling to cope with Dennis' excessively affable chatter as they glided towards the village. He only hoped he could keep up a pretence of banter and enjoyment for a whole evening.

They parked on the street in the centre of the village. A man dressed as a banana was getting into a car further up the street as Dennis led the way round to the back of the shop and up a wrought-iron staircase to the entrance of the flat. Jacinta flung open the door immediately and breathlessly ushered them both into the wonderfully aromatic fumes of the small kitchen, then turned expectantly to the outside again.

'And your friend?' she said to Dennis.

'He's right here!' Dennis gave Rufus a playful slap on the back.

Jacinta's mouth hung open in horror for a moment before she rallied.

'Go through, Rufus.' She took his arm and propelled him across a narrow corridor into the sitting room whilst managing to push Dennis, who was eagerly following, back into the kitchen with the other hand. 'I'll just get you a drink.' Her large teeth glistened at him in the dimmed light as she left him alone.

Rufus sat down and looked around at the carefully styled room with its colour-coordinated furnishings, but what really took his attention was the dining alcove with its table laid for four. Immediately he strained his ears to pick up the hissed interrogation going on in the kitchen.

'You *said* you'd ask Rufus for *me*!' Jacinta was wailing. 'And you were supposed to be bringing a special 'friend'.'

'I have,' Dennis responded dolefully. 'It's Rufus. And I said I'd *ask* him for you, not ask him for *you*, as I'm the one who knows him.'

'But he's not... you know,' she whispered savagely.

'How do you know? He hasn't shown much interest in you, has he? And I thought this dinner party was supposed to give him a chance to meet people, not for you to get your claws into him!'

174

My God, Rufus thought, what have I let myself in for? I'll need a bodyguard for the evening at this rate or perhaps I can play them off against each other.

'Oh!' Jacinta sounded stunned. 'But I thought you were bringing someone else, a new face. I thought four would be ideal for getting to know each other. There's no-one else coming. What on earth can I do?'

'A drink for your guests might be a good start,' Dennis said moodily.

When they came through with a tray of glasses and bottles, Rufus was standing innocently on the far side of the room looking at a bookcase full of cookery books.

Dennis kept up a stream of chatter as he poured the drinks, to distract Rufus' attention whilst Jacinta swept away a place setting and then after downing her gin and tonic in one gulp, bravely faced Rufus with the news that all the other guests had unfortunately cancelled - some sort of bug around the village - and how nice to be just the three of them.

The nice part turned out to be the meal itself. Jacinta might be a lousy shopkeeper, but she could certainly cook and Rufus was able to lavish genuine praise on every mouthful of the beef and ale casserole, the hackle-back potatoes with their crispy sage coats and the formidable pear and almond tart which followed.

He brushed aside personal questions from both sides with the brief fact of his broken marriage, refusing to be drawn about the current state of his emotions, and then let Dennis' anecdotes of an estate-agent's life drift past him in a haze of Bordeaux, keeping his legs firmly under his own chair in case either of his companions had amorous ideas. He had only to remind Jacinta about London life in any lull in the conversation for her to range off into a sad reminiscence of cocktail parties and business dinners at fabulous restaurants. He guessed

175

that she had run away to the country to avoid being seen in her new impoverishment by former friends and she had bought the shop on an impulse, a pathetic echo of women she knew in London who had been set up by their husbands in smart little boutiques off Sloane Square.

'You never thought of opening a restaurant yourself?' he asked. 'You'd make a bomb with food like this.'

Tears welled in her eyes at the compliment and he realised in a quick flash of shame that she wasn't stupid at all, but wounded and vulnerable as he himself had been after Alison's betrayal. She'd been cut loose into a world she had no feeling for after years of security in a rich town life.

'Geoffrey chose this place really. He thought I'd be better off in a village and it was safer to take over a going concern,' Jacinta said honestly. 'Less chance of things going wrong! I've no experience at all, you see.'

She fussed around with a plate of cheeses arranged on waxed leaves.

How wrong I was, and how cruel, Rufus thought as he watched her. You ditch your wife and bury her in the country where she can't be any embarrassment to you, stuck in a village and a business she hasn't chosen for herself.

'But you've done wonders here,' said Dennis, who was reluctant to be left out of any conversation. 'Marvellous stock.'

Rufus wondered if Dennis was the only person who regularly bought things there. He suddenly wanted to make Jacinta feel better, to encourage her to hope for improvement as he had done and to know the power of choice.

'The people who run the Falling Goat in Bruford are off to Spain soon to breed horses, I hear,' he said.

Dennis' professional ears pricked up at once.

176

'Really? I hadn't heard that.'

'Shop-keeper's perk to pick up the news before it happens!' Rufus didn't want this to turn into a real estate topic. He turned to Jacinta. 'Do you know it?' He himself had lunched there a few times when he felt deserving of a treat.

'I wonder if they've made any arrangements for selling,' Dennis continued regardless. 'It's a nice old building and not a bad position at all for trade. I must pop in there next week and have a word.'

Rufus ignored him and looked at Jacinta.

'Yes. It's just the sort of place I'd...' Her red face flushed deeper. 'But I'm fine here, really.' She got up quickly, bustling round to gather up their plates.

After coffee, Rufus felt an overwhelming urge to get away. The room was stiflingly hot and Dennis' interminable bonhomie was grinding his nerves close to the bone. He was also dreading the thought of a cosy ride home in the swish car, and the possibility of having to repel advances from the little gnome made his meal shift uneasily in his stomach.

He followed Jacinta out to the kitchen on the pretext of refilling the brandy glasses.

'Thank you for a wonderful meal. I really do think you're missing your vocation here, you know!'

Her face simpered automatically but he thought her eyes were miserable with longing for a different sort of life. There was nothing he could do to help her now but he still felt guilty at sneaking away.

'But what about Dennis?' she asked when she saw he really did mean to slip out into the night alone. 'And how will you get home?'

He put a finger to his lips.

'I'd prefer to go alone. It's a lovely night and I could do with the exercise after such a feast.'

177

'You mean you're going to... walk?' she said in a horrified whisper, as if he had suggested dancing naked in the high street on a Saturday morning.

'It's good for the brain.' He gestured towards the living room. 'I'm sorry, I know it's rude of me, but I really can't face it.'

For a second, her strange mask failed to respond and she simply nodded her understanding. Rufus leant forward to give her the briefest of kisses on the cheek and then opened the back door. 'Thank you, Jacinta. I've really enjoyed myself.' He felt that this lie was the least return he could make to her for the breach of good manners inherent in his undignified departure.

She gave a tight smile and began to stack crockery to cover the noise of the door.

Cate sat on a wooden seat in her garden, shuffling through Adam's notes, extracting what she wanted from the pile. Here it was: an account of how James Quincey Liddell, master of Creech Manor in the 1860s and a self-styled "man of science", took his role in the village seriously enough to attempt to disabuse the villagers of their superstitions by having the willow tree sacred to the moon felled and burnt. He then constructed a high-walled formal garden there to keep young lovers away from the spot which legend said would test their compatibility. The ugly Victorian church in Creech stood now as a monument to Liddell piety, if such destruction was counted favourable by any form of deity.

Adam had also made careful record of his conversations with Mavis Skelton, who at a hundred years of age clearly remembered the Liddells at the manor and their determined efforts to stamp out any sign of the old ways. The old lady enjoyed talking to Adam about her childhood, when there were still those who called the gardener's house Moon Cottage, and he himself had seen an alteration in a Liddell family document of 1886, where the record of rents showed Moon altered to Mean, as if to black out a thousand years of local history with a poor excuse for a joke.

But it was not so easy, Cate thought to herself with a smile. May Day dances on the village green, Halloween traditions, harvest festival itself were all echoes of the old pre-Christian ways, celebrated unwittingly by all and sundry who'd no more knowingly hold a pagan torch than do their weekend shopping in the nude. It was all still there, the roots of things, holding fast with the strength of earth. And Rufus could pull as hard as he liked in the opposite direction, but she did not doubt that he would own the truth at last.

Outside the village shop Rufus took in deep breaths of evening air with profound relief. He had been in similar situations a hundred times in his previous London life. Drinks and dinners and parties where he felt nothing in common with the other participants, yet made polite conversation and feigned interest in a myriad of banalities simply because it was the nature of such occasions to do so. It was the essence of most people's social lives, the thinnest veneer of pleasure not quite stretched to breaking point over the rough ground of tedium and predictability. He didn't want to do it any more. He wanted to choose, to spend time with people he cared about and to share some meaningful communication for a change. He didn't imagine that Cate or Tara accepted - or indeed received - such invitations, although he grinned to himself at the image of their presence at Jacinta's doomed dinner party. And what about Lily? Did she willingly spend time with those she didn't really like and play the social games expected with good grace? He didn't think so, but then, with Lily, who could say? He hadn't even begun to define her for himself, to dare to presume he had the knowledge or the understanding to attempt an act of such intimacy.

He groaned with the sheer frustration of it all as he strode along the main road towards the bridge.

Behind him there was a sudden noise - he feared that it was Dennis' voice, cross and urgent, echoing down the deserted street. A car door slammed and the purr of an engine coming towards him sent Rufus swiftly across the bridge and into a mad dive down the steep bank. He crouched down in the weeds by the water's edge, heart thumping, half-amused at his own folly - he surely didn't think Dennis would pursue him under the bridge like a sniffer dog? The car passed by and veered left down the lane that led to Mean Cottage. Rufus wondered how on earth he would get home now, if Dennis intended to mount a vigil outside the house. Then he looked down helplessly at the noisy little stream dashing by and was struck by an idea. What if he followed the course of the water back home instead of risking the road? A sort of path led away from him along the bank, overgrown but passable from the tread of fishermen or children. It was only half-past ten on a warm summer evening, the sky still light with faint stars gathering to await the rising moon. He thought he could manage to pick his way through the nettles and brambles without too much trouble. It would be a refreshing adventure after his stifling evening.

Rufus smiled to himself and set off. Despite whacking his head against the first low willow branch and feeling the keen prick of nettle stings around his ankles, he felt no discomfort, but only an airy satisfaction and the pleasant awareness of the soft green life all around him settling down for sleep.

The smell of wet rocks and mossy soil reminded him suddenly of the stream near his childhood house where he had spent so many hours happily playing alone, his solitude seeming easy in an environment crowded by nature. Rufus sat down on a fallen tree-trunk and closed his eyes. He felt again the sensation of running very fast through the long grass of the meadow, the pounding of his legs and rushing of blood in his ears drowning out echoes of his father's strictures and his mother's bitter sarcasms until the energy of his movement became free and joyful as he approached the water and leapt onto the big rock in the middle of the bed.

He always spent as much of the school holidays as he could out of doors, away from the noise of bickering that pierced his bedroom walls so effortlessly. He was never missed on those long summer afternoons. His parents didn't seem to need his presence or require him for hours on end, although he was likely to be told off for something entirely unconnected to his absence as soon as he came back through the kitchen door. Once when he heard his mother calling his name across the meadow, he kept very still so she wouldn't see him kneeling on the bank tending to the dam he was building right across the span. She gave up very easily after a couple of yells, although he thought he heard a 'sod you, then' before she turned away.

He had never understood why he was a disappointment to them. He couldn't see anything particularly wrong with himself. He wasn't ugly or malformed, he wasn't stupid or cruel or violent, but somehow nothing he did was quite right and for years he clung to the notion that there was some course of behaviour that would satisfy them if only he could find out what it was. But he never did. A naturally loving child, he grew less and less sure of his own instincts as time went on, and later, as a sensitive boy, thought himself less and less important in the great scheme of things. By the time he was an adult, Rufus did not expect to be listened to or consulted or valued, but to be useful to fill up space or as the recipient of conversation. He had seen Alison's initial interest as the stirrings of a real rapport, but over time those hopes faded to a quiet disappointment and the renewed assumption of his own inconsequence.

But since coming to Creech, things were changing. He had a sense of people actually seeing him and listening to him at last. He felt it with Cate despite her grave demeanour and in every syllable of Tara's forceful communication. And with Lily? Yes, Lily with all her teasing hypnotic presence. Rufus looked around at the shadowy trees, breathed in the sounds of the birds' last night chorus and listened to the trickling of the stream. It was like hearing and seeing for the first time, as if he had shed an alien skin and was at last in the right place, more fully alive, more fully himself than ever before. And he was not at all surprised, when he emerged from the willow trees into his vegetable garden twenty minutes later, to see a large blue dog regarding him impatiently from the bolted lettuces.

'Sorry I'm late,' Rufus said softly as he followed obediently through the long grass.

No blinding shaft of light greeted him when he stepped through the round entrance. Instead a silver mist hung over the moon garden, swathing the plants in luminous webs of light, blurring the edges of stone into vibrating particles like moondust. Rufus hesitated. It struck him that this was the first time he'd been in here at night without being paralytically drunk, although the wine and brandy from dinner were still warming his bloodstream. In the centre of the garden he could just discern shadowy movement, the same tall dark shapes he had seen before, but there was none of the joyful flow of dance from the first occasion. The figures moved sombrely, in a slow lugubrious circle, round and round without pause. Where he had seen limbs there were only white flashes of bones.

Now was his chance to probe the mystery of the garden and find out the reality of all his strange experience there. He went forward towards them. Fingers of mist crept all around, swirling drowsiness over him. He could not draw his eyes away from the mesmerising motion of the circling joined hands. A great wave of emotion washed right through him and tears welled up in his heavy eyes. Stretching out his arms towards the circle, 'I want Lily,' he called out loudly, 'I just want to see Lily.'

Perhaps he had had too much to drink at Jacinta's. He suddenly found himself outside the kitchen door and yet he had no memory at all of walking back to the house. Shaking sleepiness from his head, he let himself in and padded in darkness through to the living room. From the window Rufus could see a glimpse of metal in the road beyond the front hedge. It was Dennis' car, sleek and expectant. Rufus smiled to himself at the thought of leaving his admirer to a very long fruitless wait.

He turned towards the stairs and then gave a little cry of fear at the sight of a tall dark figure standing by the fireplace watching him. For a mad moment he thought Dennis had left his car by the gate and come exploring, but the figure was silent and still, two achievements way beyond Dennis' powers. It was also about a foot taller.

He had a sudden fleeting image of one of the figures he had seen dancing in the moon garden, but a split second later Rufus knew with a leap of his heart that it was Lily. He stepped forward just as she did the same. Her midnight-blue cape swirled softly as she came close, hair swinging around her shoulders. It never occurred to him to ask how she had got there, or what she was doing in his house so late at night, so perfectly natural to his hopes did it seem to find her there.

'A good evening, Rufus?' she said softly. It was both a salutation and a question.

'A strange one,' he said, 'but it's getting better all the time.'

Almost before he had the words out she was in his arms, touching his cheek with her long fingers, her eyes searching his in an invitation of desire. He could not resist kissing her once and then again more searchingly, but then he forced himself back, breathing heavily, his heart hammering under his ribs.

'Wait,' he said indistinctly. 'Just a minute. I have to ask you...'

It was true. He didn't want to ask but he had to. He avoided her beguiling eyes as he spoke.

'I mean, it's complicated. You're not exactly free...'

She interrupted him swiftly, putting her hand to his mouth, and smiling.

'It's quite simple, Rufus.' Every time she said his name he was more lost. 'I am precisely free. As you are.'

It was a supreme effort of will to ask the question, whilst his body screamed at him to be quiet, but he knew he must rid himself of his half-guilty half-triumphant anxiety.

'But what about Ged?'

There, he'd said it, managed to get out the dread name, risked ruining the spell that had brought her here, but she seemed to ignore what he'd said and continue her own line of thought.

'We are all free to make our own decisions. The only question is what decision you are going to make now.'

Rufus could not have resisted her had he wanted to. He

drew her towards him again and now kissed her as avidly as he had been cautious before. The sensation was all he had imagined. He allowed his mind to follow where his body was leading inexorably.

Hand in hand, they went quietly up the stairs in darkness to make love in Rufus' bed whilst Dennis unwittingly stood guard at the gate.

Chapter 12

In the morning there was no sign of Lily, not even the residual warmth of her body in the bed.

Rufus was keenly disappointed at first. He felt bereft and cheated of an affirmation of all that had happened between them. It was no dream this time, however, and he knew it. He was not so surprised at her departure when he realised to his astonishment that it was nearly nine o'clock and he himself should be on his way to Bruford. Instead he closed his eyes again and lay luxuriating in the memory of the night. From the moment by the stream when he felt at the end of a personal journey to the intimate touch of Lily's skin under his fingers, he knew that at last the world had shifted so that he would no longer run hard to keep ahead of its bowling roll but skip along behind directing its course for himself. He was proud and satisfied. He was alive. He was also very late for work.

The house was quiet. Joe rarely worked all day now that the basic comforts of the house were sorted out. Rufus let him come and go as he pleased, but he was glad not to have to face Joe this morning. He lay for a while longer, secure and comfortable, eyes closed in happy recall, at last accepting of the realistic fulfilment of what had seemed his hopeless love for Lily.

He got up eventually and went off to the shop, singing merrily to himself as the car wound through the green tunnels of tree-lined lanes, his heart full and grateful. He beamed at everyone he passed as he made his way up through the streets from the free car park on the edge of Bruford.

Even Neville King, leaning over the rusty railings opposite his shop and staring morosely down into the river below, got a cheery hello. He turned round blankly and the misery in his face jolted Rufus out of his own euphoric haze.

'Are you OK?'

Rufus braced himself to accept whatever sarcasm winged back at him with the good humour this day merited. But King did no more than look startled, and stare, his lips moving oddly as if trying to form words without knowing what to say.

'Are you feeling ill?'

Again no response. Rufus began to wonder if he should take some decisive action like leading King by the arm to a seat or calling an ambulance, but the other suddenly seemed to recover his own resources.

'Bloody old world, isn't it?' he said with a mournful smile and strode back across the road into his shop.

Tara and Joe were just leaving the flat when Rufus got to The Craft Shop.

'Hello there,' he said bouncing in with too much jollity, before Tara's savage sneer stopped him in his tracks.

'H...how's things, Joe?' he plunged on nervously. 'How's your mother?'

'How's your mother?' Tara mimicked derisively. 'You should know, seeing she spent the night with you.'

'What?'

'You're not going to deny it, are you, you gutless bastard?'

'Tara, come on...' Joe interrupted.

They both ignored him, Tara flushed with hostility and Rufus angry at her unprovoked attack.

'It's none of your business, Tara,' he said as coldly as he could manage, 'even if it is true.'

'We bloody know it is. Straight from the bitch's own mouth.'

Joe looked sadly at Tara's scornful face. Then he shook

his head.

'That's enough,' he said flatly.

'But she is!' Tara protested avidly.

'No, I mean, me, us, whatever. It's enough. I've had it. Sorry.'

He was gone in a moment. Tara stood with her mouth open looking at the empty doorway and back to Rufus then at the door again.

'Go after him, Tara,' Rufus said tiredly, as he felt the happiness of the morning ebbing away. 'Go and apologise to him.'

'Me apologise!' she shrieked. 'What have I done? It's that fucking cow!'

'Oh, stop it,' he snapped, 'Joe's not the only one who's sick of this abuse hurling. You're getting too fond of it and it's a poor substitute for real communication. Whatever you think Lily's done she does *not* deserve to be spoken about like that.'

'I bet Ged agrees with me!'

'Ged?'

'Yes, you remember, Lily's partner, Ged. Joe told me what happened when Ged asked the old slag where she'd been all night.'

Rufus' insides crumpled. His romantic images of last night were dashed by this overdose of sordid reality. Somehow he didn't doubt what Tara was telling him. He was shocked that Lily should flaunt her unfaithfulness, but then, hadn't he been quite ready to quieten his own uneasiness about Ged for the chance to sleep with Lily. It was his fault too.

Tara was still glaring at him, taut and vicious. Wounded as he was, he was not prepared to help her this time.

'Whatever you think, Tara, it really *isn't* your business and it's not as simple as you seem to think.'

'That old con!' she scoffed, putting on a silly grown-up's voice. '"It's too complicated for you to understand. When you're older, you'll know what I'm talking about." That's what they always say. It's all shit! shit! shit! You just do whatever you want and then try to talk your way out of it. You're as bad as she is, as bad as everyone else...'

'And Joe?' Rufus asked maliciously and suffered for it at once as Tara burst into noisy tears and ran upstairs to the sanctuary of the flat.

Customers at Neville King's bookshop drifted in and out all morning, browsing and buying. They got little encouragement from the owner, who sat at his table alternately doing a series of frenzied calculations on a sheet of paper and staring across the room, eyes unfocused and disregarding of his surroundings. It was so crashingly unfair, to find himself in this position at this time. He'd very nearly blurted something out to that idiot from The Craft Shop who'd been so solicitous this morning. Part of him longed to unburden himself, but it was the habit of a lifetime to keep to himself and he did not intend to change that so easily.

The problems and pains of old age were a cruel joke for any creator god to foist on his unsuspecting children. Just when the daily struggle for a living was over and there should be a time of ease and pleasure, the crippling torture of arthritis would set in, or bowel cancer, or, if you were lucky, a swift case of heart failure. But Altzheimer's really was the bitter twist to end them all.

His feelings towards his mother were not in question. He would look after her willingly, and motivated by love rather than a sense of duty, but how would he cope with the pain of her empty eyes and the daily silence of lost communication? How would he stand it, day after day in that house they'd shared since his childhood, now alone to attend the shell of an intimate companionship. What on earth was he going to do?

The bookshop had kept them both for the last fifteen years, since his mother had given up work and enjoyed the bit of rest she deserved after struggling to bring him up single-handed. She'd loved being at home all day, cleaning and tidying, getting his meals ready, chatting with the neighbours and the local shop-keepers, always as cheerful and full of kindness as could be and now... How ever were they going to manage, on any level, from money to sanity? He looked at all the figures again and still didn't have a clue, but there was no question of handling this in any other way. At home his mother stayed and he would be the one to tend her night and day, despite her indifference or less frequent but more horrific outbreaks of rage when she looked at him as if she simply hated him.

King put his head down on the table in the mercifully empty shop and wept silently.

Rufus had plenty of time to think things over during a long, quiet morning in The Craft Shop. Every time the door opened or the phone rang his heart leapt with expectation. Surely Lily would make contact with him today after leaving without a word? He needed to see her, to know that everything was the same between them, to find out what she had really said to Ged and Joe, and how they would go on together now.

He was just about to go and buy a sandwich for lunch when Jacinta Jacobs came in hesitantly. She flashed a nervous glance at the stands and shelves of strange goods.

'Hello, Rufus. Gosh, it's very... alternative, isn't it?'

He laughed.

'Yes. I didn't know that when I agreed to look after it.

One of life's little jokes, though it hasn't turned out too badly, I suppose.'

Her mottled face smiled politely as her eyes darted around taking in the huge revolving clutch of witches' broomsticks which Rufus had hung from a hook in the ceiling. He was rather pleased with this bold display, having carefully peeled off the Made in Taiwan labels.

'I'm closed on Mondays,' Jacinta said. 'One has to have some free time, a life of one's own, you know.'

He grinned at her sympathetically. 'I know.'

'I usually come into Bruford, do some shopping, have a bit of lunch. I can't stop thinking about what you said - you know, The Falling Goat closing. I don't suppose...' she stopped, and turned her head away to gaze at some huge zodiac earrings.

Rufus came to her rescue.

'I was just thinking about going out for lunch,' he said. 'Let's go and spy out the land. It would be nice to have company for a change.'

'Just friends, of course.' The old archness peeped out at him from under raised brows.

'Absolutely,' said Rufus, turning the sign on the door to read Closed.

During his lunch with Jacinta, Rufus found that his mind constantly strayed to thoughts of Lily and when he might see her again and he had to make a conscious effort to concentrate on his companion. They talked about the menu as they sat at a table beneath one of the paintings that had given The Falling Goat its curious name. Two men in a small boat at the foot of a cliff, red-faced and wielding blunderbusses, were glowering avidly up at a large mountain goat perched nonchalantly on a rocky cliff ledge high above their heads. Apparently there had been a companion picture showing the scene a minute later as the blasted goat hurtled down into the

191

water. This masterpiece went missing on the night the place opened, leaving only a brass title plate and chipped plaster where its fixture had been ripped away. The owners had not seen fit to change things since.

'It'd be a great pity if the name went when it changes hands,' Rufus said as they ate.

'It's certainly memorable,' she agreed, 'which would be useful in advertising.' She looked wistfully around the small bright dining room with its French doors leading onto a walled garden rich with lavender and nasturtiums. They had not been early enough to get a table out there. 'Such a lovely place! I wonder how much accommodation they've got upstairs?'

'There's two more floors, back extension as well, so it must have two or three bedrooms, surely?' Rufus said.

Jacinta's eyes gleamed with possibilities and then clouded over.

'It's silly even to think about this. I've no money and no experience whatsoever of running a restaurant! And I've already got a shop.'

'Which is fast becoming a bit of a millstone, isn't it?' he asked gently.

She nodded briefly.

'It's not active enough for me, to be honest. I'd like to be in the kitchen here, just cooking. Someone else would have to welcome people and wait at tables. I'd be hopeless at that. At the shop I don't mind the ordering and arranging goods, but waiting for people to come in and buy is a nightmare. I'm terrified of what they think of me and don't have a clue what to say to any of them. I've no experience of village life. I don't fit in and I can see it in their faces. Don't *you* feel it in the village, Rufus, that there's something, well, alien, about it?'

He considered this and thought how his response had changed over the last few weeks.

'No, not any more. At first I did, quite strongly, but then somehow things changed. I sort of fell in love with my house, which is the key, I think.'

Jacinta looked at him with raised eyebrows at this novel version of love. Then she dropped her glance in some embarrassment and he cursed himself for forgetting her awkwardness.

'I've never felt like that about any place,' she said simply to her lap. 'Geoffrey thought the shop would be just the thing, but he never asked me. That's how things always were between us unfortunately.'

'Are you still on good terms?'

She laughed sourly.

'He says if I need money I've only to ask, if that's what you mean.'

Rufus missed the sadness of her observation in his anxiety to help her out of a wider plight.

'Then why not ask Geoffrey about this place?' Rufus said deliberately. 'Could he afford it?'

She looked down at her empty plate, the muscles of her face working nervously. 'Probably, but why on earth would he when I've got the shop?'

'Which he didn't consult you about.'

'That's true, but it was generous of him.'

'Was it really?'

He realised how difficult this conversation was becoming for her, unused as she was to the luxury of talking about emotional things. He doubted if Dennis was much of a friend in that respect.

'Alright, it salves his conscious about dumping me, I suppose,' Jacinta said, her eyes saddening with the admission. 'Money is something he has to spare. The only thing he can spare for me, in fact.'

Rufus leaned forward across the table. He refrained from touching her hands which were anxiously picking at the tablecloth in case he became embroiled in mis-interpretation, but he did desperately want to help this poor lonely woman if he could.

'Then ask him about this, if it's something you really do want! It's the least he can do after the way he's treated you. Find out what they want for this place and put it to him. Make a business plan, offer to pay him interest, whatever it takes to show you're serious. If you are?'

He wanted to challenge her into some action, but she seemed flustered by his decisiveness and started fiddling with her handbag to avoid his gaze.

'Oh Rufus, you're being very kind, but I really...'

She stopped. Rufus had leapt to his feet, and was struggling to extract his wallet from a back pocket whilst craning his neck at the window.

'Jacinta, I'm so sorry, I've got to go. Look, pay for us both with this. I'm really, really sorry. Forgive me!' He leaned down and kissed her cheek. 'Ask him!' he called out as he rushed into the street and deserted her.

He's making a bad habit of this, Jacinta thought, as she went up to the counter to pay, but she did steel herself to ask the very pleasant woman at the till if it was true the place might be up for sale.

Rufus ran to the end of the street where he could see along the waterfront. There had been no mistaking the russet sheen of Lily's hair against her vibrant green jacket. His chest was pounding with the excited fear of seeing her again and there she was as he hurried forward, twenty yards ahead, looking in a shop window. And there too, raising a hand to brush the gleaming hair back from her shoulder, was Ged, dark as some medieval devil beside her. Rufus ducked into the nearest doorway, clammy fingers squeezing his heart as he watched them laugh together and then to his horror saw Lily's long, slim fingers with their silver painted nails stroke gently up and down the back of Ged's leather-clad thigh in a familiar movement of caress.

'Are you coming in or just keeping out of the sun?'

Rufus swung round to see Neville King through the open shop door. Feeling in need of any sort of sanctuary, he did go in and suddenly found himself in such familiar surroundings that a wave of nostalgia threw him back to the Fulham Road.

He wandered around fingering piles of books, trying to suppress his emotions to the extent that he could have a normal conversation with King, who himself seemed uncharacteristically restrained today, sitting at a large mahogany table going through sheets of figures.

'I gather you really did have a place like this in London,' King said at last.

'Of course I did.' Rufus was stung. 'Why on earth would I tell you so if it wasn't true? And who the hell has so obligingly confirmed it for you anyway?'

King didn't seem to mind Rufus' angry tone.

'Your wife was in here.'

'Alison?' Rufus said incredulously.

'We didn't get onto first name terms, I'm afraid. Good-looking woman, slim, upright, dark haired. She came looking for you, some weeks ago now.'

He fell silent again except for the tapping of keys on his calculator.

Rufus found he wanted to talk. Anything to keep himself from thinking about what he'd seen.

'We're getting divorced. I've decided to settle in this area and she's happy in London.'

Even as he spoke he wondered at his own veracity. If Lily didn't love him, didn't want to share her life with him, what then? Would he want to stay where she was?

King looked up.

'Won't Rita be coming back to take up the reins, as it were?'

Rufus shrugged.

'I'll find something else.'

King cleared his throat roughly as if his next words were costing him some effort.

'Pity you're not free now. I could do with someone to take over here.'

'What? You're selling up?'

'No!' The response was sharp, as if the idea hurt him physically. 'No, I just need to be away for a while. My mother's... ill.'

'I'm sorry to hear that.' God, he must be desperate to ask me, Rufus thought. No wonder he looked so gruesome this morning. 'And I'm sorry I can't help you out at the moment. This would suit me a lot better than The Craft Shop.'

King nodded and went back to his papers without speaking.

'Well, I'd better be going.' Rufus shuffled awkwardly towards the door, wanting neither to stay nor to go out again into the painful world awaiting. 'I hope you find someone.'

King waved a dismissive hand without looking up and Rufus sidled out, resolutely not looking in the direction Lily had gone and took himself sadly back to his own shop.

Cate found her thoughts dwelling more and more on Rufus as the morning passed. She had not seen him since the day Lily visited the cottage and she drew her own conclusions from that. Underlying her irritation with his folly in getting into that situation, she felt an uncharacteristically strong desire to protect him, to keep him safe from the harmful influences she felt encircling him. It was not usual to act without invitation, without specific request for help and only then in circumstances where other people would not be affected. Nothing could warrant a careless, ignorant meddling in lives, though plenty had asked her in the old days for love potions or charms to make them rich, not understanding her warnings about the dangers of trying to force others into actions against their will. 'Harm none' was the guiding principle of all Cate's life and it would take more than she had ever faced before to break that rule.

But there were things she could do. A little protection, for example, would do no harm at all.

Well before five thirty Rufus had given up any pretence of concentration on work and driven back to Creech. Instead of going straight through the village, he could not stop himself from turning down the road where Lily lived and travelling quickly past her house, wanting to see but not be seen. An old lady with a piglet in a pushchair was passing the house as he glanced wildly at the open front door and noted Lily's car parked a few yards away. All it'll take, he thought, is one meeting, one close look into her eyes and I'll know where I stand and what exactly is going on between us. I must have got something wrong, either last night or what I saw today and I just need to know which.

He resisted the temptation to park in the road and wait for a glimpse of her. He wanted to go home. Mean Cottage was calling him. He could hear the soothing whispers of the willow branches, the cheerful greeting of the stream and the deep peaceful silence inside the house itself, like a welcoming cocoon. It was the reassuring invitation of an old friend, who would understand without the need to probe and promise comfort without the need for words.

A dreadful idea occurred to him suddenly. What if,

despite the evidence of his own eyes today, Lily wanted him not Ged, but she wanted him to come and live with her here in the pleasant semi-detached redbrick house and give up Mean Cottage.

He imagined his house relapsing into the subdued neglect in which he'd found it two months ago. He saw the dust settling on his furniture and the weeds entwining the vegetable patch again and couldn't bear the thought. And what about the moon garden most of all? No, it was a 'what if' not worth worrying about. Why on earth wouldn't Lily want to live in such an idyllic spot?

He turned left over the bridge and carefully negotiated the winding lane, pulling up outside the cottage just in time to see Cate reaching up towards something above his front door. By the time he got to the gate, she was coming along the path towards him.

'It's good to see you,' Rufus said, although he knew he had not sought her out lately because of his abiding sense of her disapproval of Lily. He very much did not want to know why Cate felt like that, although he was quite interested in what she had been fiddling about with above his doorway.

'How are things?' he said neutrally.

'Things, as you so eloquently put it, are what they are, I suppose.' She picked up her bike from the hedge. 'I won't keep you now as you're obviously not in a mood to tend to what I say.'

He didn't like the sound of that at all. It felt harsh and censorious, and not what he wanted at this moment when all he could think about was his uncertain standing with Lily. He had already made up his mind to phone her as soon as he got in to try to arrange a meeting.

'You're right,' he said brusquely. 'This isn't a brilliant time, Cate. I've got a few things to sort out.'

She fixed him with a perspicacious stare. 'She's not the one, you know, whatever your basil might have achieved.'

A surge of indignation overwhelmed him.

'How would you know?' he said fiercely. 'You don't really know me or her. You come round here as if you own the place and tick me off like some errant schoolboy whenever you feel like it. Perhaps it makes you feel powerful, all that mind-reading and mumbo-jumbo, but I don't want any more interference in my personal life.' He took a breath to calm down. Her eyes had not shifted an iota during his tirade and he now looked down at his own feet rather than continue to face her directly. 'I'm sorry, Cate. I'm sure you mean well, but I need to be left alone to get on with things in my own way and to have Mean Cottage to myself.'

'Moon Cottage.'

'What?' he looked up at her wildly.

'Moon Cottage. That's what I came to talk to you about, but as you're not in a receptive frame of mind, I'll leave you to it.'

She was already pushing the bike from the kerb.

'No, wait...'

She ignored this plea and moved steadily away.

Rufus was ready to snort with frustration. In one minute he had managed to alienate the only person who knew about the moon garden and seemed to understand so much else so effortlessly. He had been glad enough of her help before and it was unforgivable to have treated her as he just had.

He stopped thinking as he heard her call out without turning her head. He wasn't sure if he'd heard correctly but it sounded like 'I forgive you, Rufus.'

Chapter 13

The sound of Lily's car drawing up outside broke through Rufus' sleep and sent him racing downstairs, pulling on ill-assorted articles of clothing as he went.

He flung open the back door only to hear a light rap at the front of the house. Why on earth wouldn't Lily come round to the kitchen as usual? He went outside, puzzled, and followed the concrete path only to find Ged's unwelcome figure peering in through the living-room window.

'Can I help you?' said Rufus, barely troubling to keep the dislike from his voice.

Ged straightened up and regarded Rufus coolly.

'Bit early for Christmas, isn't it?' he said, nodding at the door.

Rufus looked up and saw a star made of wooden twigs bound tightly with red thread lodged on an old nail amongst the ivy above the lintel.

'Is that what you've come to say?' Rufus struggled to keep his voice steady.

'Is Joe here?' Ged's eyes were mean and hostile.

'No, he isn't. I'm not expecting him this morning especially.'

'He wasn't here overnight?'

'Of course not. What's happened?' Rufus asked sharply.

'We're concerned about him.' Rufus in his hyper-sensitive state thought Ged laboured the 'we' deliberately. 'He's had a bust-up with Tara and he didn't come home last night.'

'I knew they'd quarrelled,' Rufus said without thinking. 'I was there in the shop when it happened.'

'And not exactly blameless, according to Tara.'

'What?' Rufus was horrified.

'Come on, mate. She's told me all about it.'

'That's nonsense!' Nevertheless, he was stung by Tara's betrayal.

'Is it? Strikes me you're causing a bit of trouble for my family one way or another.'

Ged took a step forwards, chin raised aggressively, but Rufus, burning with indignation, was surprised to find himself without fear.

'I don't think Lily would see it like that,' he said with a haughty confidence designed to annoy.

An unpleasant smile spread over Ged's sharp features.

'A sympathy fuck's nothing, mate. You're not the first and you won't be the last. She's got enough to go round.'

Rufus hurled himself forward at Ged in a clumsy lunge with no clear intention of what he hoped to achieve, and they grappled together ineffectually for a minute before Ged shoved him aside and stepped back, rubbing his brow where their heads had clashed on the first impact. There seemed no eagerness on either side to prolong the physical conflict.

'Just watch yourself on my patch,' Ged said thickly, 'and send Joe home if you see him. Understand?'

Rufus nodded, mutely miserable at his own descent to mindless idiocy, and watched the car shoot away with a squeal of tyres. He went on standing outside in the pellucid morning air wondering what on earth had come over him, flailing and scuffling with his lover's partner like a child in a playground losing his rag over a chance remark. Was this the quality of his new life, that he had moved so far from reason that all self-control was lacking? How was it possible in this beautiful setting where he had felt so peaceful and contented? He felt like apologising out loud to Mean Cottage for his folly, but his insides were still churning with outrage at Ged's taunts. Turning to go in, he caught sight of Cate's charm above the door and tore it down in a final act of petulance.

Rufus went back inside to find Joe coming down the stairs yawning.

'What the bloody hell are you doing here?'

Joe blinked in dozy surprise at this rude attack.

'I slept over. You did say I could, ages ago.'

Rufus remembered that he had said something of the sort in a flush of gratitude at all Joe's efforts to improve the comfort of the house. 'Maybe, but I expected you to ask me first! When did you arrive?'

Joe's pink quiff shook with the effort of calculation.

'Yesterday some time. I heard you talking to Cate outside, then I sort of fell asleep.'

'Joe, that was fourteen hours ago! Does Tara know you're here?'

He shook his head.

'I need some space from all that. It's finished anyway.'

'Come on, Joe, it'll all blow over. You know how easily she flies off the handle.'

Joe shrugged awkwardly.

'It's not just that. I just don't feel...' he stopped and glanced around the peaceful sitting room. 'I like the quiet here.'

Rufus should hardly have been surprised that Joe too would see Mean Cottage as some sort of sanctuary. That was one thing in all this upset he could understand.

He decided to leave the difficult subject of Tara and put a friendly hand on Joe's shoulder.

'Come on, we'd better get you something to eat. But then you should go home and see your mother. She's worried. Ged was here just now looking for you.'

'I heard.'

A window in the second bedroom was just above the front door. Rufus felt himself redden with shame at the thought of Joe overhearing his awful exchange with Ged.

'I'm sorry, Joe,' he said humbly and meant it.

'Yeah, right. Got any eggs?'

The bookshop was empty at last. Neville King had had a busy morning with coach-parties of Americans keen on local history and customs that might give them some tenuous links with their ancestors.

He sat down at his table, the only form of counter the shop had, with a cup of coffee and went back to brooding on his situation and the narrow range of options that faced him. He would have been reluctant to hand his precious shop over to that oaf Rufus Keene, but at least he knew the business and would presumably have been a safe pair of hands for a while. An advertisement might bring in any sort of slime who would either rip him off or ruin through carelessness what he had built up so painstakingly.

But King would not let his mother go into a home and the only way she could stay in her own house was for him to be there too full-time. There was no way they could afford a twenty-four hour nurse, even if he had wanted a stranger in their family home at such a time. One or two loyal neighbours were manfully coping with daily shifts at the moment, but he *had* to be there permanently soon. He had loved his mother dearly throughout his life, even giving up his marriage nearly twenty years ago when his wife tired of the unequal competition and forced him to make a choice of moving away or managing without her. Now, he was happy to give his mother every care in her last days, however long it took.

Suddenly his distant troubled gaze vanished and his eyes focused cleanly for a moment on the busy open-air tables of the riverside café. A slow grin pushed aside the worry lines on his craggy face and he got to his feet to have a closer look. An expression of triumphant pleasure softened his features.

'Well, well, well,' he said softly to himself. 'Look who's here. Maybe there is something in this witchery after all.'

The phone in the flat rang for ages but it was clear that Tara was either out or unprepared to answer it. Rufus sighed. He had decided to abandon the shop for one morning as, according to Joe, Ged was going up to London for the day for some unspecified purpose and Rufus intended to take full advantage of his absence. It felt a bit like skiving, but he hoped to be there to open for the afternoon and in a considerably better frame of mind. But when he reached Lily's house, Joe answered the door to say his mother had just gone out and he had no idea when she'd be back. In a state of fierce frustration, Rufus drove rather too fast back through the village, ignoring Jacinta as she waved frantically to him from outside her shop, and passing Mean Cottage in a cloud of dust. He came to a sharp halt outside Cate's house and then banged loudly on the door. No answer. Grinding his teeth and swearing fulsomely under his breath, Rufus went back to the cottage, only to find himself unable to sit still or concentrate on anything purposeful. In the end there was nothing for it but to take himself into Bruford and get on with what he was supposed to be doing down here. How fitting, he reflected bitterly: I'm in love with another man's wife and I mind someone else's shop. It's only a matter of time before the real owner of Mean Cottage turns up to claim it from me.

From the back garden Cate heard the car arrive, the knock on the door and then Rufus's retreat. Had he waited, been less impatient or in a less insistent mood than these noises suggested, she might have responded.

As it was she came into the house when she was ready, and sat down at the davenport where Adam's folder of papers lay. She was strangely hesitant to give Rufus sight of them, although she wanted to share the story of the moon garden with him. Part of her regretted that Rufus had not searched out the answers for himself by now, but she had seen only too clearly the frustrating ferment of emotions he was struggling with the day before and she knew that those issues would need resolution before he could concentrate on things of more lasting importance. She would not prevent events taking their course as they must.

Cate wondered if Rufus had spoken to anyone else - and to one person in particular - about the moon garden, but somehow she doubted it. There was a connection between Rufus and the house, Rufus and the garden that he recognised as a special bond which had become precious to him. His strange experiences were a personal possession, not easily shared, impossible to explain.

She turned away from the desk and knelt to rummage through the cupboard under the stairs, where she found a cardboard box containing a few leather bound books and a pile of pamphlets which she had chosen to keep from Adam's vast library after he died, as much for the memory of seeing them in his hands as for their contents. She selected one of the books now and took it out, the rich, damp smell of the binding reminding her of those first moments in the empty cottage, the abandoned settlement of his existence lending its weight to the crushing sense of loss she had endured when he'd gone.

They had been companions of a sort for forty-five years, all of Cate's adult life, the unequal friendship between mentor and pupil developing into a relationship sealed by experience and understanding far beyond most ordinary couples. Physical love was a rare part of their communion, some instinct always keeping her clear of the sort of constant emotional involvement that would sap the energies she needed for her work.

Cate sighed and shut those memories out as she closed the cupboard door. She had chosen the solitary path without regret. And it was Rufus she needed to concentrate on now.

The shop door was locked and no lights showed in the interior. It was too much to hope that Tara might have bothered to open up this morning but Rufus could not help noticing the lucrative number of coach parties on the loose in the town that morning.

He went in quietly and took two paces across the floor before he heard a noise in the back room. Its door was ajar and there were definite sounds of movement. He thought of the float locked in the safe and the contents of the stock room - was this a burglary in progress or was Tara down here making herself a cup of instant coffee? Neither seemed very likely. He tiptoed nearer and bent forward to listen more carefully. As he did so the door swung open and a woman stepped out briskly, making him jump.

She regarded him with a light smile and cool eyes.

'You must be Rufus,' she said and outstretched a hand regally as he nodded.

There was a moment's pause to size each other up. At a glance Rufus took in the skinny figure, unevenly dyed thin red hair straggling down to the waist, high cheekbones and sharp nose. He recognised the strong features that had managed to bleed beauty into another generation, but where Tara was striking, Rita just looked tough.

Rufus thought of all his prejudices, the preconceived ideas about this woman he'd had for the last few months. He looked her in the face and knew that he was right. He didn't like her one little bit and from the distasteful expression in the narrow eyes, the feeling was mutual. Little darts of hostility winged their way backwards and forwards between them like hornets. Of course, he was probably contaminated in her eyes by his friendship with Charlie, but she still seemed pretty unimpressed with her unseen choice of shop manager.

Rita looked at her watch ostentatiously.

'Interesting opening hours you keep.' He opened his mouth to retort, but she was too quick for him. 'I had a look at the books while I was waiting.'

I bet you did, he thought, seeing that you're entitled to draw a share of the profits for your time of absence.

'You'll have noticed book sales are up then,' he retorted.

She smiled a humourless acknowledgement.

'Just as well they are, considering some of the other lines.'

Rufus was not prepared to take this from her. He adopted the sarcastic tone Neville King did so well.

'Perhaps if I'd been told what sort of shop this was, or had a chance to benefit from some "managerial training" at the start, we would both have been better off now.'

He could see that his ebullience had taken her by surprise, as if she was not expecting an energetic retaliation, but she remained unmoved by it, shrugging off his complaint.

'I understood you were experienced in buying and selling. There's no great mystery to it, as far as I'm aware.'

Rufus, who had been mildly annoyed by her sudden appearance and gentle aggression, was truly angry now.

'And just how far is that?' he sneered. 'As far as Belgium? Glastonbury? Or your next port of call? Let's ask Tara, shall we, how far you're aware? You remember Tara, your daughter? The person you might say goodbye to next time you drift off to something more worthy of your time and attention.'

'What's going on?' said a wary voice behind them. Tara must have come down at the sound of raised voices. Rufus wondered how much she'd heard. He hadn't seen her since her quarrel with Joe and was shocked at how pale and totally washed out she looked.

He was about to speak to her when Rita intervened.

'Keep out of this, Tara.' Rita spoke over Rufus' shoulder. 'And I think you'd better leave now,' she said to him. 'Your usefulness seems suddenly to have come to an end.'

She spoke with apparent indifference, but he could hear the suppressed anger in her voice. He looked at Tara, who regarded him sullenly, but said nothing.

'Fine,' he said simply. 'That suits me just fine.'

He turned round and walked straight out of the shop. There was nothing of his to take with him, not even a biro or a mug. He had never been settled there, never tried to personalise the place, just coming and going without baggage.

He walked along the alley and over the bridge to the abbey park without noticing his surroundings. When he sat down to gather his wits he realised that, although shaken by his bruisingly fleeting encounter with Rita, he wasn't actually particularly upset. If it hadn't been for Tara and worries about money, his predominant feeling would have been one of relief. He did wonder how he was going to manage financially in the immediate future. Charlie had brokered the agreement whereby Rufus had drawn a regular wage from the shop's account and any further profit would be split between him and Rita when the year was up. But it was essentially a casual arrangement with no provision made for their early return and Rufus' subsequent loss of the income he had been relying on. He had no idea what to do about that now. He could hardly appeal to Charlie and he had nothing written down to force Rita to adhere to.

Still, he'd worry about that later. He might even have to think more seriously about Neville King's grudging need of assistance, although working for someone else again was the last thing he wanted after this debacle.

At least he was now a man of leisure today and could look for Lily until he found her. His feelings for her were a great deal more important than those for The Craft Shop. If he could only work things out between them for a lasting relationship, he was sure that everything else would fall into place.

But it was Tara's forlorn features that stayed with him as he drove back towards Creech.

'Are you back for good now?' Tara asked charily, as she watched her mother making a salad in the kitchen.

Rita grinned.

'For good or ill,' she said and went on slicing tomatoes.

Tara fiddled with a tin-opener. She seemed to have lost the knack of talking easily to her mother, forgotten the rhythms of their life together in just a few weeks. She was also unused to another person in the small flat, apart from Joe. She remembered with a pang that she hadn't seen or heard from him for forty-six hours now. She wanted to talk to Rita about that, to pour out all the frustrations about her own behaviour and her fears that Joe wouldn't ever forgive her for the way she'd kept on about Lily. But Lily was her mother's closest friend, which only complicated things more and when Tara had tried to explain the situation last night on Rita's return, her mother just laughed and said she'd get over it and that it was about time Tara moved on, whatever that meant.

In fact, the only adult who ever really listened to her and at least made an effort to understand was Rufus and she hadn't stood up for him earlier.

'He's tried very hard with the shop,' she burst out suddenly.

Rita turned round and looked at her.

'Well, the money isn't exactly rolling in!' She waved the knife she was using in the air. 'Unless he's been fiddling the books, I suppose.'

'Mum! He'd never do that!'

'Really? You seem very sure of his integrity. Astonishing in one so young and usually so cynical.'

'Rufus is different.'

'Tara, none of them are different when it comes down to it. The sooner you realise that the better.'

'That's crap, to say just 'cause he's a man he's capable of anything underhand. Rufus isn't like that. He's... he's a decent bloke,' she finished lamely.

Rita looked at her closely.

'You don't fancy him, do you?'

Tara reddened angrily.

'You always have to do it, don't you?' she shouted. 'Bring everything down to your sordid level. I love Joe and you don't even care that my whole life's ruined because of you going off and...' She broke off in tears and ran up to her room.

Rita smiled grimly as she went back to her salad.

Everything back to normal then, she thought.

Lily's car was outside the village shop as Rufus drove by and then screeched to a halt.

She was talking to Jacinta when he went in, laughing as she loaded packages into her woven basket.

They both turned to him in greeting.

'Rufus!' Lily put a hand on his arm and kissed his cheek warmly. He moved to return the greeting but she had already stepped back, leaving him gaping and flustered.

He tried to greet Jacinta with a semblance of normality, but his voice shook and she only looked open-mouthed from him to Lily and back again. Christ, it's that bloody obvious, he thought. Yesterday Jacinta regarded me as a firm, decisive human being, in charge of my own destiny, but now she can see at a glance that I'm reduced to a squishy jelly by the mere sight of this beautiful woman. She won't be looking to me for advice any more.

He followed Lily out of the shop with a desperate and apologetic face at Jacinta over his shoulder.

'I was hoping to see you,' he said quickly before Lily could get into her car. 'Have you got time for a cup of tea or something?'

A man carrying a stuffed badger stared at them curiously as he passed.

She looked at her watch.

'I don't know, Rufus. I've got a client this afternoon...'

'Please.'

She glanced up and down the street as if searching for inspiration. Two old men were staggering down the steps of The Green Man.

'What about a quick drink in the pub?' Lily said.

There was no-one else in the little room where lunches were served and they sat down at a table set with Victorian scene place-mats and plastic ketchup bottles.

'So how did you get on with Rita?' Lily said as she shrugged off the loose green shirt she was wearing over a sleeveless coral-coloured dress. Rufus tried to keep his eyes from the fair skin on her shoulders and the mole on her neck he had kissed with such delight.

'So you know she's back again then?'

He was playing for time, wondering how to answer her original question. They had already quarrelled once about Rita's behaviour and he could not afford to be so obviously censorious again, but he was aggrieved about the casual

211

way he'd been treated and he longed to be soothed and comforted by Lily's warmth.

'Of course. I went over there last night to see her. She was looking forward to meeting you today.'

He carefully adopted a light tone.

'Was she? I think you could say the event did not go brilliantly.'

Lily was surprised.

'Why, what happened?'

He told her, briefly and accurately what each of them had said and made no comment on his feelings.

To his amazement, Lily laughed when he'd finished.

'You shouldn't take offence so easily, Rufus! She's bound to be concerned about the takings, it's her livelihood, after all, although I expect she was only teasing you.'

It was the last reaction he had expected, so out of touch with his own perceptions of the situation.

'You mean I'm out of work because I had a sense of humour failure?' he said tersely.

'No, Rufus! Come on, it's not as bad as that. She'll come round. You mustn't take everything so seriously.'

He was stunned into silence, and sat there with every muscle in his body tense, resisting a terrible urge to pick up his glass and throw it at the exposed stone wall behind her head.

'Truly,' she went on, smiling at him gently. 'If you were out of The Craft Shop, it's not as if your life's over! No single thing is so important that everything else can be lost with it.'

He struggled to get to grips with this statement. Would she apply the same assessment to everything?

'Even the other night?' he asked.

Lily looked genuinely bemused for a moment and Rufus' heart sank.

'The other night when we slept together, if you

remember,' he went on bravely. 'Was that so unimportant too and not to be taken seriously in your great scheme of things?'

She wasn't smiling now.

'Was it a happy experience for you?'

He banged his glass down in exasperation.

'Of course it was. You know...'

She leaned towards him and took his hand on the table.

'But you're not happy now. You look angry and disappointed, as if someone has let you down in some way, or taken away something you want to keep. But it's your own expectations that are causing you problems.'

'What do you mean my expectations? Wanting a chance to see you again? Is this a roundabout way of telling me you're not interested in a relationship between us?'

'Oh, Rufus!' Lily withdrew her hand abruptly and sat back to put the physical distance between them that his words had already achieved.

She spoke resignedly as if she knew what she had to say would not help.

'We have a "relationship", a connection, already. It may grow or change or cease in time, I can't say. I don't think about it in that way. You want to tie something down through definition, force its contours into a shape you can identify. Just let things be what they are, Rufus.'

He looked at her face, all the shades and planes and colours he knew so well, and for a split second saw beyond all that to something he did not recognise. He realised how little he knew about her, her past, even her present in the brooding form of Ged was a mystery to him.

'Is that how Ged sees it?' he asked bitterly.

Lily stood up.

'Leave it, Rufus. I'm sorry, I really must go now. I've got a client at five.'

She put out a hand to lift his chin with her familiar light

touch.

'If it's any consolation, Rita will come round. She's not planning on hanging around in Bruford for long anyway. Someone will have to mind the shop.'

'Well, it won't be me,' Rufus retorted, although he was actually wondering how Tara would take another rejection.

Lily was already turning away.

'One other thing,' he said urgently. 'Do you know why Joe and Tara have split up?'

She turned and pulled a face.

'Just some teenage tiff, I expect. Don't worry about them.'

Then she was gone.

So you don't know everything after all, Rufus thought.

Weariness of body and spirit washed over him. He felt disconnected, cast adrift in a sea of imperceptions. This meeting with Lily had answered none of his questions and done nothing to salve the wounds inflicted by his earlier encounter with Rita. The room was airless, with strong residual smells of roast meat and vinegar, but he sat on over the rest of his beer, musing vaguely, his mind numbed by doubt and fatigue. He had handled everything badly as usual and Lily's forthright assertion of her independence only confirmed a growing suspicion that his feelings were of little real consequence to her. That familiar sense of being on the periphery of life settled over him once more as he hunched his shoulders over his glass and wondered what on earth he had to do to break into the charmed inner circle which had eluded him all his life.

Chapter 14

He came home to find a package lying on the bench outside the back door. A note on the outside of the old brown envelope said simply 'This might interest you' and was signed 'C.' He looked for a moment at the bold black slashes of Cate's writing, before extracting a leather-bound book. He read the title and his heart sank. Memoirs of the Reverend Lionel Grubbe, 1786-1843. He was slightly surprised that Cate of all people assumed, like so many others, that as a book-seller he enjoyed an endless curiosity about the minutely printed pages of any ancient tome, regardless of the degree of dullness or incomprehensibility of its contents. This one looked a pretty good contender as he flicked through, dislodging a small paper marker which fluttered to the ground unseen.

Rufus flopped down disconsolately on the bench. He felt obliged out of respect for Cate to have a proper look at Grubbe's musings, although he hoped she didn't want a valuation. Such books weren't as rare as people thought and invariably only of localised interest. The Reverend appeared to have been a traveller, like so many of his contemporaries, and managed to spend as much time on his horse as in ministering to his congregation. On a quick sample, his style was about as appealing as the minutes of a council meeting. His main interest appeared to be in legends connected to the particular localities of his ramblings. Most were around his native Northamptonshire, but he had made an extensive trip around the south of England in 1820 and Rufus had just begun to glance at place names that were more familiar to him when the phone rang inside the house and he went in, leaving the book on a side table as he passed.

'Jane!' he said with real pleasure. At last he could have a conversation that was not fraught with difficulties from the outset.

'I've got some news, Roo.'

'I only want to hear it if it's good.'

'Oh dear, things as bad as that?'

'Nothing to worry about. I appear to have lost my job and... well, things are not going brilliantly on other fronts.'

'Lily?'

'Lily.'

There was a pause in which he could almost hear her deciding not to say "I told you so" or to delve too deeply.

'You can always run away to London again, if the searing pace of the country gets too much.'

'That's a comforting thought, thanks, but I'm not quite down and out yet. So what's the bad news?'

'What bad news?'

'Isn't there always bad news to cancel out the good?'

'Rufus! I thought you'd broken out of that carapace of cynicism. Back to nature and all that pure and simple living. Although I suppose you could say there was bad news in a way.'

Rufus groaned.

'I knew it.'

Jane laughed.

'I've had a visit from Alison and the awful Brian, who's apparently re-instated.'

That news came as no great surprise to Rufus.

'What did they want this time?'

'Let's just say our garage is full of furniture again!'

'My God, they brought it back?'

Rufus immediately began to imagine where he'd put it, visualising his room complete and even more familiar.

'Indeed. Must be the old Samson syndrome at work.'

'What?'

'Chopping off the locks leads to weakening of power - I'm sure you know the story.'

'What are you talking about?'

'Alison. Had all her hair cut off. I hardly recognised her. Typical though, it usually takes years off a face, but makes Alison look about fifty. *Very* severe.'

Unaccountably, Rufus felt a strange pang at the thought of his wife with short hair, a new person, moving further away from him and the person he had known with every day.

He covered up this sentiment bravely, knowing the short shrift it would get from Jane.

'As long as the old basset hound approves, that's all that matters.'

'Huh,' Jane said. 'I don't think his opinion is much sought after on any score.'

'No change there then.'

There was a moment's pause, then Jane sounded thoughtful.

'Might have been different if you hadn't always taken the line of least resistance, Roo, although I'm very glad you told her where to go in the end. I don't really think Brian's got the gumption.'

'But it was his drive and energy that attracted her in the first place!'

'I know, but he's had the stuffing knocked out of him now, I reckon, after a year of her vaunting ambition.'

'At least he's involved in her world, where she wants to be, where the things that matter to her are,' Rufus said, realising this clearly for the first time. 'I never wanted to get into all that. It seemed to be something quite apart from the world I inhabited. Schools are a pretty closed order in their way. He understands the language and the territory, which is more than I ever did.'

217

'Is that why you were so keen to find your own brave new world?'

Rufus laughed at the aptness of this.

'At the moment I feel more like a contestant on a survival gameshow - a whole series of baffling open-air challenges that leave me rolling face down in sludge and wondering if it's worth getting up again.'

'I've got my Guides orienteering badge if you ever need help in that respect.'

'Jane, why didn't I marry you all those years ago!'

'Because I'm much too smart and sassy for you. What you need's a gentle little flower who'll flutter her eyelashes at you and make you feel like the big strong boy you really are.'

'I withdraw my last remark. I'm very glad I didn't marry you and have to submit to all your misanthropic insights at every turn. David deserves a medal.'

She laughed.

'I certainly won't tell him that! Listen, we'll sort something out about getting a van to bring the furniture down to Mean Cottage as soon as possible.'

Moon Cottage Cate had said, Rufus remembered suddenly. What did she mean by that?

'That's fine,' he said. 'It'll be great to have it back whenever.'

After a bit more general chat, Jane rang off and Rufus went into the kitchen to make some supper, heartened by the re-establishment of his identity their connection had given him and completely forgetting about Cate's book.

One evening later in the week he strolled about the neglected paths of the moon garden before sitting down on a stone bench in the niche at the far end. He noticed for the first time a date stone in the wall beneath the ivy - 1855 it said - and suddenly wondered who had designed and built a formal garden in such an informal spot well away from any major building. Perhaps he really ought to do some research about the history of the cottage. He had plenty of time on his hands now.

He shifted uncomfortably on his hard seat. The light felt oppressive and was the colour of bile. He could almost smell the promise of a storm in the atmosphere. Sitting there soberly, he wondered again how the trick was done, what unnatural quirk of light trajectory breathed life into this garden under the moon's eye and what stirrings of particles played the moon's music in the lifeless plants and empty water basin. Time seemed to have pared down his memory: it was now impossible to securely distinguish fantasy and fact in what had happened there. His own words and thoughts were clear enough but the life in the garden ebbed and flowed before his mind's eye. It was sensations, rather than physical details, he could recall.

Part of him recoiled from Cate's acceptance of some supernatural naturalness behind all this. What he could believe, empirically, was that there was something in the place - whether the ground or air he didn't know - but something in the earth itself that gave rise to these phenomena. He likened it to strange feelings of other times and events evoked by castles and ancient sacred sites. He had experience of this: the sudden anachronistic whiff of flesh singed over an open fire, a strange echo of sword blades clashing or simply the awareness of lives from different times on the self-same spot, their singular otherness suddenly sheered away in an empathetic moment.

In this way he could make sense of the moon garden.

Weren't metaphysicists drawing conclusions leading towards a fifth dimension these days? Or a sixth, a seventh? The possibilities were endless once you accepted the basic tenet that perhaps there is more than we know. And why shouldn't there be? He did not believe in the infallibility of science any more than he believed in god. He would *like* there to be more - men on Mars, species eluding the tight little prescriptions man saw fit to nail them by.

But the concept of magic power and the fulfilment of wishes - if he understood Cate correctly - was where he felt obliged to draw a line, scared though he had been of her mind-reading originally. It was something in the nature of a party-trick, he reckoned now, learnt and then practised by a clever system. He was giving her clues or she was making astoundingly good guesses from his body-language or aura or something. He would not have been at all surprised to be told his body was surrounded by a halo of murky blotches lately, the way things were going. He wondered if Lily would respond to a request for help with a bad-aura day.

Lily again. It was always the image of Lily that his mind scurried back to at the first opportunity. Thoughts of her bright face and welcoming touch had been a refuge of hope a few days ago. Now Rufus tortured himself by going over and over their conversation in the pub, replaying his lines with fresh responses, grasping for incisive straws of persuasion and cajolery. But however hard his mind worked it, things always came out with the same grim realism in the end. What was there of commitment on her side except to their friendship? And was their one passionate encounter just a confirmation of that, not a development? But why the hell had she come to his house, late at night, and waited for him with the sole purpose of sleeping with him, if it was no more than that? It was not a casual meeting that had naturally led to bed: she had sought him out and not for the chance to talk about Joe's handiwork around Mean Cottage.

Moon Cottage, he automatically corrected himself. Presumably Cate called it that because she knew all about the garden and its numinous transformations. But how? And how was she aware of the detail of his encounters? He was curious now to hear what she had to say and wished he had been more welcoming when she came to talk to him.

Had she herself experienced the phenomenon? She had talked of him "drawing down the moon" in much the same matter-of-fact tone as one might say "I saw you throwing up in the gutter after closing time". True, it was weird about Alison turning up like that after his drunken ramblings, but there were other things that might account for it. A sudden fit of remorse for the way she'd treated him, the quarrel with Brian that made her run to where she assumed she'd be wanted, both were natural enough explanations. And the sickness in the village he did not even bother to consider as his own work, though he couldn't deny the tempting usefulness of such a skill.

He decided to go and see Cate the next day and fudge his way through returning the book without offending her. It would fill up his now empty days and get him out of Gordon's clutches for a while. Perhaps Cate would have advice about his new predicament and share his scorn for Rita's shabby behaviour. Whether he would mention Lily remained to be seen, although she continued to fill his thoughts unless he fought to dispel her image as soon as it appeared.

That night, however, he dreamt of Alison, newly shorn and severe, writing a set of reports at their old kitchen table, her mouth fixed in the thin, grim line it took on when she was completely immersed in a task. He had a sudden awful conviction that it was his name at the top of the white slip, that she was analysing and assessing the performance of a husband not a child. He approached

221

her entreatingly, but she looked up and her face softened so he saw at once the traces of the woman he had loved for eight years of his life. His heart swelled and he opened his mouth to speak, to make some sort of overture, before he realised she was looking over his shoulder into someone else's eyes and had never really noticed him at all.

'I'm sorry about the other day,' Rufus said.

He was sitting in Cate's kitchen, warm with yeasty aromas from the stove. She stood at the table crushing something in a large wooden mortar and did not respond.

'Is that eye of newt or wing of bat?' he asked.

He thought she suppressed the glimmer of a smile as she tilted the bowl towards him and he saw nothing more than salt crystals.

They remained silent for a while before Rufus went on.

'Things haven't been too easy just lately. Rita's turned up again and been pretty unpleasant about things, so I'm not at the shop any more.'

Cate said nothing, her silvery coils of hair bent over her work.

'Don't know how I'm going to manage really with no livelihood. But I expect something will turn up,' he said with forced brightness. 'I could always beg Neville King to take me on. His mother's ill apparently.'

The lack of response was starting to unnerve him.

'What's that you're cooking?' He gestured towards the oven.

'Bread.'

'Oh.'

Silence.

'What sort of bread?'

She raised her head at last. Rufus quailed at the exasperation written in every line of her face.

222

'Well, it could be wholemeal or sunflower seed or granary,' he said defensively. 'I don't know.'

'Rufus,' she said sternly, 'you are not the least bit interested in what I'm doing or my bread. You want me to comfort you in the face of all your problems and perhaps offer a few suggestions, or better still solutions, while I'm about it.'

They glared at each other for a minute, before Rufus began to laugh.

'Yes, that's about the size of it,' he said. 'What's wrong with that? We're friends, aren't we?'

Was that surprise in the grey eyes?

'Yes, I suppose so.'

Rufus felt emboldened by this moment of empathy.

'Then you won't mind me returning your book without reading every single word, I hope.'

He laid it on the table between them.

Cate looked at it thoughtfully.

'I thought maybe you'd come to talk about that,' she said.

'It's not really my sort of thing, if I'm honest, Cate. I used to read all those 18th century memoirs as reverently as if they were illuminating channels of history, but often they're just downright boring, I'm afraid. Sorry.'

'I agree with you entirely. Never had time to waste on other people's memoirs myself and Lionel Grubbe seems a particularly fine specimen of tedium.'

'But you thought I might like it?' asked Rufus, genuinely puzzled at her forthright dismissal of the book.

She looked at him despairingly.

'Rufus, did you read the page I marked?'

'No. I didn't see any marker.'

He snatched up the book and flipped through the pages. 'It must have fallen out.'

'In your zeal to devour the contents, no doubt,' she said,

grinning.

'Sorry. Was it important?'

Cate pushed aside the pestle and mortar and sat down opposite him at the table, putting her hand out for the book. She found the page and began to read.

'"...dined and spent the afternoon at Creech Inn with Mr Lovelace and Captain Pridham. The inn is kept by one Webb, who tells of an enchanted moon grove. I find nothing to remark in the spot but a fine willow tree. We had for dinner a fat haunch of Venison and a plum tart."'

'You mean, it's a reference to the moon garden?' Rufus ventured.

She nodded. 'The Green Man was called Creech Inn in those days.'

'And, well, strange things happened there as long ago as that?'

Cate frowned at him as if he'd said something more unintelligent than usual.

'And long before. The legend's a lot older than that bore Grubbe, but I thought you might like a solid piece of historical information to start you off,' she said.

'But it's still an old folktale,' Rufus protested, 'unless you're going to tell me the dancing and moon worshipping themselves are well-documented. What was Grubbe expecting to see - naked witches doing a moon dance? Are there any eye-witness accounts - "What I saw one night by ye olde willow tree" - or something like that?'

She shot him a hard glance across the table.

'You of all people should have more respect than that.'

'But how come there's no willow tree in the garden if it's the same place?' he persisted.

Cate waved a hand impatiently.

'If you'd listened properly you'd remember that Grubbe said a grove, not a garden.'

'So what makes it the same place?' Rufus was losing

track of the argument now, half keen to unravel the full story, half scornful of a load of old wives' tales. 'Come on, Cate,' he said crossly. 'You've been tantalising me with these hints ever since I came to Creech. It must make you feel very powerful to wrap everything up as some great mystery to totally flummox me.'

Cate's eyes narrowed at his tone. She lit a cigarette and looked out of the window at the sunny garden, and remained silent. He saw the grim set of her face in profile and decided to leave it alone for the moment, although why she should be so sensitive about all this he couldn't imagine.

'I expect your bread's done,' he said instead and she leapt up to remove a high domed loaf from the oven. There was no invitation to stay for lunch to share it, so he left with only a brief goodbye.

Rufus walked back down the lane with his brain buzzing. He had gone to see Cate in the hope of finding some respite, but round and round his thoughts went in a morass of legends, love, Moon Cottage, bankruptcy, Lily, marriage, mothers, Tara, Rita, Alison. All was in a huge melting pot of hopes and fears and he couldn't for the life of him imagine what solid result was to come out of any of it.

It seemed to Joe that it was nearly time for his mother to move on.

All his life they had migrated from place to place and it was natural for him to see this as her way of dealing with any situation that became too much of a hassle or too difficult to handle. They had left one town when he was unhappy with school, another when a close friend died and yet another when his father walked out, although Joe would much rather have stuck that one out with people he knew and a familiar environment to give a sense of stability when the ground seemed suddenly unsteady under his feet like the premonition of an earthquake. For weeks he hardly spoke, petrified of pouring out his desperate feelings about losing his dad and so making life more difficult for his mother. He clung on to this habit of reticence afterwards as his own protection from the world and somehow Lily never tried to snap him out of it.

He knew that she was quick to tire of routine and the settled patterns of a community. They had been in Creech for nearly four years now and he thought he recognised the signs of imminent departure in her restlessness and uncharacteristic irritation over minor domestic trivia. As far as he knew, his mother had never owned a house, but moved from one town or village to another, renting or house-sitting for her wide range of friends spread all over the country. It was fortunate that she had skills which travelled well and that amongst those who quickly gravitated towards her in each new place, there were always new patients to give them an income of sorts.

It seemed to Joe when he was younger that an hour with his mother would be enough to make anyone feel cheered and better able to cope with life, although he could never put his feelings into words. He'd been slow to speak as a child and talking became something he distrusted after his father left, full of cheery promises never fulfilled, and Joe's own silent thoughts seemed to offer the greatest security.

He had never longed for independence as his contemporaries did. His mother's warmth and tolerance made him comfortable around her, although her strong commitment to personal freedom meant she didn't pry or interfere with his life. It was an uncomplicated and undemanding relationship. If he sometimes wished for more direct involvement, he knew that he had only to initiate it himself and Lily would respond.

But he couldn't now talk to her about Tara. How could he explain the cause of their quarrel? He didn't want to appear to question his mother about her sex life. There'd always been men around, after his father left and even after Ged, who, although a fixture in their lives, was always taking off for unspecified periods of time. But this was messier and made more complicated, it seemed to Joe, by his own regard for Rufus.

He could see the change in him that Mean Cottage had wrought: Rufus had found something solid and settled to build his life around, the sort of foundation Joe himself was beginning to think about. He wanted to make furniture, to gain the skills to do it and even set up his own business in time. He thought he would do best in working for himself. The whole thing with Tara had begun to bother him, even before all this crude nonsense about his mother had started.

It was odd that Rufus was the catalyst for both the clarification of Joe's own ambitions and the realisation that he and Tara had no future together. Whilst he still felt the same physical attraction and cared very much what happened to her, he just couldn't hack the wild mood shifts and impetuous temper any longer on his own account. He longed in his heart for an easier life, for the sort of steady certainty he felt when concentrating on practical projects. There he could communicate confidently through his hands, beyond the need for words which always seemed to let him down.

Apart from anything else, Tara's heart was set on travelling after college - one reason she had been so angry about her mother's fling with Charlie was simple jealousy at her exclusion from their ambitious travel plans - and then moving up to London where things happened naturally, unlike Bruford where any small excitement had to be manufactured from inadequate materials.

But Joe really liked Creech and Bruford and had decided that he was going to stay put no matter what others did. His mother would understand, but Tara, never. No, it wasn't going to work between them on any level and he would have to tell her so, despite the hurt it would cause them both.

Chapter 15

When Joe phoned to suggest a meeting, Tara felt the smallest flicker of triumph.

Her attitude to him had hardened over the last few days, as the pain of his shockingly sudden desertion dulled, and she was no longer quite so desperate for the tearful reunion she was anticipating. She still didn't understand what had made Joe go off like that so decisively - quite out of character - when he knew what her temper was like, and that she couldn't help over-reacting a bit sometimes.

It all felt so out of her control, this situation with Rita. The problem was that Tara really didn't know how to regard herself. At seventeen she should be wavering on the cusp of adulthood, not being forced over into premature independence by a parent's absence. The freedom to live without physical restrictions palled after a while and she felt herself surprisingly unready for all the decision-making and responsibilities of living on her own.

She had no close friends apart from Joe to run to with troubles. In her experience, friends let you down, usually running a mile or turning into taunting assailants when they found out your mother claimed to be a witch and ran a shop for weirdoes. They'd come into the shop readily enough for a good laugh, but no-one felt comfortable up in the flat, even though Rita did nothing more outlandish than wear long swirly black skirts and sport earrings in the shape of runic symbols.

'I'll be there,' was all Tara said to Joe and hung up.

She was prepared to concede that she might have gone a bit far about Lily lately, but she'd been badly hurt to find out from Rufus that Lily was so dismissive of her feelings. It made it worse that Tara had always admired Lily fervently: she was all colour where Tara felt herself a simple, un-interesting contrast of pale and dark, and easy-going where Tara's own mother was inclined to be changeable. Now the sense of betrayal drove all her appreciation of Lily's past kindness into a murky corner of bitter resentment.

Why did no-one seem to care what *she* wanted? It was true that Joe and Rufus had both been good to her, but they didn't really know what it was like to be a casual appendage in your mother's life.

Rita came out of the kitchen with two mugs of herb tea.

'I'm going out in a minute,' Tara said. 'That was Joe on the phone.'

'I see.' Rita sat on the sofa and curled her legs up beneath her. 'Is it all on again, then?'

Tara shrugged.

'Dunno yet.'

'Listen. I want to talk to you about something.'

Tara stiffened at once.

'You always say that when it's something I won't like. You're not running off again, are you?'

To her horror her voice sounded wobbly and tearful.

It was true that those were the very words Rita had used a few days before flitting off with Charlie, and Tara remembered other occasions when they had been the harbingers of one of her mother's selfish schemes. Usually it meant she was off to some festival or other, depositing Tara en route at a reluctant friend's house like a piece of left luggage.

Rita sighed heavily, but ignored her daughter's petulance.

'I met some people in Amsterdam...'

'Here we go,' Tara folded her arms huffily, 'I can't wait to hear this.'

230

Her mother continued in the same mild tone.

'They're having a big festival for Madron, and I thought I'd go.'

'I knew it,' Tara screeched, 'you don't give a shit about me, do you?'

'You too, if you like,' Rita added beneath the resounding decibels.

Tara was in full flow of indignation.

'I'd just like to know what I've ever done for you to treat me...' She hesitated. 'Me too, what?'

'Come with me - travel, meet people. You've finished college now and you're always saying you want to.'

'Would you really take me?'

'Tara. Don't be so dramatic! I've taken you to lots of places - Glastonbury, for instance.'

Tara snorted.

'Yeah, like when I was ten! And then you dumped me in the crèche most of the time.'

Rita eyed her angry daughter wearily.

'Do you want to come or not? We can go on after, see some other places, if you like.'

'Do you really mean it?'

Rita nodded.

'What about it?'

'But what about the shop?' Tara said hesitantly.

'Oh, we'll get Rufus back, as you seem to have such a high opinion of him! Now, will you come to Amsterdam?'

Tara got up, stumbled over to the sofa and collapsed on top of her mother, laughing and crying at the same time.

They lay there in silence for a long time, Rita's arms clasped around her daughter, each absorbed in their own thoughts, until Tara began to shake with silent giggles.

'What's so funny?' Rita asked.

Tara looked up, her eyes still wet with laughter.

'Since you felt obliged to call me after a pagan festival,

231

I'm so glad you didn't choose Madron.'

They both began to laugh and laugh until they were too exhausted to do more than lie down again with their arms entwined. Rita brushed her daughter's black hair away from her eyes and gazed down at the imperious profile.

'That's better, my beautiful Ostara,' she said.

Rufus was wandering aimlessly round the garden, closely followed by Gordon, when he heard the phone. It was Tara, breathless and excited, words spilling down the wire like the rush of small stones foreshadowing an avalanche.

'Rufus, I just wanted to tell you you can come back. Rita's fine about it. She's taking me to Amsterdam, and then we're off travelling. So everything's OK. You'll still have a job. And I'm going to meet Joe now. He phoned! Do you think he'll come with us? I'm going to ask him. It's all going to be fine. I didn't want you to worry about work and that, and you've been so brilliant about the shop and everything. How will you manage without me, though? Ha, ha! It's so great, isn't it, Rufus?'

That was about the last word he would have chosen to describe what she'd said, but he couldn't bear to disappoint her.

'Great,' he agreed and was rewarded by a quick contented sigh at the other end of the phone. It was all she had time for.

'I've gotta rush now. See you, bye.'

The sudden silence in the room was overwhelming. Rufus sank down into his armchair and put his head in his hands. It had never even occurred to Tara that he might not greet her triumphant news with any pleasure whatsoever. On the contrary, he feared for her, going off on a long trip at the mercy of her mother's brittle whims.

He did not think there was much chance of Joe being one of the party either and a nasty shock to Tara's pride was probably imminent on that score.

For his own part, Rufus had no intention of going back to The Craft Shop after Rita's rudeness and ingratitude. It would be a nightmare, constantly waiting for her to swan in again and pick a fight to get rid of him. Working together in harmony was not something he could begin to imagine.

He also felt a growing determination to spend his time doing something he had some affinity with, and, before his endless ruminations could persuade him against it, he leapt up and grabbed his car keys to set off for Bruford.

The town was busy with tourists as usual and Rufus walked back and forwards past the bookshop several times, waiting impatiently for it to be free of customers. When an elderly couple carrying a framed print bulkily wrapped in brown paper finally emerged, he elbowed his way past them in the narrow entrance and plunged into the shop.

'I've come to see if you still need a temporary replacement.'

Damn, he hadn't intended to sound so belligerent about it.

King, looking even more fatigued and drawn than before, did not seem to mind.

'You find yourself unexpectedly available, I dare say?'

Rufus swallowed back a sarcastic rejoinder.

'Let's just say Rita's idea of running a business is not mine.'

'I'm very glad to hear it. I wouldn't want to come back here and find the place stocked with novelties for Christmas.' He didn't directly engage with Rufus, but went on flicking through an ancient card index box on his table. 'I shall want a proper agreement, you know.'

'I'm very glad to hear it,' said Rufus firmly.

King looked up then with his sardonic smile.

'Have a seat. Let's discuss it. The main problem as I see it will be the timescale. My mother's condition is unlikely to improve, but she may remain as she is for many months. On the other hand, things could deteriorate very rapidly. You see my difficulty?'

It's not easy to plan for your mother's death, Rufus thought, and I've no interest in trying to make things hard for him.

'I'd be prepared to accept a renewable three month contract, with a month's notice on either side,' he said. 'That gives me a minimum of security and won't keep you out of your shop for long when you're ready to come back.'

King raised his eyebrows in surprise, as if re-evaluating Rufus.

'That would suit me very well. To be honest, I didn't expect anyone to be satisfied with less than six months.'

'I'll take my chance,' Rufus said, 'if we can agree a reasonable wage. But there are two conditions.'

'Oh yes?'

'I want to work a full week with you to get to know your systems properly and I'll follow them to the letter when I'm on my own, but I shall want a free hand in the day to day running of the shop, without interference. You'll have to trust me to make good decisions. I'm an experienced bookseller and I'm not prepared to be just a cipher filling in for the boss.'

There! He had managed to say what he had been thinking all the way into town in the car and what he should have said firmly to Rita at the start of their strange business relationship.

King was looking at him, Rufus hoped, with increased respect. He took off his glasses, wiped each lens on the

234

sleeve of his shirt and then put them on again. Rufus waited.

'I'll take my chance,' King said at last.

Rufus didn't want to hang around in Bruford in case he stumbled across Tara and Joe's tryst or, worse still, met Rita. But he didn't want to go home either and be on his own. He felt full of himself for an up-lifting change, pleased with his handling of the situation, powerful and decisive in getting hold of his life and taking a positive grip. He wanted to tell someone about it while this euphoric mood persisted. Of course, it was Lily he longed to share it with, but after the way they'd last parted, he could hardly breeze round to her house and boast about getting a new job at the expense of her closest friend. He was not a priority for her in the way she was for him, although it hurt him to acknowledge that to himself. He impinged on her life only marginally, it seemed, and his life of fleeting significance continued.

Rufus felt his melancholy rising again and gave himself a severe mental shake. This was a good day and he was not going to spoil it by being miserable. He'd go back to Creech and buy something for supper in the village shop so he could have a chat with Jacinta. It was strange to think that a few weeks ago he was energetically avoiding her and now went cheerfully to seek her out.

He threaded his way through the market stalls, side-stepping little dogs on leads and old ladies' shopping trolleys in the narrow aisles, half-listening to the bantering yells of traders with their barbecue specials and soft fruits, while inside his head he was reliving his negotiations with King and enjoying the relief of the bookshop's sheer normality after his colourful interlude at The Craft Shop.

Taking the last few steps towards the mouth of a

narrow high-walled lane leading to the car park, he came face to face with Lily, who was approaching from the opposite direction, carrying a basket full of produce.

'Hello, Rufus!' She gave him such a smile he thought his heart would stop.

'You've got a good haul.' He indicated her purchases.

'Can't resist the fresh stuff - and I have to say it's a lot cheaper than the village shop.'

She seemed amused as he insisted on taking the basket and then followed close behind her down the lane which was not wide enough for them both to walk abreast. He could smell her meadowsweet perfume and the herbal fragrance from her wonderful hair, springing with vitality a few inches from his face. He thought what a splendid reward for his decisive behaviour it was to be near her again.

When they got to her car and put the shopping in, Lily locked the boot and turned to look longingly at the cool green of the abbey park across the river. There was a wooden pedestrian bridge about a hundred yards away.

'Do you fancy a walk?' she said, turning the full force of her clear eyes on his face. 'If you're not in a hurry?'

Rufus felt that this was definitely the best day he had had for a very long time, although he did resolve to try to avoid the subject of The Craft Shop or Neville King for fear of spoiling their time together. No, he was determined to make the most of this piece of rare good fortune and, learning his lesson from the last time, not over-burden anything with expectations and emotional demands. Light-hearted pleasure was very much what was called for here and for once he felt in the right place at the right time and ready to respond. It seemed the most natural thing in the world to take her hand as they went off together towards the river.

'I don't believe you!'

Tara was shaking with surprise and anger.

'I'm sorry,' Joe said for what felt like the hundredth time. He squirmed uncomfortably on the plastic seat in the café booth where they'd sat and made plans so many times in the past. He had not had the sense to choose somewhere else for this meeting, somewhere without the associations of their previous close connection. He was making a pig's ear of it all round really, the main error being his strong conviction that simple honesty was the best way of dealing with the end of their relationship. All it had achieved so far was to make Tara mad as hell and drive them both round and round in painfully tight circles.

'Look,' he tried again desperately, 'you're going off with Rita now for maybe months, you'll have other stuff going on, new places to see. It's a good time for this.'

'What!' she howled as if he had plumbed new depths of insensitivity. 'A good time to discover I've wasted more than a year of my life and put my trust in a devious, callous bastard! I suppose you've been planning this for ages...'

Joe was helpless in the face of Tara's withering sarcasm and injustice. For some time now he'd had no confidence in his abilities to support or comfort her in the increasingly frequent crises she suffered. He couldn't cope with the constant verbalisation of every small feeling any more, it wore out and depressed him.

He made a last supreme effort.

'For Christ's sake, there's no plan. We're not close like we were, that's all, we want different things in the future, so what's the point?'

He suspected that in the bottom of her heart she actually agreed with him, and with the lure of a trip abroad with her mother ahead, she'd get over it pretty quickly. How many other people from school had stayed together right through college and beyond? But it would deny Tara her drama to admit it.

Her face was whiter than ever now and stiff with scorn.

'I suppose dear Lily's pleased,' she sneered.

'Tara,' Joe said angrily, standing up. 'I don't need this. I thought we could, I don't know, talk, but you won't listen. You never do listen to anyone else, not properly. It's time to grow up a bit' - he went on talking over her protest - 'both of us, yes, I agree with you. Enjoy Amsterdam. See you.'

He went out miserably and slouched down the street towards his motorbike. As he was strapping his helmet on, Tara came running up, her pale face mottled and stained with tears.

'I'm sorry, Joe. Please don't just go off. It's a shock, you know, coming out with this after all the time we've been together. Let's go for a walk or something and talk. It's not as bad as you say.'

He sighed and shook his head.

'I never said it was bad at all. It's not easy for me either...'

She put a hand on his arm.

'Then don't...'

'No,' he interrupted her quickly. 'It is over and I'm really sorry, but talking won't make any difference. Let's just leave it.'

He started the engine and she withdrew her hand and stepped back onto the kerb, biting at her lower lip. He rode off without another glance, but shaking with sadness inside.

Cate looked up at the lowering sky, and felt tension in the movements of the air. She listened to the rustling of leaves in the fine ash tree above her head and heard the

238

whisperings of discord. All along the filaments of the web, forged connections were breaking. Her own guardian spirits were agitated and kept peace from her mind, flooding their channels of communication with harsh reedy utterances she could not distinguish.

She should not have been so short with Rufus when he came seeking information. He knew nothing about her personal history in this place, nor about Adam and the light in his eyes as he showed Cate a poem he'd discovered after weeks of painstaking historical research, nor the hours he'd spent listening to the stories of Mavis Skelton. For Cate herself, such things were less important than the verity bounded in her own heart and spirit, but she knew that Rufus was different and more like Adam in this respect. He needed the academic structure of fact and interpretation to underpin an imaginative bound that would lift him clear of all the trammels of outside influence and make him free at last. She would have to be more patient, more understanding of his situation and put the sort of trust in him that she had urged him to exercise himself.

Rufus skipped up the steps into the village shop, his heart light with happiness. He smiled cheerfully at a man waiting outside with a ferret on his head. An hour with Lily had restored his spirits and his optimism, an hour of pleasant conversation, shared laughter and not a hint of Rita or Tara or Ged to mar their enjoyment of each other's company. He was pleased with himself for successfully avoiding all controversial subjects, although it had been something of an effort. They had talked at random, more, he realised in retrospect, about him and his life in London than Lily's own past, but that was partly because he had been afraid to ask questions that might elicit answers he wouldn't like - about Joe's father, for instance, or Ged or any other part of her life in which he had no share. He had not minded telling Lily about his mother's awfulness and she had both laughed and been sympathetic in wonderfully appropriate measures. She had talked to him about her instinct for healing and her commitment to the path she had chosen in that respect. He had not realised the length and complexity of training required for homeopathic practice and he felt humbled at the strength of her vocation, compared to his own drifting competence.

'You look cheerful,' Jacinta said.

She herself was smiling as she finished serving a customer and turned to greet him.

Rufus shrugged.

'It's a lovely day.'

'And?'

'Must there be an and? Although I have just spent a very pleasant afternoon by the river with a beautiful woman.'

'Aha!' Jacinta exclaimed. 'I knew it.'

'And what about you?' he said quickly to forestall questions. 'Have you spoken to Geoffrey?'

Her eyes gleamed.

'I have as a matter of fact.'

'And?'

'We had a jolly good talk.'

'I see I'm not the only one who can be maddeningly obtuse. What did he say?'

Jacinta laughed and turned away, calling seductively over her shoulder.

'Come through and have a cup of tea and I'll tell you all.'

They sat in the little cubby-hole at the entrance of the stockroom. Rufus was right that there was a change in Jacinta. She seemed to have acquired a new confidence that stripped away the need for all her annoying mannerisms.

'So? Is he going to lend you the money for the restaurant?'

'No.'

'No? But you said you'd had a good talk. He hasn't tried to persuade you that you're better off sticking where you are, has he?'

'No.'

'Then what? Come on, spill. You're looking very happy about something.'

'I'm going back.'

Rufus was stunned for a moment.

'Geoffrey's asked you to go back?'

'Oh no, not to him, not in so many words, but it's better really. I'm going back on my own terms...'

'Wait, wait. Start from the beginning. You did tell him about the restaurant?'

'I did, but not at first. He said as soon as I rang that he may as well tell me that the girl has gone, and won't be coming back. It's all over between them.'

That one may be finished, Rufus thought, but there'll be others. He did not want to spoilt Jacinta's pleasure, however, with his cynicism.

'Well, I said I was sorry, of course.' She looked down at her hands. 'And I really was, surprisingly. Love's a strange habit isn't it? I don't like to think of him being unhappy.'

Rufus remembered his frequent fervent wish that Alison's life with Brian would be such hell she'd long for her marriage back. It seemed a very long time since he'd felt like that.

'Anyway,' Jacinta looked up brightly again, 'he asked how things were going and I told him straight out that I didn't like it here and was thinking about the restaurant maybe. He didn't say very much, just that he'd consider it.'

'But on consideration he thought you'd be better employed going back to look after him and iron his shirts?'

She seemed mildly surprised.

'No, nothing like that. You misjudge him, Rufus. Geoffrey's not an ogre. If everyone who made a mistake was damned eternally where would any of us be?'

'OK, fair enough. But what is it you're so mysteriously cheerful about?'

'He phoned yesterday to say he had a proposition for me. They've been thinking of opening a director's dining room at head office - there are various other companies in the building. I'm going to run it - everything from working with the kitchen designer to cooking the food. And there'll be girls to serve, so I'll have no public appearances to worry about, just good food and organisation.'

'And is there a company flat to go with this dream job?'

'Not exactly, but Geoffrey owns a lot of property and he's offered me a nice apartment - which I insisted on paying rent for from my salary, so it's the best of all worlds.'

'And do you want him back?' Rufus asked, genuinely curious.

'I'm going to see how I get on with being independent and take things as they come. There's no planning for relationships, is there?'

Rufus shook his head sadly.

'Unfortunately not,' he said.

As he drifted over to the moon garden later, Rufus reflected on what Jacinta had said and her situation. Part of him envied her bravery and the positive decision

242

she had made, whilst another part of him was sure that she would not be quite as assertive of her independence when dealing with her husband again on a regular basis. He did not put much faith in Geoffrey's conversion to good behaviour either. Did men who had abused women in that way ever really change? But for Jacinta the thought of work she adored was clearly an inspiration and maybe she was right to dwell on the positive. Rufus allowed himself to look forward to the proper job he now seemed to have secured at the bookshop. He liked the town of Bruford very much and the shop's location was excellent. He could not help selfishly hoping that old Mrs King would live for a very long time.

Rufus sighed and yet again looked in disbelief at his surroundings. Everything around him was parched and stiff with lethargy. The harsh sun was filtered through a haze of sandy cloud, which still held the heat of the day in its swathes. He could not identify this lifeless semi-wasteland with the vibrant animation of the garden under the moon. It was ridiculous, unthinkable, risible even. He would have to tell someone about it, someone other than Cate, who was plainly barmy in many ways herself, he thought, despite the friendship that had grown between them. Perhaps Jane would be the most sensible person to try, although something told him she would react with mirthful scorn initially. Why not Lily? What was it that stopped him from telling such a secret to the woman he loved? It wasn't that he didn't trust her, of course, or thought she would laugh at him - maybe it was precisely because he feared she would accept it all too easily.

Chapter 16

The Falling Goat was busy with Sunday morning brunch trade. Rita and Lily sat at a corner table talking about their plans for departure from Bruford. Neither wanted to discuss the ruptured relationship of their offspring, other than agreeing it was no bad thing. The ins and outs of the affair were no concern of theirs. The bottom line was that Joe and Tara were much too young to commit to a lasting partnership. Their mothers had both been stuck with small babies at their age and were under no illusions about the limitations it placed on young lives.

'I'm glad Tara's agreed to go with you,' Lily said. 'It will do her good to get away from here for a bit. She's a lot more curious and adventurous than Joe at heart.'

Rita agreed. She was surprised at how much she was looking forward to taking Tara to Amsterdam. Perhaps she had neglected her daughter a bit in the last couple of years, pursuing shallower and less lasting relationships instead of being around at home.

'And you don't mind Joe staying behind when you and Ged go?' she said.

Lily smiled.

'A bit of real independence will be the making of Joe. He's full of ideas and plans for making a living and he really does want to concentrate on developing his skills into a way of life here. There's been too much moving around for him. He needs to settle.' She stared into her cup for a minute. 'I shall miss him though.'

'He can visit you in Scotland,' Rita said. 'It's not the end of the world.'

Lily sighed. 'Joe's never been much of a traveller. Maybe when he's established himself here and got a bit of confidence from that, things will be different.'

'Doesn't he want to see his father?' Rita asked.

'They've nothing much to say, honestly. Plenty of good will on both sides but they don't really know each other any more. It's been too long. He'll miss Ged more, but I'm sure Rufus will be kind to him.'

'Ah, Rufus.' Rita looked slightly uncomfortable. 'I wanted to ask you about that. I'll need him back for a few weeks to cover for this trip. Do you think he'll do it ?'

Lily laughed.

'If you ask nicely I expect so. He's very willing to please.'

Rita made a face.

'I don't think Rufus is all that enamoured of me actually. Can't think why.'

They both grinned.

'Tara seems to think he'll come back, but I'm not sure. I'm not that keen on asking him myself.'

Lily reflected briefly.

'I could ask him, if you like,' she said. 'I think I could persuade him.'

If what Tara told me is true, thought Rita, that's what I was relying on.

She said brightly, 'Would you really? That'd be great.'

Rufus spent the weekend tidying the house and labouring in the garden, trying to work steadily through his deep physical and emotional frustrations about Lily. His thoughts went constantly to her, no matter what he did: what was *she* doing, what did she really feel for him, was there any possibility of a future for them together. Perhaps he should ring her? But to say what? A serious talk was the last thing she'd appreciate, but there was surely something to be said, to be discussed about the feelings they had for each other. You didn't just sleep with someone, someone you liked and respected, and then - nothing. He tried very hard not to think about the dark satanic Ged and what the sleeping arrangements were in the red-brick cottage.

Rufus was relieved when Charlie phoned to say he was going to an art fair in Huddlebridge early the next morning and suggested he'd stop off in Creech on the way if Rufus fancied a drink in the pub. Rufus was only too glad to agree and persuaded him to spend the night at Moon Cottage.

On and off during the day, Rufus thought of asking Charlie's advice. He would probably be scathing or scornful and enjoy making Rufus suffer a fair bit, but he would listen and his advice would be surprisingly sound. He had always been spot on about Alison. Let's face it, he knows far more about women than I do, Rufus thought ruefully, stretching his aching back.

He moved behind the house into the green shade of a sycamore tree to rest and let the soothing tranquillity of the day wash over him. There was not a sound to be heard. He closed his eyes and swayed gently to and fro in the depths of that natural silence, his mind stilled and empty, his limbs gradually relaxing in the warm air. There was a sudden lull in the gossipy conversations of the birds, a lull in the rustling of leaves above his head, as if he had fallen over a precipice into the very depths of silence. The thought that this was total peace registered in his brain, and then at once, as if the completeness of the silence had made room for the idea, a small voice inside his head whispered that perhaps Lily, for all her loveliness and attraction, was not right for him and could never give him what he needed to flourish and be strong.

This heresy echoed harshly throughout his system. He shook it off straight away and plunged indoors where the ringing certainty of Handel's Messiah easily silenced the voice of schism. He sang along vigorously despite having only the faintest inkling of the words, as he made up a bed for Charlie in the spare bedroom. He then lay on his bed as the glorious music soared around him and felt the remembered thrill of Lily's naked body beside his on a night of stars when wishes came true.

Cate went out into the garden. She was ready to let go of old memories and give up her jealousy of unappreciative eyes on Adam's work. Rufus could believe or not as he chose, but at least he should see what Adam had discovered, standing as he did now, in Adam's place. She was sure that he was brought to Moon Cottage for a purpose and would find the answers to his dilemmas there.

Placing an offering of anemones on her altar stone, Cate closed her eyes to concentrate and then she raised her arms to the four quarters in turn and prayed.

By the spirits of air, may his mind be open to receive
By the spirits of fire, may he be driven to succeed
By the spirits of water, may he sense his true desire
By the spirits of earth, may he know his real worth
Great Goddess, grant this
Lord of the Wild Hunt, grant this
To your honour, let it be.

A strong breeze swept through the garden where she stood, stirring the flowers and the feather on the altar. But the candle remained unmoved, its flame as straight as a pine tree, and brighter than ever.

Rufus sat happily in The Green Man, graphically regaling Charlie with the details of his experiences at The Craft Shop. Descriptions of the ambience and clientele amused Charlie no end. He felt he'd had a lucky escape with Rita, parting on reasonable terms of mutual rejection.

'Otherwise she might have turned me into some kind of toad,' he said with a grin.

'Perhaps she thought you were half way there already and not worth further effort,' Rufus retorted, downing his second double whisky more swiftly than was wise. 'I've had some personal experience of this cursing lark myself.'

'Oh yeah? I thought you were looking a bit on the warty side.'

'Ha, ha. No, I mean it, and I was not on the receiving end.'

Rufus tried to tap his nose knowingly and nearly poked himself in the eye.

Charlie laughed.

'You're a mad fuck, Rufus, and in danger of losing your last few functioning brain cells in this hole by the sound of it.'

He went off to the bar again. Rufus closed his eyes for a second and felt the room spin so he snapped them open again.

Charlie was back. 'Get this down you.'

'I mean it,' Rufus said earnestly, slurping his drink. 'I made the whole village sick!'

'Bollocks.'

'And Alison came back.'

Charlie did an exaggerated double-take.

'Wow! That must have been some powerful curse - OK, I give in. It's all true.'

'Fuck off,' Rufus said crossly. 'And I'll tell you something else. I've got a magic goon marden.'

'I won't argue with you there,' Charlie said. 'I've never seen a worse case of it in my life.'

Rufus was really annoyed now. He had not for one second envisaged broaching the subject of the moon garden with Charlie, but under the influence of this unexpected return to normality, sitting in the pub with an old mate talking about nothing very much and both generally rather pleased with themselves for no good reason, he had felt secure enough to open up and share some important stuff, and all Charlie could do was take the piss. Well, now he really would tell him.

He left out the blue dog and the dancers and concentrated on the strange effects of light on the garden and its plants, and how whatever you said seemed to happen. Even to his own drunken ears the story sounded a bit daft told here under harsh electric lights around a table mottled with tomato ketchup stains.

Charlie gave him a long cool look when he came lamely to a halt.

'You've been mixing too much with the locals, mate, if all this mumbo-jumbo's wearing off on you. Rufus Keene, master of logic and sweet reason, falling for a load of bullshit like that. It's not Tara who's been feeding you this gunk, is it? I wouldn't be surprised if all this moon garden crap wasn't a figment of Rita's weird imagination, given she's as crazy as a coot.'

'No, it's nothing to do with Rita,' Rufus said, regretting already that he had mentioned any of this to Charlie. 'I don't expect she even knows about it. Cate told me the story, well, only some of it so far.'

'Cate?'

'She lives in the nearest cottage to me, about half a mile away. She was a bit annoying when I first moved here, but now we're quite good friends.'

Charlie raised an eyebrow.

'Just good friends?'

'Come on, she's about seventy. And if you think Rita's strange, you should see Cate talking to streams and doing her mind-reading act.'

'Rufus, old son, you really are in need of a strong dose of normality. All this hanging out with witches and goblins is doing you no good at all. You need a proper woman to set you straight. What about this Lily? Is she as mental as the rest of them?'

Rufus shook his head vehemently and felt the first stirrings of a volcanic headache.

'She's wonderful. The most beautiful person I've ever met...'

His eyes filled with tears.

'Christ, don't go all maudlin on me, mate. I haven't got a clean handkerchief about my person.'

'Sorry, sorry, it's just that she seems interested in me and we get on so well and then, well, nothing, or rather we did sleep together, but then nothing again, and then I saw them together - she's got a bloke - a real wanker - and later we went for a walk but it was just a walk, and then there's her son Joe, I think he likes me and I'm really very fond of him...'

Rufus clutched at the table to ensure he remained upright.

Charlie narrowed his eyes consideringly.

'Sounds a right mess,' he said. 'But I'd go for Joe, if I were you. It's never too late to change, they say, and you've certainly had piss-awful luck with women in your short life.'

'Thanks, Charlie. I knew you'd understand.'

Rufus heard only the sympathy of a friend, tried to pat Charlie's hand and fell off his stool.

Next morning Joe mooched down the lane to the cottage without a clear idea of why he was going to see Rufus.

After waking early, he'd just felt like a long walk to get away from the house and have a chance to think, but it had turned into a dismal and constant re-run of the parting scene with Tara. Perhaps he should have stayed and given them both another chance to talk things over, but he knew full well that it would have ended badly whatever he'd done. He had drifted through the last months of their relationship, letting Tara take the lead, deciding where and when they should meet and what they'd do, while all the time his own feelings were melting slowly away. He could never compete with her fluency and strength of character to urge his own demands, and after all, it was easier to go along with her than risk the rows he loathed so much.

Joe wondered if talking to Rufus now might help, given that he knew Tara and understood what Joe was up against, but had no reason to take sides between them as Lily would. His mother wasn't the right person to share this with, Joe knew that instinctively. She would listen and sympathise, but he did not think that she would really understand the turmoil he felt inside. Especially as she had other things on her mind.

She had talked to him now about leaving Bruford and he had said he intended to stay. He'd also made a big effort to find out about courses and accommodation. He sighed. It was all so difficult. He was not at all surprised that adults so often seemed to get it so wrong.

'I've made quite a hash of my own love life,' Rufus said as he poured out the coffee. He was feeling fragile but strangely cheered after Charlie's visit. 'Personally, I wouldn't dream of taking my own advice, now I come to think of it.'

Joe thought about this for a moment.

'You mean you don't trust your own feelings?'

Not where your mother's concerned, Rufus thought and then was instantly sorry for his levity. He did not enjoy the sight of Joe's pained bewilderment. The least he could do was take it seriously and try to be of some constructive help. He remembered too much teenage anguish of his own to want to be frivolous now.

'No,' he said consideringly, 'I think I find it difficult to act honestly on them.'

Joe looked brighter at once.

'That's what I mean!'

Rufus smiled at him.

'Making excuses for avoiding the truth, going along with things for a quiet life - sound familiar?'

'Right.' Joe smiled hesitantly back at him. 'I'm not the only one then.'

'You and a couple of million others I should think, Joe, so it's not exactly a personal flaw of character. But it does lead to all sorts of misunderstanding and dissatisfactions. I sleep-walked through the last years of my marriage, refusing to stand up for myself or face the consequences of my own unhappiness. I liked the idea of being married, having a settled life and all that and I certainly didn't want to be a divorce statistic. But for that I paid a price and would have gone on doing so - out of my own weakness, I hasten to add - if Alison hadn't had the courage to go off with someone and give me the boot. She was right, although at the time I thought the world had ended and felt excruciatingly sorry for myself.'

'Yeah,' said Joe sympathetically, 'I know what you mean.'

They drank their coffee in thoughtful silence.

'So you think I was right to finish with her?' Joe said eventually.

'If that's what you really feel inside, yes. It's no compliment to her to keep on with a relationship if your heart's not in it. You say you tried to talk it through calmly, so it's not as if you wrote her a note or just got another girl behind her back.'

'But she was so...' he fumbled for a suitable word.

252

'So Tara?' Rufus suggested.

'Yeah, right,' he said gratefully. And then he added, 'I really do like her, you know, and care what happens to her and stuff.'

Rufus liked him even more for that thought.

'So what are you thinking of doing next?' Rufus asked.

Joe's face flushed.

He mumbled something in which Rufus thought he caught the word 'reference'.

'Are you applying for a job, Joe?'

'It's a course at Huddlebridge.' He looked round the room, anywhere rather than at Rufus.

'And you need - what? Someone who can vouch for your ability, something like that?'

Joe nodded with relief that he hadn't had to ask outright.

Rufus was only glad that he could do something to help Joe so easily. It was Joe's efforts that had made Moon Cottage a pleasant place to live and through his instinctive response to the fabric of the house, taught Rufus to stop and look before panicking and giving up on it.

'Why don't we take some photos of what you've done here? I have some photos of how it was originally - we could take some more and make up a folder with before and after shots, and I'll write a glowing account of your application and skill in making my life here viable.'

Joe managed to look both embarrassed and pleased at the same time.

Rufus slapped him affectionately on the shoulder, making the lurid quiff wobble.

'That's no problem, Joe. I'll be glad to do it.'

Joe was now looking at some spot on the wall high above Rufus' head. He gave another long mumble.

'Something else? Rufus asked.

More mumbling. Another reference figured somewhere, but this time he had to question Joe more carefully to extract the meaning.

Apparently Joe wanted to rent a flat in Bruford and needed a personal reference for the landlord. There was a whole street of these units out by the old railway station in Bruford, studio flats each over a lock-up garage, most of which were rented by artisans - Joe knew a jewellery maker who lived there and his girlfriend who was a potter. He would be able to use his garage as a workshop as they did and try to build up clients for his furniture-making, whilst getting a proper training for paper qualifications at college.

Rufus thought it was a brilliant idea. He was thrilled for the reticent and unenterprising Joe to be showing such initiative. How pleased Lily must be!

'I expect your mother'll miss you at home though,' he said, thinking of Lily there in the redbrick cottage alone. Ged seemed to have mysteriously disappeared from the picture in his imagination.

'No,' Joe said, still glowing from Rufus' enthusiasm for his plans. He forgot momentarily that Tara had assured him Rufus was madly in love with Lily and that she was stringing him along. 'She won't be there.'

'What do you mean?'

Rufus' alarm sounded a warning bell in Joe's brain, but he was not adroit enough to extricate himself now.

'She's moving on. Leaving here. They're going to Scotland next week.'

Chapter 17

Joe left quickly, aware that he had made a terrible blunder but quite unable to gainsay his words or offer Rufus comfort. He was beginning to think that relationships with all their subtle complexities were beyond him and resolved to concentrate on his work which was far more simply satisfying.

Rufus went back into the house, slumped into his favourite chair in the sitting room and gazed vacantly at the wall. He did not want to be outside in the sunshine any more. He had been stunned initially by Joe's bombshell, but he didn't disbelieve him for one moment, didn't feel any inclination to pick up the phone or rush round to Lily's to demand an explanation. It was true. She was going and she felt it was nothing to do with him.

Now Rufus just felt heavy, lethargic and empty. He sat there for the rest of the day, unaware of the changing patterns of light in the room and the clammy closeness of the air which heralded a storm, immersed in a misery that seemed to spread back from this moment right to his childhood.

He remembered his mother saying 'Where's that bloody boy?' in tones of the most profound irritation, as if he were deliberately hiding at the bottom of the garden or shirking some duty, instead of in his room doing his homework. Rationally he knew that people cared for him - Jane and David, Charlie, other friends from the London days, maybe even Cate in this strange new Creechian life - but why did it seem as if all those he most loved treated him with total disregard, as if his feelings were of no account and not to be weighed in any balance of decision. It wasn't the actual narrow fact that Lily was leaving that hurt him most, but the way in which he had heard, casually and unexpectedly, from someone else. If only she had come to see him, to make some explanation, however tenuous, as if he was deserving, an acknowledgement of his status as a part of her current existence, even if there was no future for him there.

Is that really all I expect, he asked himself grimly. Would a pat on the head before departure rather than a kick in the teeth make things better? That was so much crap. His low expectations were all part of the problem: he wanted to stay comfortably married so he put up with shit from Alison, he wanted Lily so much he was prepared to share her with Ged.

Rufus leapt up and stormed about the room, shouting, causing Gordon to skip excitedly around his tether peg on the grass outside the window.

'No, no, no,' Rufus yelled, waving his fists in the air.

'That's not what I want! That's not at all what I bloody well want!'

He stamped his feet in exasperation, his face contorted with effort, bobbing his head up and down like an inelegant Indian brave performing an inept war dance. He found it was surprisingly liberating to rant and rage and was just beginning to feel he might come to enjoy this sort of thing when an amused voice interrupted.

'So what is it you *do* want?'

Rufus stopped his tirade abruptly and turned to face Cate in the doorway.

'How did you get in?' he said.

She was unperturbed by his rudeness.

'The door was open. I heard strange noises and what sounded remarkably like cries for help.'

Rufus struggled for a dignified response.

'I appreciate your neighbourly concern, but as you can see I'm perfectly alright.'

Cate's mouth twitched into a smile.

256

'Indeed?'

'Oh, alright, I'm a complete and utter mess, but it's a private and incurable matter and I've no need of any more potions. Thank you very much for your concern. Goodbye.'

Cate sat down comfortably on the sofa and took out her tobacco.

'You can do something about it, if you seriously want to bring about a change,' she said amiably, 'but it requires focus. Give some thought to what you *really* want, Rufus. Think about it very carefully, in as much detail as you can.'

'Like make a shopping list of my ideal woman's qualities?' he sneered.

'Certainly.' Cate was not the least bit rattled by his sarcasm. 'Good idea to write it down. Then concentrate all the power of your mind on it and ask for help.'

Rufus gave a caustic laugh.

'Out in the bloody moon garden, I suppose?'

'Naturally.'

'There's nothing natural about it,' he shouted with a sudden burst of angry frustration. 'That's the trouble, it's a veritable freak of nature!'

Cate regarded him calmly.

'You mean you're afraid of something because you don't understand it,' she said.

The haze of blue smoke was building into a layered wall between them.

Rufus' bravado suddenly deflated and he sank back down into his chair.

'I'm afraid of lots of things,' he said sadly. 'That's been the problem. I didn't want to be on my own in a world full of couples, so I married Alison without much thought at all about whether we were really suitable for each other in temperament, and I stayed in the marriage after it got unpleasant because I couldn't face trying to start all over again alone or stumbling into another ill-matched relationship. Although I think what I really couldn't face was the idea that I'd been found lacking and inadequate. If Alison didn't want me, no-one else would.'

'The right person would,' Cate said.

Rufus gave a hollow little laugh.

'That's what I thought when I met Lily. She was so beautiful, so alive...'

'So unsuitable,' she finished the sentence for him.

'You mean someone like that would never fall for someone like me.'

Cate gave a puff of indignation.

'Rufus, you really are ridiculous sometimes. Stop trying to make yourself so important, it's nothing to do with you. Lily's just a grazer, she flits in and out of people's lives.'

'She helps people,' he said quickly, determined to defend Lily from the unpleasant attack he was expecting.

But Cate only nodded mildly.

'She has a gift of healing, it's true. But there's a lightness in her, and her giving goes only so far. She'll never be happy with one man, Rufus, and I can't see *you* happy in that situation.'

Rufus couldn't argue with this. His heart sank with the weight of it.

'She's moving up to Scotland,' he said. 'With that dreadful Ged, and Joe's father is up there already.'

And a lot of other men who'll come under her spell, he suddenly thought.

'Rufus,' Cate said sternly, fixing him with a cool grey gaze. 'You need someone who needs you. Someone who'll take from you emotionally, rely on your support and judgement. You need to share love, Rufus, to be an equal, not the underdog. That's my advice. Take it or not, but think - what is it you really want? And then don't settle for less.'

258

Cate reached over and grasped his wrist. Rufus felt a spurt of energy shoot up his arm like a pleasurable electric shock and looked up in surprise.

She smiled and gave him a reassuring nod.

'The energy is there for you to use,' she said. 'It's inside all of us and it means there's always potential for change.'

She released her hold quickly and got up to go, pointing to something she had left on the table beside him.

'I hope you'll find that interesting,' she said. 'It may even be instructive!'

When he heard the back door close, Rufus glanced at the green folder with its sheaf of papers and then reverted to his wall-gazing with an incurious sigh.

Lily went around the village, organising final consultations with a few of her clients. She had made arrangements with a practitioner near Bruford and wanted to reassure them all about ongoing treatments. She walked along the high street, moving with her light gait, hair gleaming in the sun, smiling at everyone she passed.

Inside, she was happy to be going. There was now too much that was familiar and predictable in Creech, a place she had found full of endearing eccentricities four years earlier. She knew the long haul didn't ever seem to suit her, the grinding routine of sights and faces, and she had stopped feeling good-natured amusement at her next-door neighbour's garden gnomes, tidy hedges and assiduous car-washing. There was nothing Lily felt she would miss here, but she would be very sorry to say goodbye to Rufus, of whom she'd grown tremendously fond in a short time and who had been so good to Joe. The stimulus of a new environment was what she needed, and, thinking of recent rifts with Ged, now at home stacking tapes and books into cardboard boxes, perhaps the potential of a new relationship.

Three dogs sitting upright in a line in the middle of the road jogged over to lick her hand and trail saliva joyfully across her long scalloped violet skirt. She brushed them aside pleasantly and they returned to their obstructive posts, sentimental eyes following Lily as she crossed to enter the shop.

She expected to find their white-haired, irascible master inside, but the shop, as so often in her experience, was resoundingly empty. Lily selected a few vegetarian salads and a jar of manuka honey before telling Jacinta of her impending departure.

Jacinta's eyebrows shot up on hearing the news. Wide-eyed, her heavy face flushed as all the muscles worked overtime in her struggle to refrain from asking Lily about Rufus. Her voice came out in a strangled squeak as she wished Lily well and handed over her change.

Lily wondered what on earth was the matter with this strangely gauche woman who seemed so upset about losing a customer. Perhaps business really was as bad as people said.

Tara was in her room, sorting out clothes. Garments of all shapes and sizes in varying shades of black littered the small space. As she burrowed and pounced among the heaps, tossing chosen items into a large hold-all, she tried not to think about Joe or at least to remember what her mother had said, that Joe would still be in Bruford when they returned and who knew what would have happened before then. She was truly excited about the coming trip and would not want to miss it, even for Joe.

She went over to the mirror and checked out her image. Did she look older, she wondered? Was she a woman now that she had survived her first real relationship rather than when she'd had sex for the first time? Half of the jet black hair fell down flat over her face today, whilst the other half stuck out from her head in thickly jelled spikes like a starfish. She turned her head this way and that, critically regarding the length of her nose and the deep sockets of her dark eyes. She could see her mother's face in there somewhere, although their colouring was very different. It pleased Tara that the dramatic contrasts in her physiognomy were original and all her own. She refused to see the minutest trace of her father.

Rita came in and sat down among the chaos on the bed.

'We'll get off as soon as the shop's sorted,' she said.

Tara began to rifle through the box of heavy silver jewellery by the mirror.

'I must see Rufus before we go,' she replied. 'When's he coming in?'

'Not sure.' Rita was rearranging clothes in the hold-all. 'Lily's going to have a word.'

Tara swung round sharply. 'But *I*'ve already told him he can come back,' she said. 'It's nothing to do with Lily.'

'Tara, for goodness sake stop being so prickly about Lily. She's been a good friend to us.'

'And Rufus has been a good friend to me.' Tara's chin jutted forward crossly towards her mother. 'He stood up for me when you and that cow were treating me like shit. He doesn't think much of your maternal instincts.'

Rita laughed icily. 'I don't think much of him at all,' she retorted. 'He's a man, so hardly the best judge of motherhood - or anything else for that matter.'

Tara sensed she'd touched a nerve and persisted.

'He knew I was unhappy. Fat lot you cared, swanning off with Charlie like that.'

Rita got up. 'Tara, let's face it,' she said, 'you're a teenager. Of course you're unhappy, it goes with the territory.'

She saw that her daughter's eyes were filling with

261

tears.

'Fine,' she said, 'cry, scream, tear your hair out, whatever you like, but don't expect it to change the world.'

Rita was careful to close the door quietly behind her and not slam it as she would have liked. But as she went down the stairs she was thinking hard and Rufus would not have liked it if he had known her thoughts.

As the evening sky began to dim, Rufus still sat in his chair, thinking of his first sight of Lily in his makeshift kitchen all those weeks ago and how she'd fancifully appeared as an angel sent to save him. That was how she'd always seemed to him, with her lustrous hair and radiant smile, her warmth and responsiveness - a shining being who had lighted up the stony path of his new rural life. Falling in love with her had given the whole messy transition a point and allowed him to think that there was a purpose behind all the hardships he felt he'd suffered.

Rufus jumped as a tap on the window roused him from his reverie.

He knew at once that the dark silhouette in the glass was Lily and, instead of obeying his instinct to leap up to welcome her, did no more than give a wave of his hand to summon her in.

The first thing he noticed was that she was wearing the dress she had worn the night they went out to dinner. He pushed aside the memory of that evening and the hopes it had harboured, and said nothing to greet her.

Lily must have sensed that something was not right and sat down opposite him, with no more than a warm smile.

'Are you OK?' she then asked with her customary tone of concern.

'Have you come to tell me something?' he countered, trying to keep all anger from his voice.

She was surprised by his response and looked at him quizzically.

'More to ask you, I suppose.'

'To ask me?' Rufus echoed feebly.

'Well, it's not exactly a favour, because it benefits you as much as anyone.' She smiled winningly.

Rufus said nothing. He felt tired and betrayed, far too enervated for guessing games. There was no way in which her departure from Creech could benefit him.

Lily shuffled in her seat, crossing her legs and lifting one foot to examine the sole of her green suede sandal. A curtain of springy auburn waves fell between them like a barrier in the darkening room.

Suddenly she tossed back her hair and laughed.

'I can hardly see you over there. Shall we have a light on?'

Rufus shook his head. He knew his only power lay in silence. If he spoke, all his anguish would spill out in a fountain of bitterness and recrimination.

'Alright. I can see I've come at a bad time,' Lily said. 'Are you sure there's nothing I can do for you?'

He swallowed back a retort and merely shook his head again, keeping his eyes fixed on her face as if to memorize it for all the weeks and years of his life that he was now to spend without sight of her.

His lack of communication was beginning to get to Lily. She straightened up, one hand on her bag ready for departure.

'Rita really needs you to start back at the shop,' she said crisply. 'She and Tara want to get off as soon as possible. You can imagine how Tara's looking forward to it!'

Rufus felt momentarily winded by her sheer audacity.

263

She was planning to leave Creech without telling him, but had undertaken to get him back in the shop before she left as a last favour to her good friend Rita. Not one ounce of concern for his feelings about her departure or for his well-being as a friend.

'Is that what you've come to say to me?' he demanded incredulously. 'That I should go running back to that awful shop just because bloody Rita's chasing off after some new rainbow, "kindly" condescending not to actually forget her daughter this time but to drag her along too as long as it suits her!'

During this outburst, Lily stood up. Rufus knew he had blown the small advantage he'd had and now felt the recklessness of impending defeat.

'Still, you'll be up in Scotland, won't you, so none of it matters a damn to you in practice. You can do your Lady Bountiful act and sort everyone's problems out, then just fuck off somewhere else and to hell with us all.'

She was taken by surprise.

'How did you know about Scotland?'

'Joe came round this morning to tell me his plans and yours just happened to slip out in the process.'

He stood, breathing heavily, waiting for some sort of explanation.

Lily took a pace towards him.

'You seem to have an expectation of me, Rufus, as if I owe you something. But I never promised you anything - far from it, I made it quite clear that I couldn't have the kind of major starring role in your life you seemed to hope for.'

'So why did you go along with it?' Rufus was beside himself now, roused by her coolness. 'Why did you go out with me and, if I'm not mistaken, make the first advances if you weren't interested in me. Why did you sleep with me if it meant nothing?'

Lily turned away in annoyance and went over to the window.

'Life isn't black and white like that. I like you, I was grateful to you for helping Joe...'

'Grateful!' Rufus shouted. 'Shit!'

Ged's barb about a sympathy fuck rang in his ears. He had not believed that such a thing was possible, but she seemed to be confirming it. He gripped his head with both hands as if to hold on to his sanity.

'I wanted to help you,' she went on as if he hadn't spoken, 'you've been badly hurt, Rufus, by your wife, your friends...'

'Jesus, I don't believe this.' The sense of being patronised made him feel vicious with rage. 'Do you go round sleeping with everyone you're grateful to? What, like someone who helps you with your bags, or maybe the postman who delivers a parcel you've been waiting for? Do you sleep with all your clients to heal their wounds? I expect it's more effective than those little white pills under the tongue ten times a day.'

'You're being ridiculous now,' she said angrily. 'I wasn't talking about sex. That hardly needs explanation. You're an attractive man, we get on well, why not sleep together - but it doesn't mean total commitment or one true love. It's not how I am, Rufus, and not what I want. I'm sorry you feel differently and I'm sorry you found out from Joe about me leaving, but I've never deceived you.'

'So leaving without a word isn't a form of deceit?'

'Rufus! I was going to say goodbye to you, of course. There are things to sort out. We're not going tomorrow or the next day - I don't know exactly when, but certainly not before saying goodbye to good friends.'

'Just good friends, eh. That's an original concept. A bit sad when I'd hoped...'

'I'm not responsible for your hopes,' she said coldly. 'Sorry, but I'm not. I've never lied to you or said anything to give you the wrong impression. So those hopes really are down to you and I can't help you there.'

He swallowed hard, his brain racing over previous conversations to see if he could prove her false or dredge up more telling accusations.

Lily came up to him and took his hands.

'I really am sorry, Rufus. I care about you a lot, but there are other people in my life. You won't let things between us stop you seeing Joe, will you? He needs your support and friendship more than ever. You've done so much for him already.'

Rufus' bitterness choked in his throat. He shook his head.

'I'll always be pleased to see Joe,' he said, 'and I'll help him any way I can.'

Lily reached up and kissed him swiftly on the lips.

'Thank you,' she said softly in his ear before kissing it too.

He closed his eyes, overwhelmed by her touch and the scent of her skin.

Their lips met again. Part of Rufus wanted to push her away, but he could not forget the intimacy of their last night together in the cottage, when he had thought his world was complete.

'We can't,' he said, breaking off abruptly. 'There's no point. We can't.'

Lily smiled at him from beneath languorously lowered lids.

'Why ever not?' she said, stroking her arms around him, drawing their bodies close, easily arousing him against his will. He pulled away a little, but one look at her face, her mouth warm and inviting, was enough to break his resistance. He lunged back into the embrace, kissing her again with all the sudden imperative of hopeless love.

Why not, he thought, why not after all?

They lay on the bed afterwards, Lily with her back to him in the crook of his arm. Rufus stared at the ceiling, feeling empty and miserable inside. Despite the willing treachery of his body, he had not enjoyed making love to her. What could be sadder than sleeping with the woman you loved whilst knowing you meant nothing to her and might well never see her again? But it wasn't quite that, he realised, that had left him so dissatisfied. He remembered his conversation with Cate earlier in the day. Here was the perfect and painful illustration! Yet again he'd done something, or gone along with something that was not what he wanted. He had settled for a much lesser thing.

Lily stirred and turned over to face him.

'You could come up to Scotland and see us sometime, you know. Bring Joe up with you.'

Rufus laughed.

'What's funny?' She was puzzled.

'You never think of me without appending the thought of my usefulness to Joe.'

'Oh, come on, Rufus. Don't let's start that again. I thought we were through all that.'

She ran a hand lightly over his head.

He shook it off and then hauled himself to a sitting position.

'I don't want to start anything,' he said and was amazed to hear the firmness of his voice. 'On the contrary, I think we've finished all there ever was.'

She stroked his face.

'Rufus,' she said, her voice soft and compelling, 'Let me...'

'No!' He pushed away her hand strongly. 'Really, it's no good. I can find answers and sort things out for myself, and I won't be in need of remedial sex again, thanks all the same.'

'I see.'

She sprang off the bed and began to gather her clothes without looking at him.

He watched as she pulled the lovely emerald dress over her head and it slid down, covering the exquisite skin inch by inch, clinging to the outline of her body as it hid the essence. While she scrabbled for her shoes under the bed, he got up and quickly flung on his jeans.

They went downstairs in silence and with unconscious formality Rufus led her to the front door where they faced each other on the doorstep.

Lily looked uncomfortable and unsure of her ground.

'You won't forget about the shop?' she asked.

'I'm not going back there, Lily.' He allowed himself the last luxury of saying her name. If she had been thinking of him, she'd never have suggested that he return to The Craft Shop: as ever, he was a low priority on her agenda. 'I've got another job, something that suits me much better.'

'Good for you.' She didn't look particularly pleased, nor did she ask what it was, he noticed. 'Well, despite what you said earlier, I really do hope you'll consider coming to visit us in Scotland.'

Rufus smiled wearily.

'Those are your hopes,' he said. 'I can't help you there.'

After she'd gone, he wandered about the cottage aimlessly, picking things up and putting them down again, drumming his fingers on the furniture and meaninglessly re-arranging the contents of the bookshelf. He lifted and discarded Cate's folder without even registering what it was.

He was feeling a bit light-headed, airy and vacant, but not particularly unhappy. He went upstairs and sat on the bed in the spare room, wondering if he wouldn't make this his room in future. He pushed the bed over to the window, from where he'd be able to see the vegetable garden and the goat's shed when he woke up, and flung open the casement.

He gazed out at the stars. Something was moving across the garden. Rufus knew that even Gordon couldn't work the lock on his pen, so it wasn't him. The shadow came closer and raised its head.

Rufus grinned broadly.

'I thought you'd deserted me,' he said, as the first blood-curdling howl hit the night air. 'Welcome back.'

Chapter 18

The big blue dog bounded ahead as usual, despite Rufus' calls. He wanted to make it stop and approach him like any normal dog, although this was perhaps a trifle ambitious, considering that it was clearly a law unto itself, appearing so rarely, disappearing so easily, with its coat the indigo blue of a star-filled midnight sky.

When he reached the entrance in the brick wall, Rufus stepped straight into a silvery mist that seemed to gather him in and propel him towards the heart of the garden. A flat film of smoky silver lay like a dinner plate over the stone basin: above he could see the upper half of three lithe figures undulating in jubilation round the circle.

This time Rufus was not thinking about himself, nor was he drunk, but only entranced by the spectacle before him. He took a step forward and the image of the dancers retreated, keeping him at bay, an isolated spectator unheeded by the performers. They did not dance for him, he realised this time, as he watched long-fingered hands raised to the fulsome moonlight which glimmered over their mask-like faces, but for the huge silver disc above the garden.

He looked up. The moon seemed to grow larger as it held his gaze, reflected light extending in a new rain of silver, enveloping him from head to foot. A curious sensation of numbing spread through his limbs as it fell on him. The white flower music faded, and he lost sight of the dancers. An opportunity seemed to be slipping away from him and there was something he wanted to ask for, if he could only think...

He turned around in the confusion of coiling mist, and then round and round again, searching for a way out, thrashing his arms in movements like a swimmer in difficulties. A huge shape swerved past him, paws skittering on the paving stones of the path, then stopped not far away. It gave a single deep bark and Rufus stumbled his way blindly towards the sound. They moved like this in turn until he felt the rounded edge of brick beneath his hand and instantly was plunged into the darkness of a normal night, to be greeted across the orchard by the frantic calls of an indignant goat.

It was unfortunate that the next day Rufus was to start his apprenticeship with Neville King. He overslept, waking disorientated and dishevelled in the spare room, and had to rush from the house without a proper wash or breakfast to prepare him for the day. It was not until the relative calm of his short car journey to Bruford that memories of his parting with Lily flooded back.

'You're late,' King said incredulously. 'On your first day.'

'I know,' Rufus said. 'I'm sorry. Something happened last night. I overslept. That's it.'

'Nothing serious, I trust?'

Nothing that's going to keep me from running your wretched shop, you mean, Rufus thought. Shall I tell him about sleeping with Lily or spectral dancers in the moon garden?

'Just something that needed resolving. It's sorted now. Let's get on with business, shall we?'

They worked all day with files, accounts and systems. Rufus was horrified to discover that, although King had a computerised ordering and stock system, he kept none of his other records in this way. Card index boxes stacked under the table held all the day to day business information. Putting that right should while away the lonely hours without customers, he thought resignedly, although an endless, tedious chore was probably just what he needed to get through the next few weeks.

The shop was much busier than Rita's had been and Rufus was quickly absorbed into the routines so familiar to him from the London days. He ate sandwiches in the back at lunchtime to avoid the risk of seeing Lily or Rita around in Bruford and spent quiet, reflective evenings at home in the garden with only Gordon for company. No-one came to visit him and he kept his phone switched off, content to have this reclusive lull after recent traumas.

After they'd been through everything at the shop, there was little point in King hanging around any longer. Despite the difference in their characters and outlook, they were pretty well agreed on how the place should be managed and he seemed to have no real anxiety about leaving Rufus to get on with it.

'I hope your mother will... well, you know.'

King looked embarrassed and shook Rufus' hand without meeting his eyes.

'Yes, yes. Phone on Saturday evening then, or before if there's any problem. I don't want things left to...'

'It's OK,' Rufus said gently, 'I promise not to spare you any disasters.'

He saw the alarm flare in King's eyes.

'That was a joke,' he said. 'Honestly. You have nothing to worry about. Nothing bad is going to happen.'

Joe turned up the same evening, ostensibly to tell Rufus of his progress, but his discomfort and jittery manner suggested that there was more to come. Rufus' heart beat a little faster as he imagined what it might be.

They were sitting together on the garden bench, drinking beer and watching Gordon nibbling the brassicas.

'You can tell me about it, Joe,' he said finally. 'I'm not going to fall apart.'

He was rewarded by the sudden release of tension beside him, as Joe blew out a sharp breath of relief.

'They went this morning.'

Rufus looked at Joe's profile. For all his bleached hair and eyebrow studs, he had the aura of a small lost boy.

'Are you OK with that?' he asked gently.

Rufus saw Joe's adam's apple going up and down like a yo-yo.

'It's a bit weird, the house being empty and that,' Joe managed to get out after a moment.

On impulse, Rufus said 'Do you fancy staying here until you can go into the new place? End of the month, isn't it?'

Joe's face brightened.

'Yeah?' he asked.

'I could do with the company,' Rufus lied, 'and you're a useful sort of bloke to have about the house.'

'Yeah,' said Joe happily.

Let him sleep in that bed, Rufus thought. I don't want to ever again.

The news of Lily's departure had given him an intense pang of loss, but deep inside he was relieved that it was really over, that his feelings were not to be revived by a chance meeting in town or a nocturnal visit when his defences were weak.

Joe was fidgeting nervously again.

'I'm sorry about you and L...'

Rufus put him out of his misery.

'It's OK, Joe. We'll miss her, won't we?'

Joe nodded.

Rufus put his arm round his shoulders and gave him a brief hug.

Then they sat together companionably on the garden bench, both blinking hard.

'What about Tara?' Rufus asked eventually. 'Have you seen her again?'

Joe shook his head.

Rufus thought about it. 'I might give her a ring myself. It would be a shame not to say goodbye.' He stood up. 'Everyone's leaving, Joe. I hope the ship isn't sinking.'

Joe nodded his agreement as he polished off the contents of his bottle.

'I can't swim,' he said.

When he woke the next morning, Rufus knew at once that change was in the air. It had rained in the night, washing away the yellow gritty atmosphere after several weeks of almost unbroken sunshine. The vegetable garden was preening itself, vivid greens restored by the brief downpour, and he could smell the syrupy scent of ripening apples. Despite the clear blue sky and sun rising red over the trees, he could feel the very first taste of autumn in the freshness of the air and the tiny skittish swirls of mist in the field beyond the stream.

Appropriate for a new start, he thought. First day alone in the bookshop, first day without the hope of seeing Lily constantly at the back of my mind, first day of taking Cate's advice and thinking about what I really want. He remembered for a minute that he had not yet looked at the folder she'd left him and felt a twinge of guilt. Tonight he would definitely go through it.

There was a mid-morning lull in the shop after he'd unpacked the deliveries, phoned some customers and greeted a few browsers. It was market day and business in the town was thriving despite the end of the main holiday season. Being in Bruford somehow made him think of Lily again and their happy afternoon in the park by the river. They had been so easy together then: it was incredible to think of what had happened since and he wondered how long it would be before the thought of perhaps never seeing her again stopped hurting like hell.

'Well, well, here you are! So good to see you again, dear boy.'

Dennis Braithwaite's galling bonhomie seemed to fill the shop, despite the puny stature of the man.

'Hello, er, Dennis,' Rufus greeted him reluctantly. 'Looking for a book?'

Dennis faked a moment of alarm at the suggestion.

'Far too busy, far, far too busy for reading, I'm afraid. No, business calls, my young friend, as ever, and here am I! Cometh the man, and all that.'

Rufus had no intention of asking him to elaborate on that and fussed about with papers in a pretence of busyness. He wondered if this old shark had got wind of King's mother's illness and was hoping to put his marker down for selling what must be quite a valuable business.

'It's nothing to do with me,' he said, following his own train of unpleasant thought.

Dennis was puzzled.

'But who else, dear boy? You surely can't be fixed up already?'

Rufus looked at him blankly.

'Mean Cottage?' Dennis went on. 'It is still yours?'

'Of course it is,' Rufus retorted. 'I don't understand what you're getting at.'

Dennis switched into confidential mode, taking Rufus' arm to lead him into the psychology corner.

'I got a buyer for you if you want to sell,' he said in hushed tones.

'What?' Rufus almost shrieked.

'It's exactly what my client is looking for - old stone house, perfectly habitable thanks to your sterling efforts, good size land and, absolutely at the top of the wish list, a stream all around!'

He beamed at Rufus in triumphant complacency, like a magician holding up a rabbit.

'Moo - Mean Cottage is not for sale!' Rufus managed to stutter in dazed response. 'Whatever made you think it was?'

'But it's ideal,' Dennis went on regardless, 'and, best of all, money is NO OBJECT! That's the point, old thing, you can ask whatever you like!'

Rufus took a deep breath.

'In that case, please get out of my shop,' he said firmly, giving Dennis a gentle little push towards the door.

'Now don't be hasty,' Dennis protested, trying to wriggle away. 'At least think it over and let me know. We could discuss it over a meal...'

'Over my dead body,' said Rufus as he propelled him out into the street with a final satisfying shove.

Alone again, he sat for a few minutes as the strength of the revulsion he had felt at Dennis' proposal filtered through him. It wasn't just the man himself, but the mere idea of selling Moon Cottage and losing all that he had found there filled Rufus with horror. He had found his home and nothing was going to separate him from it, least of all an oily little worm like Dennis Braithwaite. He didn't care about the money. He was OK for now and the future would take care of itself.

To take his mind off the unwelcome intrusion, he picked up the phone to call Tara, hoping she'd be up, and planning to cut the line if Rita answered.

He was in luck.

'Hello?'

'Tara, it's Rufus. How're things?'

'Where are you?'

'At work.'

'Yeah, where?'

Her voice sounded tight and strained.

'At the bookshop on the quay, just round the corner...'

The line went dead.

'Hallo? Tara?'

Puzzled, Rufus replaced the receiver and then redialled. The phone began to ring, but he had to put it down almost at once as a couple, obviously retired and at leisure, entered the shop and began to butter him up with questions about local history before beginning to recount their own memories of Bruford thirty years earlier. The wife, permed blonde hair bobbing as she enthused, was just describing how they'd started their married life in a flat over what was now a bookies, when the shop door burst open and Tara, in full purple face paint and a painful-looking selection of black bondage gear, stormed in.

Fortunately Rufus was behind the wide mahogany table with his customers ranged one on each side like defensive knights. She had to content herself with leaning across the paper-littered surface, craning forward to hurl abuse at her bemused audience.

Rufus managed to decipher the words 'trusted', 'shit', 'miserable' and 'you' in various embellished configurations.

'Shall I call the police?'

The man's hand hovered over the phone.

'No,' said Rufus quickly, 'it's OK, she's a friend of mine.'

Three pairs of eyes regarded him with amazement. Then the couple exchanged nervous glances.

'In that case, I think we'd better be going,' the blonde woman murmured, moving behind Rufus to grab her husband's arm and manoeuvre him in as wide a berth as possible around the still snarling Tara.

When they'd gone, there was a second of silence.

Rufus perched on the edge of the desk, well within range.

She opened her mouth to start again, but he was too

quick for her.

'Well done, Tara,' he said unpleasantly. 'Now you've driven my customers away, what's this all about?'

She glared at him, still breathing heavily.

'You were supposed to be coming back to our place, so we can go to Amsterdam,' she said petulantly.

'Who says?'

She was mystified.

'But I said you could come back! I phoned you to say it was OK!'

'OK for who?'

'But you needed a job!'

'All of that's true, Tara. But it's not the point. The Craft Shop was never my idea of work, you know that perfectly well, and your mother's attitude to my achievement there was, frankly, rude and ungrateful. I've no reason whatsoever to help her out of another spot. I'm really sorry about your trip, but you can't expect me to run my life to suit others against my own wishes.'

Tara seemed to have run out of steam. She stood silently, biting her mulberry-lipstick plastered lower lip, avoiding his eyes.

'Is there really no-one else?' he asked reasonably. 'Couldn't she advertise?'

'She's going to see someone this afternoon. I've got to look after the fucking shop.'

He bent his head to force her to look up at him.

'I know you think I've let you down, but I've got my own life to think about. You didn't exactly appreciate me needing you to help out in the shop, did you? But you feel I ought to take over the place again because it suits your plans. Is that fair?'

A reluctant shrug. Rather than concede the point, Tara changed the subject. She looked around the bookshop.

'Are you staying here for good?'

278

'Not sure yet. For a good while, I hope. You must look in and see me when you get back from Amsterdam.'

She looked at him in astonishment.

'You don't hate me now? Causing a scene and that?'

He shook his head and, held out his arms.

'I'm really rather fond of you actually.'

First Joe, then Tara, he thought. Perhaps my true vocation is to be an agony-uncle.

The rest of the week passed quickly. Rufus was pleased with steady sales and his own sense of confidence in dealing with things he knew about. When there was no-one in the shop, he browsed the stock, familiarising himself with the range of second-hand books in the upper gallery and the collectors' items in their locked cabinets. He made a long overdue start on creating a customer database. It was all routine, but satisfyingly so. He looked forward to phoning Neville, as he was trying to think of him, with a positive first report at the weekend.

Whenever thoughts of Lily leapt into his head, he sang snatches of 'Someone who needs me' under his breath like a mantra and mentally began listing the qualities of his ideal partner. Someone who wouldn't run off to Scotland with another man would be a good start...

The shop always closed for half-an-hour for lunch, between one and one thirty. Today he felt like getting out for some fresh air and intended eating his sandwiches - made from some rather dubious sausages he'd found at the back of the fridge - by the river, but well away from the park where painful memories of a happy afternoon might overtake him. He fetched his jacket and came back through the shop to find Rita waiting for him.

Rufus was foolishly scared for a moment when he came face to face with her, thin-lipped and angry as a snake. Tara he felt he'd got the measure of by now, but Rita was a different matter altogether. Despite the warmth outside, the temperature in the shop seemed to have plummeted.

'So this is where you're hiding,' she said with a nasty smile.

'This is where I work,' said Rufus, trying not to shiver openly. He waved his hand around. 'Oh, look, it's a proper bookshop!'

She glared at him balefully.

'You didn't have the guts to come and tell me!'

'Excuse me,' Rufus retorted, determined not to cave in cravenly, 'but you didn't actually have the nerve to ask me to come back yourself. I seem to remember you sending a messenger.'

'And she did everything she could to persuade you, didn't she?' A cruel smile spread over her thin face. 'Lily must be losing her touch.'

Rufus flushed with anger at the thought of Lily recounting what had happened between them to this harpy.

'But then she did say it was the maternal feelings you always brought out in her,' Rita went on. 'I hope you'll be able to cope on your own now she's gone and left you behind.'

Rufus turned away, as casually as he could, to hide the pain in his face. He could not bear to give her the satisfaction of wounding him so easily.

'I expect so,' he said, striving to keep his voice steady. 'I've had the chance to watch Tara coping with abandonment, after all.'

'You leave my daughter alone,' she said in a dangerously low voice. 'The last thing she needs is the advice of selfish bastards - so that rather lets men out!'

Rufus laughed with genuine amusement.

'That's right. First kind, affectionate Joe, who couldn't

280

do enough for her, and then there's me listening to all her troubles, trying to comfort her when she was down - poor Tara really has suffered badly at the hands of men lately.'

She took a step towards him, face twisted with menace, although her voice was still low.

'I know your sort of cleverness, Rufus, and, believe me, it's really no sort of match for mine at all.'

He went for his walk as planned when Rita'd gone, but he was disturbed by the encounter and glad to leave the chilly atmosphere of the shop for a bench near the bridge bathed in warm sunshine. His hands were still shaking as he unwrapped his lunch and began to eat. The sound of water gently trickling over a fall of ancient stone steps below did something to calm him, but hunger and his earlier sense of renewed confidence had both deserted him.

It was ridiculous to feel distressed by what had happened. He had to stop being so sensitive about such things. He owed Rita nothing whatsoever - in fact, her levels of irresponsible behaviour made his drunken purchase of Moon Cottage seem quite a sensible move in comparison. All he'd said to her was fully justified by her hypocrisy, pretending to be so concerned about Tara when it suited her and then just turning her back. He wondered why on earth Charlie had got mixed up with Rita in the first place, but then there was no pattern, no reason to be discerned in Charlie's long list of conquests. He'd given up trying to understand what drove them all into his friend's arms. All physical types, all backgrounds, even all ages of females seemed to fall for him with the least encouragement. But I don't envy that, Rufus thought. I'm not cut out for all that chopping and changing. It doesn't excite me in the least. Cate's right - perhaps it is time I was honest and sorted myself out.

He looked around as he made his way back to the shop, ready to take avoidance measures if there was any sign of Rita, but all he saw were the usual shoppers and market traders. Visitors poured out of pubs and cafes, fortified for an orgy of spending. He anticipated an active afternoon in the shop.

But he was wrong. He opened punctually at half past one and an hour later was sitting in unbroken solitude. Several times potential customers studied the window displays and once even put a hand on the door handle but no-one actually came in. He became restless, striding over to the door to peer out at regular intervals for any possible cause, but if anything the town grew busier as the afternoon wore on, with the advent of numerous parties of visitors to the abbey.

It was a mystery, but similar unaccountable things had happened occasionally in the London shop, so he gave up trying to think of a plausible explanation and sat down to use the time more profitably by beginning the dreary task of data input.

After half an hour of this, Rufus began to feel decidedly queasy. The sausage sandwiches stirred uneasily in his stomach and his fingers stuttered unsteadily over the keyboard. His head was hot and light, although the shop seemed surprisingly cold. His first reaction was that he could not afford to be ill now of all times, laid low by some virus when he had finally begun to settle to a congenial occupation. Deciding that boredom might be contributing to the malaise, he searched for something of greater interest to do and ransacked the local history shelves for anything relating to Creech. He only learned what he already knew, that the village, which was mentioned in the Domesday Book, had for a short time in the thirteenth century been the property of Bruford Abbey and later the scene of an unremarkable but bloody skirmish in the Civil War. Nothing to distinguish it there from a thousand other villages, he thought. No highwaymen, no ghostly apparitions, not the slightest hint of a legendary moon garden...

'Aaah!' Rufus dropped the book he was holding as he was seized with an unbearable shaft of pain in his stomach. He clutched the table for support and, after a few deep breaths, eased himself gingerly into a chair. He rested there for a while, trying to regain his equilibrium but it was no good, he really did feel sick. Cursing himself for his feebleness but longing for home and bed, he closed the shop at quarter to five and drove very slowly back to Moon Cottage. He *had* to be well enough to work normally the next day.

It was better, just being home. All he needed to do was take things easy. He had a cup of tea and two paracetamols and fell asleep in the chair downstairs. He dreamt that he was locked in an ice-box, counting down the minutes to paralysis as his system shut down inch by inch. Something woke him soon after half past nine. His sleep-filled brain could not readily identify the noise but it made him uneasy. Rain spattered on the window and it was nearly dark outside, but he thought he had heard something in the house. He listened carefully, but all was quiet. Perhaps a bird had flown in and out again, as the downstairs window was open, or maybe Joe was in, moving something around upstairs.

Rufus stood up slowly. He could see nothing untoward in the sitting room, but he went to check the kitchen and the bathroom anyway, unsure of the source of his own tension. They were empty and untidy as usual. But with this small degree of physical effort, the waves of nausea were re-surfacing and he decided to go straight upstairs and have an early night. He glanced into his old room, but there was no sign of Joe.

In the spare room, Rufus fell asleep at once, breathing noisily. It felt like many hours later that he was roused by an awareness of people in the room. A group of angry faces surrounded him as he lay helpless, large white sexless blobs, mouthing words he could not understand, grimaces puckering and distending, a ripple of censure spreading from one to the other, round and round in a Mexican wave of menace.

They disappeared suddenly, to be quickly replaced by features and voices that were more familiar, whirling around him with the random speed of a kaleidoscope. There were his mother's strident tones, a splash of crude orange lipstick, a snort of derision, Alison's dark hair brushing over his face, stifling his breath. He pushed and kicked to wriggle free, summoning the benign spirit of Lily's beloved face, only to see it turn on him, unthinkably ugly with rancorous fury. He gave a half sob of horror, as that distortion gave way to Tara's pale image, smiling irately and spitting venom in a purple stream. He was thrashing around on the bed now, sweating with fear, battling the sleep that was tormenting him. He tried to sit up to regain the reality of the room, but the wall seemed to melt and lose substance before his eyes as a final figure appeared before him. Clad in a long robe, Rita approached his bedside and stood over his defenceless form. In her right hand was a large wooden staff carved with arcane symbols. She raised it high and began to chant, the words a string of meaningless babble. He put his hands over his ears as the noise began to hurt his head and then screwed up his eyes in fearful anticipation as the staff fell towards his midriff. His hands countered futilely and when the blow came it was agony. He screamed aloud and then descended into the black emptiness beyond pain.

Chapter 19

Someone was lifting him up and a slow, calm voice spoke close to his ear.

'Drink this, Rufus.'

He opened his eyes. Joe held him in a sitting position, whilst Cate leaned over him with a glass of liquid. He drank obediently, spluttered at the bitterness of the taste, but finished it all.

'Joe heard you and came for me,' Cate said as she put the cap back on one of her brown glass bottles. 'Can you tell me what's wrong?'

Rufus tried to concentrate, to remember the sequence of events.

'I ate something that didn't agree with me,' he said. 'I was in the shop, then I felt ill and came home. It seemed better but when I went to bed I had this terrible dream about - well, various people - and at the end Rita was about to club me with this wooden baton thing...'

'Rita! Have you had anything to do with her recently?' Cate spoke urgently, her face full of worry.

Rufus was alarmed by this uncharacteristic anxiety.

'She came in the shop today, yesterday rather, and we had a row.' The pain in his stomach was returning, but he forced himself upright. 'My God, I have to open the shop...'

Cate pushed him back onto the pillows.

'Sssh. Don't be ridiculous. It's four o'clock in the morning. Just relax.'

'Actually, I have to go to the bathroom now,' Rufus said anxiously.

Joe followed him there protectively and waited outside.

'Sorry, Joe,' he said with some embarrassment when he eventually felt strong enough to emerge after a violent spell of vomiting.

Back upstairs, Cate was brisk and business-like. She questioned Rufus closely about what had happened in the shop, then his symptoms and the nightmare he'd had. Finally she got up and moved to the middle of the small room, closed her eyes, and stood with the stillness of a marble statue, facing the door for a few moments before tracing the outline of its frame in mid-air with her fingers.

'What's she doing?' Rufus spoke in a hushed voice to Joe who was still standing awkwardly by the bed. He shrugged, eyes fixed on Cate.

After several more minutes, she opened her eyes and came over to him.

'Do you think the doctor might come out here in the morning?' Rufus asked. His limbs were aching and he felt as if he'd never get up easily again.

'You don't need a doctor, Rufus. You're not ill.'

'Oh, thanks very much,' he said crossly. 'It feels as if a weasel's eating my insides and you say I'm not ill. I'll just get up and do a few laps of the local swimming pool, shall I?'

'Hush, hush,' she said impatiently, without a hint of amusement. 'You must stay here in bed, in this room. Joe will be nearby. I've got work to do. If the pain's too bad, you can take more of this, but try to put up with it.'

Rufus recoiled at the sight of the brown bottle and pulled the sheet around himself defensively.

'Wait a minute - what's all this medicine and meditating or whatever, if I'm not ill? Why are you going to all this trouble for an idle malingerer?'

He was rewarded at last with a quick smile as she paused at the door.

'You're not ill, Rufus,' Cate said firmly. 'You've been cursed.'

The air beneath the willow tree in Cate's garden was laden with the scent of frankincense. She was angry with herself for not taking better care of Rufus and miscalculating the real source of trouble for him, but she breathed deeply and steadily to maintain the balance of her energies. Nothing would be gained by acting in haste or without due thought for the consequences. She watched the black candle flame for a time, silently invoking the aid she needed, and then took up a cord which lay on the stone before her. Slowly she tied a knot in its length, intoning softly: 'May what you do rebound on you'. And then another knot: 'Bound with this twine, you'll harm not mine,' she said. The third knot was the last. 'But if your harm shall cease, may your good increase.'

Cate wound the twine into a tight ball and closed her hand over it as she sent a silent blessing on the object of her spell, that malice should be replaced by kindness.

Somewhere deep in the vortex of his psyche, Rufus caught the end of a thread and was trying to follow it. Hand over hand he went along the woven strands, moving uphill, his footsteps hesitant over a slippery surface he couldn't see. All the time he feared the tenuous filament would break and he would crash back down into the unknown, but he laboured on, inching forward through the gloom, keeping his eyes fixed on the dimly apparent summit ahead. When he reached the top, there was nothing there and the thread hung limply from his hands. He peered over the brow of the hill, and found himself on the edge of a low cliff, looking down on green water lapping placidly below. Further out, beyond the white tipped swell, he saw a boat, a wooden fishing skiff painted carmine red. Fixed to the mast in the middle was a large white flower, unfurling like a flag in the breeze. Two women in loose blue shifts were casting lines over the side, whilst a third lay back in the stern, trailing a net behind the little craft. As Rufus watched their slow, rounded movements, the deepest peace descended on his own limbs, spreading warmth and ease throughout his body. He felt his mind empty of anxiety and his heart unfolding, layer by layer of protection peeling away to reveal a naked core. His eyes became fixed on the flower, which seemed to grow and grow, blotting out the women, the boat and then the whole scene, dazzling him with its whiteness, a huge disc of light filling him to the brim.

Cate was there in the bedroom again when he woke in the morning. Rufus noticed how tired and old she looked, as if exhausted by some ordeal.

'How are you feeling?' she asked him.

He levered himself up slowly.

'Better, I think.' He rubbed his sore stomach muscles. 'I knew I shouldn't have eaten those sausages.'

She shook her head pityingly and produced another bottle of medicine for him to take.

'You shouldn't underestimate Rita,' she said. 'She'd be a formidable witch if she could focus her powers for long enough.'

Rufus suddenly felt a rush of fondness for this staunch old woman and took hold of her hand affectionately.

'We're never going to agree about this, are we?'

'So it was just the sausages?' she said. 'Nothing else? Nothing odd about the shop or the house when you came home?'

Rufus shifted uneasily, releasing her hand. He did not want to argue with her, especially after the sort of night he'd had.

'No,' he said decisively, and then stopped short.

Cate looked knowingly.

'Except?' she asked.

'Except that no-one came in the shop all afternoon, although there were plenty of people about. And it felt cold. Then there was something odd in the atmosphere here when I got home.' He looked at her in amazement. 'Is it really possible?'

'Stop fighting it, Rufus,' she said, kindly in victory. 'I'm tired of telling you. The power is there if you can harness it, for good or ill.'

'But,' he protested, 'if Rita went round cursing everyone she didn't like, the population of Bruford would be decimated.'

Cate shook her head.

'She's not stupid. What you do to others will rebound on you eventually. She obviously feels you were worth the risk.'

'She only lost it because I sided with her daughter against her, although just being a man is probably enough to qualify for extermination.'

'It's not funny, Rufus. None of this is a joke.'

'No.' He thought about Rita for a while. 'It's amazing that someone like Neville King should fall for her... Shit! The shop should have opened hours ago!' He began to scramble out of bed, but Cate restrained him.

'You're going nowhere,' she said. 'A few days rest is essential for your spirit to recover.'

'There's not much point my spirit recovering if I lose that job in the shop and can't keep body and soul together,' he said crabbily.

'Leave it to me,' Cate said. 'I'll deal with it.'

'What are you going to do?' he asked anxiously. Neville King was not the sort to appreciate any unknown influence at work in his beloved shop and he'd certainly blame Rufus whatever happened.

He said as much to Cate, but she brushed aside all his objections.

'Nonsense. He's a very *reasonable* man, more's the pity. His mother, on the other hand, is one of us.'

Rufus laughed at her analysis. 'I didn't realise you knew them.' He felt Cate would never fail to surprise him.

'Sixty eight years ago, Rose Matthews and I started school together. I've not seen so much of her since they moved away, but the bonds are there.' Cate stared reflectively out of the window and then back at Rufus. 'And now she's dying.'

'You sound very matter of fact about it.'

Cate shrugged.

'It's perfectly natural. When your time has come, you die. There'll be plenty of other lives to come. And you should try to make the most of this one,' she said as she stood up. 'Now, do you still want me to fetch you that doctor?'

Rufus thought it over. His body felt as weak as wet paper, the usual aftermath of a virus, but the savage stomach pains seemed to have subsided with the night.

'No. I think I'll put my faith in you,' he said.

She returned with soup for his lunch and verbose messages of sympathy plus a promise to visit later from Jacinta, recited by Cate with ironic exactitude.

Rufus laughed and told her of Jacinta's decision to join the mass exodus from Creech and Bruford.

Cate shrugged.

'This is a place of transition,' she said. 'The earth energies are strong and active. It takes a special person to make a permanent home here.'

'I'm sure it's wrong for Jacinta,' Rufus replied. 'She's never been happy in that shop. I just hope she's doing the right thing, going back to London.'

Cate wrinkled her nose.

'That one's always pretending to be something she's not. It's put her under a great strain here - the spirit will only stand that sort of thing for so long.'

He nodded.

'She's brave to try to make an old situation work for her in a new way. I wish her luck, especially as I misjudged her so badly when we first met.' He grinned. 'And you too, I suppose.'

She pretended a casual unconcern about this.

'Whereas I daresay you were right about me,' he went on, 'from that very first moment on the bridge!'

Her eyes gleamed.

'On the contrary, I had no idea what hard work you were going to turn out to be.'

They continued this vein of banter until she stood up to go. Then she regarded him silently for a moment, her face serious.

'I don't think you've anything more to worry about from Rita.'

'Great! It's just all the rest of my life to sort out then,' Rufus replied.

'It doesn't have to be such a struggle, you know,' Cate said dryly.

'Don't tell me you're going to grant me three magic wishes to transform my life!'

'Very good, Rufus, you're improving. That's *exactly* what I'm suggesting, although it's not me who'll see them through for you. And it's usual to make one for the world, one for someone close and only one for yourself.'

'We're talking about the moon garden again, aren't we?'

'That's why you're here,' she said simply. 'I've felt it for a long time now. Can you deny that something draws you to it?'

He felt that an admission of some significance was being drawn from him, but resistance to Cate was a battle long lost.

'No.'

'Then use it. Take the power while it's there. You may be the last.'

In his enfeebled state, he could hardly remember the invigoration he'd felt when the garden sprang to life.

'What would I do?'

She shrugged.

'Be clear and simple. There's no mysterious ritual you have to adhere to. Ask, ask truly for what you want in your heart. If it's right, you *will* shape your future.'

'If it's *right*?'

She shook her head vigorously.

'I don't mean some grim moral judgement from on high. There is a principle of harmony in the universe, however unlikely that seems sometimes. If you attune with the energies around you and respect their powers, you will work magic for yourself and transform your life. But it's up to you.'

'But how...?'

Cate gave him a parting smile of complicity.

'Start by making a list,' she said.

'Wait,' he called. 'One thing I want to ask you. What about the blue dog? How does he fit in to the story?'

She gave him one of her old looks of incomprehension.

'You'd better take some more of that,' she said, nodding at the brown bottle. 'It should settle the hallucinations.'

'But...'

Cate continued on her way downstairs.

Joe came up looking puzzled shortly after she'd gone, with a notepad and pencil, and the green folder Rufus had forgotten all about.

'Cate said you needed to make a list or something,' he said.

Rufus fell back on the pillows with a laugh that made him clutch at his sore ribs.

He lay in bed all afternoon, thinking and dozing peacefully. It was dull outside but the house felt warm and comforting around him again. Every time he opened his eyes he saw the green folder on his bedside table. Finally curiosity got the better of him and he hauled himself upright to examine the contents. He read right through Adam's notes, from vague fragmented memories of local stories to the evidence of Liddell's attempt to destroy the moon grove, recorded with matter-of-fact amusement by a contemporary in a letter of news to his wife in London. At the bottom there was a torn half-sheet of the thick rough paper which was blank. Rufus was about to put it back in the folder with the others when he caught sight of impressions of letters on the surface as the light caught it from behind. He held it up carefully towards the window and managed with difficulty to make out a single sentence of Adam's distinctive hand-writing. 'Research and personal experience have taught me that this is truly a place of love.'

The remark was strikingly intimate after the careful objectivity of the recorded research and Rufus suspected that the paper on which the original words were written had been destroyed on Adam's second thoughts. Something told him it was not to spiritual love that the words referred.

Was that really why *I've* been drawn to this strange place of history and legend, he wondered? Is my need for love so strong even after all my failures? I feel I've found my resting place here, but is there more to come?

He picked up the notepad and wrote confidently at the top of a clean page: Moon Cottage is where I want to live. It was true; he felt a strong sense of rightness here. It had been a supreme folly initially, then gradually a place of quiet refuge. Now it was the base on which he would build a new and satisfying life. Grow vegetables, he continued. Restore the moon garden. That should take care of his leisure, even before he started spending quality time with Gordon. He would collect information and draw up plans in the long winter evenings ahead. The garden would emerge as if from its long chrysalis state in the spring.

He was happy with that picture. Hard physical work that was productive was just what he needed and the research needed as a basis was his natural metier.

Thinking of that took the list on to his professional occupation. He would be content at the bookshop if it was his own, but that was an imponderable for the moment (and he had yet to explain this current blip satisfactorily to Neville King). Another idea that had been simmering away for years was a possibility to be investigated. There were no small independent publishers in the area and it was something he had always thought of doing. The details - minor points like raising capital, he thought frivolously - didn't matter now as long as he had a plan to work on and an idea to fire his imagination.

What else did he want? A friend of the female persuasion, a companion, lover, wife? All of that, but this time he was determined to get it right. He made another hopeful heading: The Ideal Woman. He was still scribbling when his mobile rang downstairs and Joe came running up with it.

To Rufus' horrified surprise, it was Neville King.

'Sorry to hear you've been ill. Rotten luck, that. Just thought I'd ring to see how you were. No need to worry about the shop. I can pop in tomorrow if you still feeling dickey.'

Cate really was a marvel, Rufus thought. It must be she who'd turned King into a carey-sharey sort of chap, almost unrecognisable from his former self.

Rufus gave assurances that he'd be fit enough to go back after the weekend. It was true that all this writing was starting to make him feel a positive glow of health and well-being, although Cate had insisted he stayed in bed another day.

On impulse he asked King if he thought a small independent publisher could stand a chance of survival in Bruford and was surprised to hear an almost eager endorsement of the idea. It was clear even from that brief exchange that King himself might, in other circumstances, be interested in such a project. Perhaps a partnership would make it viable.

Rufus put down the phone, amazed at King, at himself and at the whole prospect his future was taking on.

'It's only me!'

Jacinta came quickly up the stairs the next afternoon, almost hidden behind an enormous bunch of flowers and a huge basket of fruit. 'Thought these might cheer you up!'

Rufus smiled at her jolly bedside manner and the typically excessive gesture of the gifts.

'You shouldn't have bothered, really, but thanks. It's good to see you.'

'I've closed up a bit early. Thought you'd be bored stiff here on your own all day.'

'Yes,' he lied, and then thought better of it. 'Actually, no. I've been quite busy. I decided to make a list of the qualities of my ideal woman.'

Jacinta flushed scarlet.

'How very... interesting.'

'Well, I don't want to make any more mistakes.'

Her face took on a sympathetic expression as she sat down on the edge of the bed.

'I heard Lily had moved,' she said. 'I'm sorry.'

He waved a hand airily.

'Don't be. It's over - painful, but finished. I'm concentrating on the future now.'

'You are brave, Rufus!'

'That's something I've forgotten to put on my list of essentials - flattery!'

Her silver and black curls bounced up and down as she shook her head insistently.

'But I *do* admire you!' she exclaimed. 'You seem to know what you're doing, whereas I just flounder around and achieve nothing.'

'Nonsense! In the past I've been the biggest flounderer since flatfish first floundered, but things are changing now. I do feel more in control.'

'I wish you'd tell me your secret,' she said wistfully.

'Do you believe in magic?' he asked, eyes playful to conceal a serious question.

'What like conjurers and fortune-tellers? No, of course not.'

'What about something more mundane like being in the right place at the right time?'

'Serendipity? But that's just chance, surely?'

'I'm beginning to wonder,' he said lightly, as he saw that Jacinta looked bewildered and uncomfortable with this subject. 'Now, do you want to hear my list?'

She sat up straight and clasped her hands.

'Oh, yes please!'

'Here we go.' Rufus cleared his throat dramatically. 'My ideal partner must be affectionate, bounteous, compassionate, delightful, edifying, faithful, gentle, humane, imperfect, joyful, kind, lenient, mild, nice, optimistic, perceptive, quiet, receptive, sympathetic, tender-hearted, understanding, vulnerable, warm, and... that's as far as I've got.'

'But it's brilliant, Rufus. You must finish it!'

'Short of desiring a xylophone-playing, yellow zebra, I'm a bit stuck.'

Jacinta was completely nonplussed for a moment, before the light slowly dawned.

'Oh... I do see now. How stupid of me! Alphabetical! How clever! I wasn't thinking, she sounds so wonderful...'

'Doesn't she just,' said Rufus longingly.

Jacinta wrinkled her brow in thought for a moment.

'What about zealous?' she suggested eagerly.

He shook his head firmly.

'No,' he said. 'Nothing so potentially overwhelming. And before you suggest 'zany', I've already rejected it, for similar reasons.'

She laughed.

'Point taken. But you do really want to find another partner then? Your experience hasn't put you off?'

Rufus sighed.

'As long as I avoid making the same mistake and just settling for something because it's there. Whilst I'm lying here, I should be writing out a hundred times - I must be more demanding, I must be more demanding... And so must you, while we're on the subject of marriage.'

He looked at her big, heavy face, conditioned to over-expression and yet so true to her feelings with the constant welling and fading of colour.

He put a hand over hers.

'I really do hope everything works out well for you, you know.'

Tears filled her eyes at this unaccustomed sympathy.

She nodded dumbly and then got up, fussingly straightening her skirt and jacket.

'I'd better be going,' she said, without looking at him. 'Dennis is coming round for a drink.'

'Don't tell him I'm ill, will you, for goodness' sake,' Rufus said in alarm. 'Don't even mention my name if you can help it.'

She smiled and raised her eyes.

'I'll pretend I haven't even seen you, if he asks,' she said eagerly. 'My lips are sealed on the subject.'

Rufus hoped she wouldn't overdo it and create such a mystery that Dennis hot-footed it to Moon Cottage as fast as his Mercedes could carry him.

'Thanks.'

She seemed to hesitate about going and was blushing furiously again.

'Rufus, I hope we can keep in touch when I go back to London, I mean...'

'Of course we can,' he responded quickly. 'One thing I'm certain about is that I'm not going anywhere. You'll always know where to find me, if you need a friend.'

She bent forward to give him a clumsy kiss that glanced off the side of his head, and clumped off without another word.

Rufus lay back wearily and closed his eyes. He thought he heard muffled voices below as Jacinta left and, by the sound of it, this latest visitor was male.

'Please, please don't let it be Dennis,' he repeated under his breath over and over again, but silence was restored downstairs and he wondered if he'd imagined that there was someone else in the house. Settling down into a comfortable position in the mass of pillows, he let his mind go back to the list still clutched in his hand and began to consider the physical appearance of this ideal partner.

He had just decided that he'd had enough of tall, slim women lately, when a noise disturbed him. Was that someone in the kitchen? Yes, definitely a chink of glass and cupboard doors opening and shutting. Joe must be back early from college. He began to drift off again. Didn't he really prefer brown eyes...

'Ideal woman, eh?' a well-known voice said, as the paper was snatched from Rufus' hand. 'I hope that wasn't her I met downstairs.'

Charlie was holding a plate of sandwiches and a bottle of scotch. Two glasses stuck out of the pockets of his leather jacket.

'Jacinta's a friend,' Rufus said defensively. 'She brought me a lot of fruit.'

'So I see,' said Charlie, knocking a pineapple to the floor as he set the glasses on the bedside table and poured out two large shots. 'This is what you need - purely medicinal purposes and all that.'

'I don't think I will.' Rufus refused to take the glass. 'I've been quite ill, actually.'

'Just a touch of food poisoning, according to the old boot.'

Rufus ignored this slur on Jacinta.

'Either that or Rita's revenge,' he muttered. He felt some of his new-found confidence ebb away at the contrast between his own state and Charlie's rude good health, coupled with that raffish air that was so irresistible to women. I'd better change compassionate to Charlie-proof on my list, he thought; it'll be a much more valuable quality in the short term.

'Christ, you're not still harping on that cursing crap, Rufus. Let's face it - what old shit could she throw at you that you haven't tried for yourself already?'

'Thanks, *mate*,' Rufus said sulkily.

'No worries, cobber. Sandwich?'

Rufus shook his head.

'What are you doing here anyway?'

'Just passing.' Charlie carried on munching and swigging his scotch nonchalantly. A little too nonchalantly for Rufus' liking. He didn't need to believe in magic to know there was no such thing as coincidence where Charlie was concerned.

'Who is she and what's the problem this time?' he asked.

Charlie grinned.

'Haven't a clue what you're on about. Now, let's see what lurid fantasies have been filling your feverish brain, shall we?'

He read through the list, grimacing at every word as if someone had spiked his drink with cat piss.

'Rather you than me, mate,' he said. 'She doesn't sound a barrel of laughs.'

'Great,' said Rufus. 'I've finally got something right then.'

'No, I'm not kidding. You need to lighten up, get out and have a bit of fun, meet some totally disreputable women while you've still got the energy.'

Rufus laughed.

'We're thirty-six, Charlie. I've got a bit of time left and I'd like to spend it with the same person, not an endless procession of changing names and faces. Don't you ever get tired of it?'

Charlie shook his head.

'Give me the thrill of the chase every time, as long as I'm still standing.'

Rufus tapped his list. 'My perfect partner must exist somewhere.'

'Well, with a bit of luck,' Charlie said, 'someone'll put a curse on her and she'll get you as a punishment. And

300

while you're sitting around waiting for Miss Right to drop out of the sky, there's something you could help me out with.'

'No,' said Rufus.

Charlie ignored him.

'I bumped into Louise at the Ravens bar a couple of weeks back. You remember her?'

Rufus' heart sank. It was a good while since Louise had been on the scene. The first time Charlie introduced her, he had a black eye courtesy of her ex-husband. The second time they all met up, Louise herself was sporting a shiner and a broken wrist from the same source. He knew he wasn't going to like what was coming, even though all that must be five or six years ago now.

'How is she?' he asked coolly.

'Fine. Still looking good, though she must be the wrong side of thirty now.'

Charlie was on the second glass of whisky.

'All her limbs intact this time then?' Rufus asked distastefully.

'Funny you should remember that. She's having a bit of trouble with that mad git of a husband at the moment. She needs a place to hide out for a bit.'

Rufus began a sympathetic nod for the split second it took him to register the significance of this. Then he gave a shout of horror.

'No! Forget it!'

Charlie threw up his hands and shoulders in a great shrug.

'Come on, man. It's no big deal, just a couple of nights. He won't have a clue where she is, you'll have a good-looking nurse for a few days - everyone's happy.'

'ABSOLUTELY BLOODY WELL NOT!'

Rufus was struggling to get up out of bed.

Charlie leapt back out of his way in mock fear.

'You're not going to hit me, are you?' he said, grinning as Rufus swayed for a moment on his bare feet.

Regaining his balance, he stepped right up to Charlie and thrust his face forward so they were eye-ball to eye-ball.

'I just want to be on the same level as you to say this,' Rufus began, 'because I *am* on the same level as you. My feelings and ideas and ambitions and relationships are just as important as yours, though you don't seem to respect them and you enjoy mocking my attempts to sort my life out, but involving me in your sordid little schemes with women without any regard for my interests has got to stop. I'm really happy here and just about ready to start living at last, so please, if you have any concern for me at all, please let me get on with it without any of your habitual complications.'

Charlie's eyes sparkled with amusement.

'Is that a no, then?'

Rufus laughed weakly and relaxed his offensive stance.

'No,' he said adamantly. 'Louise cannot come here, at any time, under any circumstances. I'm sorry, but that's it.'

'Fair enough,' Charlie replied, 'I hear where you're coming from. Just answer me one question though.'

Rufus was surprised by his serious tone.

'What is it?'

'You do still love me, don't you?' said Charlie and puckered his lips for a kiss.

Chapter 20

Thanks to Cate's medicines and Joe's faithful ministrations, Rufus felt steadily stronger, although he allowed himself to enjoy the complete rest while he could. There were no more strange dreams and he lay comfortably in his small warm world, allowing thoughts to come and go gently, without anxiety for the past or future. When he was well enough to get up, his first action was to wander out into the garden to Gordon's great delight. Just stroking the smooth dark muzzle raised Rufus' own spirits as he revelled again in the sense of connection he felt in this place after such an inauspicious start what now seemed light years ago.

He settled down in his favourite spot on the old bench and thought of all that happened since and the chain of events that had brought him to this moment here and now. He was beginning to feel the strength of the present in a new way. The past was well and truly finished for him: he felt no lingering pangs for Alison or city life, and old resentments against his parents' indifference had gradually disintegrated in the face of all he saw and felt around him since he woke up to the world.

What was to come would unfurl naturally without the hindrance of his old vague fear of the unknown. He'd wait and see what the future brought, and deal with whatever it was when it happened. He had proved himself in his own eyes over the last few months - the cottage, work, Alison, Lily. Things that would have reduced and distressed him beyond measure before, now seemed manageable. The pain he had felt over Lily was less sharp, more bearable. He allowed himself to feel the full sensation of being used and let down, acknowledging the emotions, letting them run their course inside him. Lily's desertion could destroy him or not - it was up to him and he had chosen to accept it and move on. He was in control of himself, and the sense of strength and power over his own destiny made him hot with happiness, as he sat in his true home with all his life before him to be enjoyed.

After some lunch, he decided to stroll along the lane to see Cate. It was a cool, clear, almost autumny day, the bones of the trees in stark relief against the blue sky. Leaves littered the tarmac under his feet and he could smell the distinctive musty scent of fungi among the roots in the banks around him. He breathed deeply to take in the crisp air that circulated round his lungs like a steam cleaner, and bent to pick a mushroom from the moss at the foot of an oak, whose leaves were brittle and already browning after the long dry summer.

It was then that he heard a sudden noise and swung round to see three familiar dogs scrambling in noisy confusion down the bank about twenty yards behind him, panting with their exertions, flicking great streams of saliva into the air. Rufus stopped dead, horrified by this abrupt encounter. They were eying him now, ears up, measuring the distance for an assault, blocking his way back to the relative safety of his garden. He looked round wildly for some means of escape, and when none offered, his thoughts veered towards defence. A stout stick might be enough to fend them off, but only spindly, brittle oak twigs lay around him.

As the dogs, in a tight phalanx, started slowly towards him, he felt himself trembling. What shall I do, he thought, what on earth shall I do?

His mind went blank for a second and then a simple thought clicked into his head. He would just carry on and not bother about the dogs. He almost laughed at the sheer simplicity of the decision.

They were still coming towards him. He could see their rows of sharp white teeth gleaming against the bright red gums.

'Get lost,' he shouted sternly, taking a step towards them.

The two black dogs stopped uncertainly, whilst the other, his old assailant, continued to advance inch by inch.

'You don't frighten me,' Rufus said to this one, gazing directly into its eyes. 'Any nonsense from you and I'll pull your master's wig off and dance on it in the high street.' He moved a foot nearer, still holding his stare level.

The dog paused, irresolute, and then abruptly turned its head away as if something in the bank had attracted its attention.

Rufus smiled with satisfaction, turned his back on all three of them and continued on his way. When he looked round at the next corner, they were following him at a distance, cautiously keeping track of his progress. He gave a sudden violent yell, stamping his feet and semaphoring his arms in a rough and ready haka. All three dogs turned tail together like synchronised swimmers and hared back up the lane, black and chestnut rumps swinging from side to side.

Rufus felt a tingle of exhilaration run triumphantly through his whole body. He had to restrain himself from skipping as he went on down the lane.

'I want to thank you,' he said to Cate, almost as soon as he entered the cottage, where he found her cleaning out the ancient range. 'I want to thank you for everything you've done for me.'

'You're a lot better,' was all she said.

'I feel fantastic,' Rufus said, spreading his arms as wide as he could in the small space.

She looked at him over the top of her reading glasses.

'Don't get too carried away,' she said. 'You've a way to go yet. A hex can carry a long tail - or are we still sticking to the sausage theory?'

'No,' he said decisively. 'No more denial. I may not understand or appreciate fully what the hell it's all about, but I accept. There are forces at work in the world unacknowledged by science and rational thought and, for all I know to the contrary, they really may be what life is supposed to be all about.'

'Good,' she said, and turned back to her work.

'Is that it?' he said.

Cate faced him again.

'What more is there? Accepting is the first step. Everything else will follow.'

'But where will it come from? I don't know who or what I'm dealing with - in the moon garden, for instance.'

She got up and put her hand on his shoulder.

'My dear Rufus,' she said, 'those are matters to be experienced, not told.'

He gave a grimace of frustration.

'OK, but will you tell me one thing I really don't understand? If Liddell constructed his garden to obliterate the moon grove, why did he make the entrance that shape, as if he was acknowledging the moon's place there?'

'He didn't. After Adam found out about the garden and its history, he redesigned the rectangular opening and made what he called the moon gate. It took him a year to learn the skills, but it was his own act of homage.'

'He didn't feel inclined to knock the whole thing down and leave it grow wild again?'

Cate thought of the care and affection Adam had lavished on the garden and shook her head.

'It would have been needlessly destructive to living

306

things. The point is that no man could change the nature of that place. Liddell tried extravagantly hard and failed, as you know only too well.'

Rufus thought of the high brick walls, designed to keep the local courting couples out of a spot that 'discovered or denied true love.' He tried to imagine Adam at the cottage, tending his vegetables and nurturing the moon garden, wondering again about the relationship Cate had had with this unusual man.

'Did he, did Adam, ever see the dancers, like I have, I mean?' he asked tentatively.

A shadow of sadness passed swiftly over Cate's face.

'I'm afraid not,' she said.

Rufus felt with sudden conviction that this was wrong, although Cate was not lying. Whatever his experience in the moon garden, Adam had chosen not to share it with Cate.

'What about you, Cate?' he probed. 'You seem to know such a lot about it.'

She shook her head.

'Neither Adam nor I chose that kind of love in this lifetime. In that sense we had no need of the moon garden, although we could not help but be aware of its latent powers.'

Rufus thought to himself that he knew better than this. Adam did find true love there, but kept it to himself for all those years to leave Cate free to follow the path she was born to. He felt a sudden strong connection with the man who had lived in Moon Cottage all those years, whose secret he had discovered and would keep.

'But how did you know about what happened to me in there?' he asked.

She sighed and rested her hand gently on his arm.

'Much of what I know and see would seem inexplicable to you, Rufus. My way is a very different one from yours, though I can't deny there's a strange affinity between us. Generally I have my inspiration from the air, or to use a modern term, I'm hypersensitive to any kind of changes in the atmosphere - on that occasion, a surge of energy chaotically released. But it is *your* connection, your unique connection, with the place that's important and that will determine the nature of your participation in a very great adventure.'

Her grey eyes held his for a long time, a time in which he felt a mental mist evaporating inside him and everything clicking into place. For one tiny moment, he had the sense that all his consciousness was shorn away and he was not thinking or feeling or anything at all, but only being.

The thread was broken when she took her hand away.

They still looked at each other.

'Yes?' Cate said.

'I'm beginning to get the idea,' Rufus replied.

After he'd gone, Cate sat for a long while in a chair by the stove, smoking and thinking, gazing into the flames with unfocused eyes. Her head swayed gently from side to side, echoing the ebb and flow of decades of memories and unspoken hopes. Then, finally, she began to recite softly:

> Dance, daughters of Selene
> Weave your silver ring
> To mortals in moon's orbit
> Sweet joy bring

> Dance, daughter of Selene
> With movement fierce and free
> To mortals in your power
> Fair protector be

Dance, daughter of Selene
Fertile in embrace
May mortals in your power
Learn the beauty of your face

Dance, daughter of Selene
Spin your visions clear
All mortals in your power
Guide away from fear

Dance, daughters of Selene
Weave your silver ring
To mortals in moon's orbit
Sweet joy bring

When she'd finished, there were tears on Cate's lined cheeks, but the smile of a young girl illuminated her face like a candle flame. Sweet joy to you, Rufus, she thought, sweet joy to you.

A week later, after a pleasant day in the bookshop and a good supper, Rufus was contentedly enjoying the evening sky, leaning on the frame of the open back door of Moon Cottage. Clouds scudded across the silver-streaked expanse making the stars wink and fade like beams from a light-house. He was in a state of suppressed excitement, gearing himself up to seek out the power of transformation.

He tried whistling and calling softly for the moon dog to come, but he felt self-conscious after a while and all too aware of responsively wild grunts from Gordon's shed. Anyway, Joe wasn't in yet and Rufus didn't want any complications. It would be better to wait until Joe was in bed asleep.

The sound of his motorbike droned down the lane at

that moment.

Rufus affected a nonchalant stroll round the side of the house to greet him.

'Hi, Joe,' he called far too brightly as the black-clad figure came down the path.

'Are you OK?' Joe's quiff emerged from his helmet. He looked worried to see Rufus still up and about and alarmingly cheerful.

'Absolutely fine. Just taking the night air.' Rufus ostentatiously sniffed at the nearest foliage. 'How about you?'

'I wanted to say goodbye to Tara,' Joe said sadly, 'but there's no sign of anyone there. Just a notice on the shop door saying it's closed until further notice.'

Rufus patted him on the back sympathetically, as he led the way back into the house.

'She'll be back eventually, Joe.'

They stood talking in the kitchen while Joe drank what seemed like nearly a pint of milk straight from the carton. They were just about to say goodnight, when a howl came echoing from the garden.

'What was that?' said Rufus nervously, knowing full well that a great blue hound was sitting on the potatoes, but not much wanting to share this knowledge with Joe.

'What?' said Joe.

'That strange noise.'

Another howl from outside.

Joe looked warily at the peculiar false smile wrapped round Rufus' face.

'I didn't hear anything,' he said. 'Are you sure you're OK?'

'Quite sure,' Rufus said, feelingly inexplicably elated at the realisation that as Cate denied all knowledge of the blue dog and now Joe couldn't hear the unholy yodelling in the vegetable patch, then it really was a manifestation

310

just for him. The alternative, of course, was that he'd gone mad. 'Think I need a bit of fresh air after being inside all day.'

It was not in Joe's nature to question anyone else's agenda.

'Right, I'm off to bed.' He turned on the stairs. 'I'm here if you need me.'

Rufus wanted to cry. 'Thanks, Joe,' he said instead.

This time Rufus had a plan. He followed the dog nearly to the entrance of the moon garden and then stopped and waited. He wanted to lure the animal to him, close enough to touch it, to feel that it was real flesh underneath that strange coloured coat. Sure enough, it came bounding back through the opening seeking him out. Rufus crouched uncomfortably in the brambles, listening to the enormous paws trampling the grass and leaves in frenzied search.

Then it was on him, a sudden flash of blue, round and round his legs like a playful dolphin, spinning him up onto his feet and dancing him over the threshold of the garden. Rufus put out a hand as they whirled along, but the dog was too quick for him, skipping away and vanishing into the undergrowth, leaving him in sudden silence under an inky sky.

Disappointed, he made his way slowly forward, feeling more confident as the stone paths appeared under his feet and he began to make out familiar shapes. A small thrill of anticipation ran through him as he reached the heart of the garden and looked up for the moon to answer his silent call. Through a lace of cloud he could see the outline, slowly sharpening, preparing to burst out of its wispy chains. His heart beat faster and faster as he waited for the moment of release, eyes focused directly on the brightening disc. Then, for one split second before the blinding shaft shot out, he saw the outline of a face he would never forget, one split second that lasered every detail into his brain and tore away his doubts.

The garden lit up around him and moon music wafted through the flowers. Rufus felt for the first time entirely in tune with his surroundings and himself. He forgot about the prepared list he carried in his pocket.

Undaunted by the pyrotechnic display of silver rays in every corner of the garden around him and the face of the moon seemingly yards above his own, he felt his whole body driven with the force of intent, as he began to exclaim his three wishes to the sky.

'LET THERE BE COMFORT FOR THOSE UNJUSTLY TREATED THROUGHOUT THE WORLD.'

He said it again, relishing the round, rich echo of his voice within the brick walls.

'LET ALL JOE'S DREAMS COME TRUE. MAY HE WORK AT WHAT HE LOVES AND FIND FULFILMENT IN HIS SKILLS.'

It was a wonderful release, to shout and gesture to the boundless audience of the night sky. He felt the applause of the plants, urging him on to the heights of his own wish. It all came down to one simple desire.

'LET ME FIND MY TRUE PARTNER TO SHARE LOVE.'

Then, determined to be perfectly honest in his petition, as an afterthought he yelled, 'SOMEONE TO PUT ME FIRST'.

Chapter 21

Rufus woke the next morning in a state of vibrant happiness and went off to the shop feeling euphoric, sure that he had only to repeat his mantras of positive thought, focus his intentions and wait for his ideal mate to appear. It was a job to concentrate on routine tasks and everyday conversation with customers, so great was his state of suppressed excitement.

In the afternoon, he was distracted from some mundane calculations by the noise of cymbals and drums approaching along the cobbled riverside road. Immediately alert, he wondered for one mad moment if it was possible that his perfect woman was being brought to him ceremonially as some wonderful divine gift.

The first thing he saw clearly as he came out into a blaze of noise and colour seemed to confirm this crazy notion. A splendidly statuesque female clad in breastplate, helmet and greaves marched staunchly towards him, leading by the hand a lithe, sensuous figure in diaphanous purple harem pants and little else. Transfixed as much by the silver double-crescent moon headdress nodding above this beauty's sleek black hair as by her more obvious charms, Rufus hesitantly took a pace forward onto the cobbles and awaited their approach in a state of some agitation. This was only increased when he saw to his horror that there were dozens of other women, all in extravagant costumes, following along behind this pair: women of all ages, shapes and sizes, as if he was expected to choose his prize from this huge cast like some ghastly judgement of Paris.

Rufus felt a trickle of sweat run down his back. This was not at all what he'd been anticipating and he wasn't sure he liked it very much, especially as he noticed with some alarm that quite a crowd was gathering to watch what was happening. It was all too brash, too public for him. What on earth was the etiquette of such a singular occasion? What should he do? He only wanted one simple straightforward partner, not this exotic menagerie. Nothing in the self-contained excitement of the moon garden had prepared him for this.

When the warrior and her companion came level with him, he gulped down his fear and stepped into their path, holding out a hand in what he hoped was an appropriate greeting. In the same split second, the enormity of his misunderstanding dawned and he tried to jump back, but it was too late to avoid one deft blow of Athena's shield as she swept him aside to a gleeful cheer from the audience.

Rufus was sent spinning into the arms of a group of onlookers, who obligingly cushioned his fall and lowered him gently to a sitting position on the kerb. There he remained, head in hands, completely mortified by his mistake, as the loud, colourful confusion of the goddess festival procession passed by.

He did not have the courage to move and draw attention to himself until the crowd of onlookers began breaking up, returning to their shopping with smiles of good-humoured amusement.

Despite this minor setback, Rufus remained quietly confident for the rest of the week that some less earth-shattering event was about to occur at any moment, secretly scrutinising every female customer for signs of attraction and compatibility. He forced himself to meet the eyes of each shop assistant who served him, and made a point of eating his sandwiches out of doors, despite the uncertain weather, just to make himself readily available for the climactic contact he knew was close at hand.

Even the uneventfulness of the second week did not quench his hopeful enthusiasm one iota. On the contrary, he waited patiently, enjoying meanwhile the small pleasures of a settled and congenial life.

He went on waiting and waiting and waiting. And nothing whatsoever happened.

Epilogue

Charlie was in Huddlebridge again, this time for an antiques fair, or pre-Christmas antique bonanza as the advertising styled it. He had spent an agreeable evening with Rufus on the way, full of admiration for the completed improvements of the cottage. A new shower-room was installed upstairs and the subdued decoration throughout reflected the simple charm of the house, with Rufus' few pieces of fine furniture looking totally at home in an appropriate environment.

There were over a hundred stands in several cavernous halls. Charlie had made half a dozen purchases within the first traders-only hour and was now standing at a stall, drinking coffee and eating a bacon roll. He didn't want to linger until the domestic punters started pouring in.

He was just thinking about organising the loading of his van when he noticed a nearby display that hadn't been there on his first trip round this section. The stall-holder was still unpacking, trying to hang a small oak corner cupboard on a metal display hook which was too high for her to reach comfortably. Charlie stepped forward quickly to assist her and received a shy smile of thanks for his pains.

He let his eyes dwell provocatively on her before examining the cupboard more closely.

'Nice piece,' he said.

It certainly was. The plainly moulded cornice sat above two panels, unequal in size, with simple beading round the base. A rich nut brown sheen emphasised the beauty of the grain. Charlie could not help noticing that it was the same colour as the woman's hair.

'How much?'

As she looked up, he saw that her eyes were also a pretty good match.

'Five fifty.'

'Four for trade?' he said with the most charming smile in his repertoire.

'It was the trade price I gave you,' she said, turning away as if there was nothing more to say.

'Shame.' He picked up one of the business cards on her table and went back to his coffee. It gave her name and a local address.

Charlie watched her arranging the rest of her stock. There was something about her that drew his attention, although he couldn't at first work out what it was. He was not used to serious thought, especially this early in the morning, but he knew there was something important within his reach here and persevered.

She dealt with a couple of customers, with pleasant efficiency. He could see that she was reserved by nature but making the sort of effort the business demanded. He observed her slow, unhurried movements, the autumn colours of her casual clothes and careful attention she paid to detail in setting out her pieces to their best effect. It was a restful picture in the midst of this busy hall.

A broad grin suddenly spread over Charlie's handsome face. He tossed his plastic cup into a bin and strolled back over.

'Can I ask you a personal question?' he said.

'If you must.'

She looked away in some embarrassment. He realised it was the worst sort of corny chat-up line for a sensitive woman like this. Unfortunately, he didn't have anything more discerning to try with.

He pointed at her left hand.

'No ring. Does that mean you're free and single?'

He saw from her flushed face and the swallow in her

throat that she was going to make a brave effort to deal with his impertinence firmly.

'It does,' she said, in her quiet, clear voice. 'But I'm afraid you're not my type.' She tried to meet his eye, but looked away again quickly as she saw his amusement at her discomfort.

'I'll take the cupboard,' Charlie said, counting out fifty pound notes, 'but I'll want it delivered.' He scribbled quickly on a piece of paper. 'To be honest, you're not my type either.'

He began to walk away and then turned. She was standing, open-mouthed, holding his money and Rufus' address.

'Happy Christmas,' he called, waving cheerily. 'To you both,' he added under his breath.